DEATH AT FOURNIER DOWNS

A BOW STREET DUCHESS MYSTERY
BOOK TWO

CARA DEVLIN

First Cup Press

CHAPTER
ONE

Fournier Downs, Hertfordshire
August 1819

The chirping of crickets was a demented symphony, unending and shrill. If Audrey listened to their song too intently, the sound would drive her to insanity. So, she made sure to keep up a one-sided conversation with Fortuna, her dappled gray mare, as she led her through the overgrown rye grassland. The fields were thick with wild carrot, red campion, and purple harebell, and the heat brought out a sweet, peppery scent from the soil. It made her think of vibrant sunrises, thunderstorms, and puffy white clouds trimmed by slate gray skies. Audrey breathed it in and sighed.

"I wish there were some way to bottle that smell and transport it to London," she said to Fortuna as the mare nosed a clump of meadowsweet and tore up the roots. She snorted and shook her white mane.

"I know, I know, you don't want to talk about the end of

summer, do you?" Audrey brought the horse to a stop along the matted deer path and let her munch on another few sprigs of meadowsweet. "Neither do I."

She and her husband Philip, the Duke of Fournier, had arrived at their country estate at the beginning of May and had been lazing about for the whole of the summer. At first, their respite had seemed doomed. Only a few weeks after their arrival, Philip had taken to his bed with a nasty malaise. Headaches, fever, coughing; he had been miserable for weeks. So much so that his younger sister, Cassandra, who had been with Philip's brother Michael and his wife Genie at a house party in Kent, had decided to travel to Fournier House and help Audrey care for him.

Cassie was supposed to have had a summer filled with routs and house parties, and even a trip to Cumbria, all in preparation for her first season as a debutante—something Cassie had been excited about for as long as Audrey could remember.

However, she'd given it all up to stay at Fournier House with Philip. Audrey suspected it wasn't just out of fear for his health either.

They had come so close to losing him in April, when he'd been accused of murdering an opera singer. Found at the scene, covered in the dead woman's blood, the duke appeared to be guilty. Audrey, however, hadn't believed it, and for good reason. Against the wishes of the Bow Street officer who had arrested Philip, she launched her own investigation. Using her irregular —if oftentimes convenient—ability to see the memories that clung to objects, she had tracked down answers in the case, item by item. From the opera singer's earbob to an opium locket used to gain entry to a gambling hell to a pocket watch, and even a pair of Philip's cuff links.

Principal Officer Hugh Marsden had eventually realized the truth and helped her to close in on the real killer. But while exoneration had saved Philip's hide, his reputation had been badly damaged—as was Audrey's. Decamping to Fournier Downs, the duke's expansive estate in Hertfordshire, had been an easy decision to make.

It had not, however, lived up to expectations.

The Duchess of Fournier dismounted into the grasses and let Fortuna amble off to munch more flowers. She crouched to pick a few sprigs of red campion, with which she'd weave into the horse's bridle. Maybe she would press some flowers to take with her to London. She might even attempt to arrange a vase back at the house and paint, though she'd never had much in the way of artistic talent. But it would at least keep her busy.

As much as she dreaded returning to London and seeing her old acquaintances, she also didn't think she could take much more of this solitude in the countryside. The boredom of it was slowly driving her mad. Cassie was showing signs of distress too. Her usual bubbly and bright demeanor had faded over the last few weeks.

The young woman had lived with Philip's great aunt Hestia in Scotland since their mother's death. With two of her older brothers being newly married, and a third, Tobias, finishing up at Cambridge, Edinburgh had been the best place for her. But now, she was ready to begin looking for a husband of her own. Michael and Genie were to take her in for the Little Season in the fall, even with Genie about to enter confinement for her first child. Still, they had agreed it would be better for Cassie to be hosted by Michael, rather than Philip. All due to the murder scandal, of course.

A few months in the countryside would not be long enough to cure the taint of disgrace, even if to Audrey it felt as though they were suspended in time here, protected and absolved.

A dash of motion across the field caught her attention as she languidly braided the stems of the flowers she'd picked. She squinted against the sunlight. The sky was nearly cloudless, leaving the sun unimpeded. Heat beat down upon her shoulders, and a fine sweat had built up on her skin, under her linen riding habit. Ahead, the field sloped toward a stone wall bordered by tall alders and an open gate that led into a stretch of woodland. A woman in a white dress popped in and out of view as she ran through the trees. She passed the mouth of the stone wall, giving Audrey a better view. Her bright red hair was unmistakable—it was her friend Charlotte, the Countess of Bainbury.

What in the world was she doing all the way out here, on Fournier Downs parkland?

"Charlotte!" Audrey shouted, but the countess gave no indication of hearing her. She kept running, past the gate and into the woodland.

Audrey lifted the hem of her voluminous skirts and called to Fortuna. The mare, of course, was all too happy to ignore her, favoring instead a patch of meadowsweet across the field. Grinding her teeth in annoyance, she stalked across the field, all the while wondering what had brought Charlotte out here. And why should she be running?

Lord Bainbury's estate, Bainbury Park, was several miles away. It did not even border the Fournier Downs parkland. Rather, it lay beyond their neighboring estate, Haverfield— Audrey's own childhood country estate.

Multiple walking paths and riding trails crisscrossed throughout all the countryside here, so she supposed it would be possible to reach Fournier Downs on foot. But it was a great distance, with miles upon miles of meandering paths. And Charlotte had never been overly fond of exhausting herself in nature.

Audrey clicked her tongue to Fortuna and grasped her traces at last. Mounting her horse, she then led her toward the gate.

Something about her friend's running did not sit well. To be all the way out here, alone, and seemingly in a panic... Audrey gave Fortuna's ribs a gentle press with her heels and increased her pace.

It felt good to have a destination for once. With nothing to do and hardly anyone to see, the days at Fournier House had passed in timeless ease. Audrey woke each morning wondering how she might be able to fill the day that lay ahead. Philip spent most of his time in his study, poring over estate ledgers and plans, while Cassie played the pianoforte or painted—with *true* artistic aptitude—and Audrey either read or took Fortuna out onto the downs for hours on end. Bringing a footman with her would have been more proper, but Audrey liked to be alone. She'd find a good spot to spread a blanket in the grass and either nap or read while Fortuna grazed nearby, her tail whipping at persistent flies. Sometimes Cassie joined her, but even though they liked each other immensely, she and Audrey didn't have much to converse about beyond the one thing they had in common: Philip. Cassie's conversation had grown thin the last few weeks, and Audrey supposed hers had as well. The imminent return to London seemed to be weighing down on the three of them like the building pressure of a wicked summer storm.

She reached the gate and turned left, in the direction Charlotte had taken. The light coming through the boughs of the trees fell in dappled sweeps of gold and slate shadow, and the cooler air was an instant relief. There was no sign of Charlotte, though she had been moving quite quickly and several minutes had passed by the time Audrey finally mounted Fortuna and started to follow. The countess could also be obscured by the thick stands of trees filling this part of the forest.

"Charlotte!" Her voice carried, and a few birds in the limbs above scattered. Fortuna huffed impatiently as Audrey held the horse still and listened. Waiting. But again, there was no response from her friend.

She and Charlotte had been acquaintances when they were younger. Charlotte, the only daughter of the Viscount and Viscountess Prescott, had spent her summers here in Hertfordshire at Greely Park, the viscount's country home near Low Heath. Though they would often see each other at gatherings and social outings, it wasn't until after Audrey broke her own betrothal to Lord Bainbury in order to marry Philip, and Charlotte agreed to marry the older earl instead, that they became closer friends. At first, the news that Charlotte would wed Bainbury had astonished Audrey. There were at least twenty years between them, and the earl had already lost two wives. The first to a wasting disease, and the second to a tragic suicide. Her maid found her dead in bed one morning, a muff pistol in her hand.

But then, Audrey had begun to understand Charlotte's position. She'd felt sorry for her, knowing she'd likely had little say in whether she married the earl or not. Audrey herself had been forced into the betrothal, which had been arranged by her mother and her father's successor—her uncle, Lord Edgerton. However, upon seeing Charlotte for the first time after the wedding, her friend had seemed content.

"We don't have a love match like you and Philip have," she'd admitted to Audrey once. "But I am quite satisfied with my situation."

For some reason, Audrey always felt guilty when people spoke of her "love match" with Philip. He'd whisked in at the eleventh hour, stealing Audrey from Bainbury with all the flair of a man in love. But it hadn't been love between her and Philip; it had been a safe agreement between longtime friends.

Besides, Philip was a duke. Even Audrey's mother could not complain...at least, not publicly.

Audrey pushed Fortuna onward, into the woodland and around trees, trying to spot her friend again. Soon, she pulled on the reins, discouraged.

"I think we've lost her," she told Fortuna. Her stomach twisted with worry. Charlotte had to have been running fast to have disappeared so quickly. Ladies never run.

Not unless they are in trouble.

A curl of unease worked its way through her, and she tried to ignore her instinct.

"Let's keep on," she said to Fortuna, leading her mount forward again. There was a trail ahead that would eventually take them back to the stables at Fournier House. Perhaps that had been Charlotte's destination?

A sudden scream cracked through the air, followed immediately by the shrill ruckus of cawing ravens. Audrey whipped around in her saddle. The ravens were still at it, their cries coming from deeper in the woods. Heart pounding, mind racing, Audrey tugged Fortuna's traces and started for the direction of the ravens.

"Charlotte!" she shouted as Fortuna wove between trees. Something had happened. Her friend was in some kind of danger. Had she crossed paths with a wild boar protecting its piglets? Or a lynx, or some other wildcat?

The ravens beat their wings, darting overhead through the thick green foliage. Audrey aimed Fortuna in their direction. Soon, the alders, pines, and whitebeams began to thin. Fortuna deftly leaped over a downed pine, and Audrey drew her to a hard stop. Ten yards ahead, the land dropped off into a craggy open pit. This was the old citrine quarry, one of Philip's ancestor's enterprises that had not withstood the test of time.

Audrey breathed heavily, the utter stillness of the wood unsettling. A single, sharp caw from a branch above jolted down her spine. A lone raven spread its wings and leaped into flight, soaring over the quarry's edge. With shaking legs and arms, Audrey dismounted. She held the leather traces a few moments longer than necessary.

"Charlotte?" Her choppy breaths made her voice wheezy.

She didn't want to go to the edge. Didn't want to look down into the open pit where, if memory served, blocks of rock lay scattered as scree at the base of the abandoned quarry. Intuition loomed like the black belly of a rain cloud.

Audrey could mount her horse and ride back for Fournier House. She could gather a group of footmen and stable boys and lead them back here, and they could then search for Charlotte together. But she knew in her heart that it would be cowardly. Last April, she hadn't backed down once on her quest to prove Philip's innocence. It had nearly gotten her killed, but that hadn't mattered at the time. What *had* mattered was doing the right thing. Even if it frightened her half to death.

"Stay," she told Fortuna, and then with as much false nerve as she could gather, went to the edge of the quarry. The drop was at least a hundred feet, and when the bottom came into view, her blood ran cold.

Audrey swallowed a scream and covered her mouth. Far below, Charlotte lay broken. Her eyes were open, but she wasn't moving. Her red hair fanned around her like a halo of radiant light in a sacred painting. Blood splashed the rocks near her head.

Behind Audrey, a stick snapped. She whipped around, the small hairs on her arms standing on end. But it was only a pair of red squirrels skittered up a tree, chirping at one another. Fortuna loped toward her mistress, perhaps sensing need. Audrey, her legs weak, gratefully took her by the traces and mounted swiftly.

"Come, hurry," she whispered, the sensation that she was

not alone in the wood crackling along her skin with rushed impatience. "We have to get help."

She dug in her heels and rode toward the path to Fournier House, her eyes stinging with tears. It would be too little, too late. There could be no help for Charlotte now.

CHAPTER
TWO

"Cor, is there anything out here that's not grass, sheep, and trees?"

Seated on the bench across from Hugh Marsden, the young street urchin stared out the carriage window with a sneer of disgust.

"Are you really complaining about the countryside, Sir?" Hugh asked, suppressing a grin. It wouldn't do to let the boy know that he found him more amusing than he did vexatious. Hugh had asked Sir to come along with him into Hertfordshire for practical reasons, but he couldn't deny that getting him out of London for a week or so would be good timing.

Not only were the rookeries in London little more than rank stink pits at this time of the summer, but over the last few months the street gangs had been ramping up in violence. Sir had come around with a few black eyes, and though the lad wouldn't breathe a word about what happened, Hugh could easily guess. Sir had made it clear he wanted nothing to do with the gangs; unfortunately, gangs didn't generally like being refused.

Sir sat back in his seat and crossed his arms. "Strange, is all. There's too much sky if ye ask me."

"And not enough pockets to pick, I imagine," Basil, Hugh's valet, muttered.

"Aw, come off it, Baz, ye know I don't do that trick no more."

Basil gave a roll of his eyes and adjusted his spectacles. He'd insisted on joining Hugh, even though he'd been told it wasn't necessary. Multiple times.

"I will not have you presenting yourself to a viscountess without a properly tied cravat," the aggravated valet had said.

After that, Hugh didn't put up much more of an argument. Basil was serious when it came to cravats. The man ran Hugh's household and small staff, which included a cook, Mrs. Peets and a maid, Greta, who came in a few times a week to tidy and do the wash. Basil also hadn't had a holiday in ages, and Hugh suspected he wanted a bit of fresh country air now that London's had turned humid and stale.

Not that this would be any sort of a holiday. A woman was dead, and her mother believed there had been some foul play.

Yesterday, Hugh, a principal officer at Bow Street, had been called into Chief Magistrate Sir Gabriel Poston's office. The magistrate slapped a letter onto his desk and gestured toward it in his rough, no-nonsense fashion.

"You've been hired to investigate a death." He'd gone on to explain what little the letter had provided.

Lady Bainbury, the Countess of Bainbury, had been found dead. Her husband, the earl, was claiming it was an accident. However, the countess's mother, Lady Prescott, refused to believe it. She had been advised to send for Officer Hugh Marsden by none other than Her Grace, the Duchess of Fournier.

Audrey.

Her name, scrawled in black ink at the close of the letter,

had loosened something inside his chest, something tight and constricted. Like a fist clenched for too long, the muscles were reluctant to release.

Hugh had set the letter back on the desk and told the magistrate to find someone else.

"This fancy lady what we're visiting," Sir began as the hired coach and four rumbled and shook down a post road toward Greely Park. "She's a viscountess?"

Hugh's pocket watch read half four. They should be arriving any moment now. He slipped the watch back into his waistcoat pocket and fought rising irritation. It wasn't Sir he was irritated with but himself.

"Yes, Viscountess Prescott. But *we* are not visiting. I am. You and Basil will wait with the carriage while I interview her ladyship."

Sir groaned and slumped down in the seat like a petulant child. If he wasn't the smartest, scrappiest, most resourceful urchin Hugh had ever known, he would have left him in London.

Basil swept away a clod of dirt that had floated in through the open window and landed on his cuff. "I sincerely hope there are acceptable accommodations in Low Heath."

Hugh knew next to nothing of the village closest to Lady Prescott's estate. Just that it was in Hertfordshire. If it was anything like the other villages along the post road, it would have a posting inn and tavern, and a stable, at the very least.

"Hopefully we won't have to stay on for long. A few days at the most to sort things out," Hugh said.

Sir Gabriel would be having himself a grand chuckle right now, he imagined. He'd refused to have another officer summoned for the job. *Your duchess is asking for you, Marsden,* he'd said. *The last thing I need is her hoity toity self, storming in here, asking why I sent the wrong man.*

Had the Duchess of Fournier been in London, there was no doubt she would have done just that. Last April, he'd had a devil of a time keeping her from getting herself killed during her unorthodox investigation into Belladora Lovejoy's murder. She'd been shot in the shoulder just before the true killer was caught, and Hugh had felt a barbed friction under his skin for days afterward. He'd been frustrated, bloody angry, and blissfully relieved.

Once Audrey and the duke left for Hertfordshire, that friction faded slowly. Arresting thieves and burglars, drunkards with tempers, and run-of-the-mill murderers had buried the memories of that remarkable case, in which Hugh had arrested the wrong man—something that still pricked like a thorn.

"No doubt you want to return by Friday evening," Basil said, arching a brow.

"Shut it, Basil," Hugh replied, more peeved than usual with his valet. He was a perpetually sarcastic snob who felt entirely too secure in his position. There wasn't another valet in all of England who would provoke his employer with a sarcastic remark about his mistress. Basil was the epitome of grace when he saw fit, and yet also managed to be as petulant as Sir at times. No wonder the two of them rubbed each other the wrong way.

Next to him on the bench seat, Sir snickered. He was probably only eleven or twelve, but that boy knew more than he should.

"Miss Friday's real pretty, she is," he said.

Hugh glared at him. "Mind your manners, Sir."

He pouted. "What? I didn't call her ugly."

"You should never mention a man's mistress in conversation," Hugh replied.

"Why not?"

"It is considered rude."

Sir rolled his eyes. Hugh fought another grin. Sometimes he felt like his own father whenever he tried imparting wisdom and manners into the young lad. Lord Leatham, the sixth Viscount Leatham, had never shirked his responsibility to teach his sons how to behave in polite society. That Hugh was not his legitimate son, and would never be required to enter polite society, had not stopped him from instilling the knowledge just the same.

Hugh had been raised alongside his half-brothers, Bartholomew and Thomas, as well as his half-sister, Eloisa, and had absorbed every last drop of wisdom the late viscount had offered. He sat back in the carriage as it trundled toward Greely Park and sighed. A hell of a lot of good it had done him.

"Maybe ye two should be spliced then," Sir said after a moment. Hugh jerked his head toward him.

"Spliced?"

"Ye know. Enter the parson's mouse trap? *Married?*" Sir said while affecting a look of revulsion.

"Marry who? Miss Hanson?" A spate of cold sweat rushed the back of his neck. Gloria Hanson was his longtime mistress, and while they had a comfortable arrangement, there was absolutely no desire rampaging through him to make her his wife. He was quite certain Gloria felt the same way.

Sir shrugged. "Why not?"

The question hung in the carriage like a miasma. Hugh met Basil's eye, but after arching a brow, the valet looked away, apparently uninterested in weighing in.

"Men do not marry their mistresses," Hugh replied, hoping it was enough.

"Your lot don't make much sense," Sir muttered.

Hugh wasn't sure he did not agree with him. Thankfully, at that moment, they turned into the drive for Greely Park.

He'd left Bow Street the day before with the beginnings of a searing headache, the stabbing pains beginning the moment he'd gritted his teeth and ripped the letter from the magistrate's desk. In the last few months, he'd been all too happy to pretend London's polite society did not exist. After the close of the Duke of Fournier's case, and his and the duchess's departure from London, Hugh had found himself parsing his investigation with the duchess, and in turn, thinking of the *ton*. And thinking of the ton only led to reflecting on his own past, which only ever put him into a foul mood. It was in that irritable, foul mood he'd stayed for a few weeks, until he'd quit thinking so much about the duchess and the case. Exhausting himself at work and increasing his meetings with Gloria from one night per week to two had helped.

However, with that letter and this assignment, the barbs of irritation had immediately set in again. She was here, in Hertfordshire. The duke's expansive estate of Fournier Downs was only ten miles or so from Greely Park. A subtle thrum of expectation had lived under his skin since he'd barked at Basil to begin packing his things.

Lady Prescott's estate was a somewhat modest neoclassical home, ivy and roses creeping up the sides of its pale sandstone exterior. The hired coach's wheels rolled over the half-moon drive of crushed gravel, which was centered by a fountain topped by a winged angel clutching a harp. Hugh rolled his eyes at it as he pulled on his deerskin gloves. Basil had insisted he wear them while presenting himself to her ladyship, the dowager Viscountess Prescott. That it was a hot, humid afternoon with a rainstorm on the horizon and his palms would be sweating buckets did not matter. Appearances and formalities were everything, at least among the Quality.

The coach came to a stop. Sir sat forward to peer out the window, his jaw loose, showing off two crooked front teeth.

"I'll return shortly," Hugh said, then descended. The front

door to the manor opened and a man who appeared to be butler came out onto the front step.

"Officer Marsden, I presume," he said. "Her ladyship was expecting you, however she has since become indisposed. If you'll follow me, Her Grace, the Duchess of Fournier will receive you."

Without waiting for a reply, the man turned and entered the foyer. Hugh's feet weren't swift to follow. Instead, a stone of weight dropped into each of his hessians. He shouldn't have been surprised that she was here. She'd written the letter on Lady Prescott's behalf, after all. A footman at the door stood patiently, waiting for him to enter. Hugh doffed his hat and kept after the butler, who moved with the elegant efficiency that all proud head servants possessed. He paused within the entrance to a room, announced the principal officer, and then stood aside to allow Hugh entry.

As if he'd been carried in on a dizzying wind, Hugh swept into a grand sitting room—and came to an abrupt halt. Audrey Sinclair, the Duchess of Fournier, slowly rose from a chair to her feet.

"Officer Marsden." Her voice was soft, her gloved hands clasping together in front of her waist. It was a nervous motion, as was the hesitant smile to touch her lips.

Warmth pooled in his stomach, and his shoulders stiffened. Momentarily, he lost his train of thought. He'd forgotten the deep cerulean blue of her eyes. The fullness of her mouth.

"Your Grace," he replied, then cleared his throat and remembered to make a short bow.

The duchess gestured him toward a chair before retaking her seat. She nodded toward a maid, who left, presumably to fetch tea.

"Lady Prescott wished to meet with you, but she isn't faring well. I hope you don't mind speaking to me on the matter?"

"No, not at all." He eyed the chair warily. He'd already been sitting for several hours in that rattling coach and his backside ached like the devil. He also didn't feel like relaxing just yet. Instead, he set his hat on the cushion and clasped his hands behind his straight back. "How may I be of service?"

As if realizing he wouldn't be sitting to converse, the duchess got to her feet again. She crossed the room, toward a pair of open French doors that led to a terrace. Her upswept hair had been styled to leave artful blond ringlets to trail down the nape of her neck and over her shoulder. Hugh took a breath before averting his eyes.

"Lady Bainbury, Charlotte, was a good friend of mine," she began, her fingers still twisting together as she looked out onto the terrace.

"My condolences." He didn't know what more to say. He'd always found the lengthier an expression of sympathy became, the cheaper it sounded.

Audrey turned toward him, her cheeks pink with a new flush. "The earl is saying it was an accident, and already the rumors are spreading that it was suicide, like the previous countess. But I know it was neither of those things."

Hugh hitched his chin, struck by the glittering intensity of her stare, at the set lines of her jaw. Last spring, she'd been just as adamant that her husband had not been having an affair with Miss Lovejoy and was innocent of the gruesome murder. At first, Hugh had dismissed her as naïve; it was a well-established tradition that married men of the ton took mistresses. However, he'd soon come to understand she was correct. The duke had been having an affair with a male lover, not a mistress, and he was indeed innocent of the murder.

Hugh stepped around the chair, toward her. "Tell me what you know."

THREE

Audrey hadn't been ready for this.

She'd known writing to Bow Street and requesting Mr. Marsden specifically would cause upheaval to what had been, so far, a placid summer in the countryside, and she thought she had prepared herself for his arrival, but the reality of it had walloped her the moment Newman had shown Hugh Marsden into the sitting room.

Lady Prescott's butler had flared his nostrils when Audrey insisted on staying at Greely Park to welcome the principal officer after the dowager viscountess took to her bed in a fit of melancholy. The butler had not wanted to permit him through the front door, but have him enter around the back, at the servant's entrance. Audrey's insistence that he be welcomed as a guest had put a sour glint in the old man's eyes. Ever since they'd been children, Charlotte and Audrey had stuck out their tongues and pulled faces whenever Newman turned his back. He was a snob, through and through—worse than some of the titled people Audrey knew.

Hugh Marsden appeared taller than when she'd last seen him in late April. His rich brown eyes and chiseled jaw and nose even more striking. It seemed her mind had done well in subduing her own memories of him. His clothing appeared finer than what he'd worn in London too.

She'd expected him to challenge her immediately, insist that she was overthinking Lady Bainbury's tragic death, and subtly scoff at her summoning him all the way to Hertfordshire. Instead, without a trace of arrogance or sarcasm, he waited for her to tell him what she knew. So, she did.

Audrey started from the beginning: seeing Charlotte running through the woods, trying to hail her from across the field without success. She recounted following her on her horse, hearing a scream and the cacophony of ravens, and then finding her friend at the bottom of the quarry.

"A scream?" he repeated, his brow furrowing.

She nodded. "It's why I know she didn't jump. Why would she scream, as if in terror, if she was choosing to leap to her death?"

He considered the question in silence as he stepped toward the open terrace. The humidity in the sitting room had turned thick and close, and though the breeze outside was weak, at least it would be some relief. They stepped onto the terrace, which was bordered by a balustrade and potted topiary.

"She could have changed her mind too late, when she was already falling," he said, his eyes narrowing on a topiary, clipped into a rabbit-like shape. "Or she could have slipped over the edge by accident. You did say she was running."

Audrey had considered those possibilities too. "The quarry drop-off is visible from a distance; it would be impossible to not see it coming. And *why* was she running? I've never seen Charlotte so much as walk briskly. She appeared panicked. Like someone was chasing her."

He turned from the rabbit topiary and speared her with a serious look. "Did you see anyone?"

She assumed his forbidding expression was because she was basing her argument on conjecture, not proof. However, when she replied that no, she had not seen anyone, but that she'd had the distinct impression someone was there at the quarry, his forbidding expression turned thunderous. He shifted his footing, bringing him a step closer.

"You believe she was pushed."

Audrey nodded.

"And you think the person who pushed her was still there? That they saw you?"

Her skin prickled as it had that afternoon in the shady wood when it had felt as if a pair of eyes were boring between her shoulder blades. A dozen times, she'd wished she'd scaled the quarry ledge down to the base, to feel for a pulse in Charlotte's neck and be certain she was gone; that she'd touched some item she wore—a ring, her necklace, anything—so that she could make sense of what had just happened. But with the stick snapping behind her in the woods, the chittering of squirrels, the cawing of a raven...and that peculiar sensation of being watched... she'd run away in fear. In cowardice.

Audrey lowered her eyes. "Possibly."

"Who have you spoken of this to?"

She knew why he was asking. And that he would not be happy with her answer. "Lady Prescott, of course, and the duke. And Lord Bainbury, naturally. But he dismissed my account, and the local magistrate did as well."

Mr. Marsden loomed closer, throwing off palpable tension. "If you are right, and whoever it was hears that you have brought me here to investigate, if they have any reason to believe you saw them, Audrey—" She snapped her eyes to his, and he sealed his lips with an expression of chagrin. "Your Grace," he corrected. "They might wish you harm."

"I didn't see anyone." Small tremors shook out along her

arms and legs. "But I don't believe she jumped, and Lady Prescott agrees. Charlotte had no reason to take her own life."

"None that you are aware of," he reminded her, moving aside, toward the balustrade.

She'd just seen Charlotte a fortnight before, for tea; she hadn't been so very out of sorts. They had discussed her stepson's upcoming nuptials, and Charlotte had seemed eager for the wedding, if only to get Lord Renfry off of his father's estate. She'd seemed a bit harried; hot and distracted, too. But the summer weather had been unnaturally humid. It was bothering everyone. Still, she supposed Charlotte could have been keeping something to herself. Audrey knew too well the masks those of polite society so often had to wear. She'd worn many herself, especially these last few months.

Audrey joined Mr. Marsden at the balustrade, looking over the viscountess's garden. It was a point of pride, with several varieties of roses and hydrangea that she was happy to say no other garden in England possessed. The poor woman was devastated by Charlotte's death. She had a son, the new viscount, but he was young and still at Cambridge. He'd written that he would arrive in time for the funeral, but Audrey found his lack of urgency disappointing. So had the viscountess.

"Lady Prescott will pay any fee you require for investigating Charlotte's death," Audrey said. At the tightening of his mouth and the shift of his footing, she wished she hadn't brought up the subject of payment.

"Money is not my concern," he said. She knew it wasn't. His father, Fitzgerald Neatham, the late Viscount Neatham, left him a generous living despite the fact that he was illegitimate. He *chose* to work as a Bow Street officer; he wasn't dependent on his wages.

"I will investigate," he continued. "On one condition."

Audrey frowned. She suspected she knew what that one condition would be.

"You will not insert yourself into this case," he said.

She hitched her chin. "I was of assistance last time."

He ripped off his deerskin gloves and turned toward her, his irritation simmering. She remembered his temper well. Oddly enough, she didn't dislike seeing it again. If anything, it assured her of some normalcy.

"You were reckless and were nearly killed."

Her shoulder tingled with the reminder of being shot. She knew she had been lucky—and incredibly rash. She'd gone aboard a houseboat, suspecting she would find proof of her husband's innocence there, and the man who'd murdered Miss Lovejoy had caught her. She'd had a narrow escape and had been shot in the shoulder before falling into the Thames. Out of pure providence, Mr. Marsden had been there to leap into the river and save her life.

The muddled memories of being wretchedly cold, in pain, and bundled into Hugh's arms as he rushed her to his doctor friend's home for treatment flashed into her mind, then out again.

"I did what I had to do." She gritted her teeth. "However, if you will take on the post, I will...stay out of your way."

He cocked his head and peered at her curiously. As if he didn't quite believe it. Audrey continued to clench her jaw. Finding the truth about Charlotte's death was more important to her than proving Hugh Marsden wrong.

He slapped his gloves into his palm once, twice, as if in thought. "Very well. I would like to see the quarry."

She brightened, though was also slightly confused. "You would like my help then?"

"In this, yes. But that will be the extent of your involvement."

Lord, she hated that tone. Hated being told what to do or not do. Especially since he knew full well that her ability to read objects had played a critical role in solving the opera singer's murder. But this was at least an opening. She would take it. And with any luck, widen it enough to step through fully.

She pasted on a forced grin. "When would you like to set out?"

~

FOURNIER HOUSE HAD ALWAYS BEEN a place of respite for Audrey.

Five miles east of Haverfield, the country estate in which she had spent summers and Christmas holidays as a child, Fournier House was a bright and cheery Elizabethan design, with clean lines, tall windows, and a pale limestone exterior. It was much friendlier in appearance than Violet House, their ducal home in London, which was a blocky and imposing monolith type design that Audrey had never truly liked. And while Haverfield was a fine home in the Grand Baroque style, memories of it left her feeling cold and lonely.

Some of Audrey's worst memories had been formed there. When she'd been just seven years old, her father and brother had died at Haverfield. To avoid catching the fever that gripped her brother, she'd been shuttered up in the nursery, a hot and stuffy prison, for over a week. When she'd finally been allowed out, she'd learned that not only had James succumbed, but her father, Lord Edgerton, had as well. She hadn't even known her papa had fallen ill. She'd never gotten the chance to say goodbye.

After that, Haverfield was a desolate place. Her neighbors at Fournier Downs were happy to see her whenever she ambled through their parkland with her governess or maid. It was how she and Philip, eight years her senior, had grown to be acquaintances, then friends.

Now, as she returned home after her encounter with Hugh Marsden at Greely Park, she felt an odd twist in the pit of her stomach. As much as it calmed her, Fournier House, the crowning jewel of the duke's grand estate, did not feel any more like home than Violet House or Haverfield. It didn't matter that she was duchess, and that this was her household to run. It did not truly feel like she had any real claim over it. Because she wasn't, in truth, married to the duke.

Oh, they had taken all the correct steps to convince the ton that she had cried off from her betrothal to the Earl of Bainbury due to a love match with Philip, and he had applied and received a special license from the archbishop, allowing them to marry within days. They had taken vows at St. George's and entertained at the wedding breakfast after, at Violet House. They had then traveled across France and Italy and Greece for four months before returning to London to enter society as duke and duchess. It had been expected that Audrey would return from their tour *enceinte*. However, not only had she not been with child, she and Philip had not even consummated their marriage. By mutual agreement, of course. And so, she couldn't help but feel as though she wasn't truly the Duchess of Fournier.

Verly, their butler at Fournier Downs, met her in the foyer. He took a short bow. "Your Grace. His Grace has asked that you join him in his study upon your return. Shall I announce you will be in shortly?"

He must have shrewdly taken in the state of her hem. The skies had split open while she'd been taking a turn around Lady Prescott's garden after Mr. Marsden's departure. She'd needed a few minutes to think and clear the jitters from her arms and legs. Her muslin gown had dried on the ride home in her post-chaise, but her hem was still trimmed in mud.

"No need, I will join him now." Philip did not care about the state of her hem any more than she did.

Audrey set off for the wide, oak stairwell, carpeted in gold and sapphire carpet. Calming shades of blue and elegant touches of gold could be found throughout all the common areas in the manor house, though Audrey's bedchamber leaned toward silvery gray.

"Verly, have Greer meet me in my chamber. I need to change."

He promptly darted away. Hugh Marsden would arrive shortly. He'd said he needed to find lodgings at the posting-inn in the village of Low Heath before meeting her for a tour of the parkland, where she had last seen Charlotte. As Audrey approached Philip's study door, a shiver of dread turned her stomach yet again.

These last two days, she had not been able to stop thinking about Charlotte, sprinting through the wood. The cawing of the crows, the terrified scream that had startled them into flight. She should have known Mr. Marsden would want to see where she'd died. *Had* known it, deep down. But she wasn't sure she was ready to return there just yet.

She rapped upon the door before pushing it open and popping in her head. Philip sat at his desk, a large, scrolled hunk of dark wood that would have been at home in the captain's quarters of a sailing vessel. It had belonged to the fourth Duke of Fournier, then the fifth, and now, the sixth. He looked up from his ledgers and the papers strewn around his elbows, his eyes heavy with disinterest and burden. His fair hair was tousled, his cravat loosely tied.

"There you are," he said. Audrey couldn't tell if the statement was neutral or if he was still perturbed.

"I was with Lady Prescott," she reminded him.

He'd still been abed when she'd left earlier, though the previous evening, when a messenger delivered a note from Bow Street's magistrate, saying Officer Marsden would be arriving at Greely Park on the morrow, Philip had been livid.

She had not shared with him that she'd written to Bow Street, or that she had requested Mr. Marsden's help. She and Philip had exchanged tense words at dinner, which his sister, Cassandra, had watched as she ate her sponge cake, eyes wide with entertainment. It wasn't that Philip did not appreciate all that Hugh Marsden had done to exonerate him; however, the officer dragged a past scandal of his own behind him, like a shadow, and Philip was of the firm belief that from here on out, he and Audrey had to divorce themselves from any scandal whatsoever.

Easier said than done.

She stepped more fully into the study. "You wished to see me?"

"How is the dowager faring?" He closed one of his books and massaged his eyes.

This last month, he had shown true improvement from the illness that had taken nearly all of July to recover from. A respiratory malaise, Dr. Ryder from Low Heath, had determined. But even though he'd been outdoors more, and finally attending to the business of the estate, Philip was reserved. It wasn't just the many repairs and improvements needed to the farms and businesses on the duke's thirty-thousand acres that weighed on him. It was the mess they had left behind in London.

"Not well, I'm afraid," she answered. "Though, I cannot see how anyone could easily withstand such anguish."

Philip sighed and pushed back his chair. "He has come?"

"Yes." A strange heat stirred low in her stomach. She didn't understand it.

"And he has taken the case?"

"He has. In fact, he will be here soon. He's asked to see the quarry. I should meet with Greer to change—"

"Audrey," Philip said, standing up as she turned for the door. But just then, the door swung open, and Cassandra breezed into the study.

"Oh, good! You're back." Her voice was sweet and vibrant, much like herself. Philip's sister, and youngest sibling, wore a pink day dress with green floral embroidery. She was just about to turn nineteen and would enter society soon. The informal Little Season in the autumn would prepare her for the courtlier and more official Season in late winter and early spring of next year.

Her bright green eyes darted between Audrey and Philip, and then narrowed. "Are you two still arguing about that Bow Street blackguard?"

Audrey gaped at her sister-in-law. "Mr. Marsden is not a blackguard."

She pouted playfully. "Pity. But I would like to meet him. Will I have the chance?"

Philip rapped his knuckles against the desk. "Cassie, the man is here to investigate a death, not socialize."

She startled at his tone, but still appeared amused by it. Cassie did enjoy vexing her older brother. Audrey often wondered if she would have taken such pleasure in nettling James if he had lived.

"Does Lord Bainbury know Officer Marsden is here?" Cassie asked next, strolling into the study, and running her fingers along the spines of books upon a wall of shelves.

Audrey crossed a look with Philip. They had argued over Bainbury the night before as well. She'd suggested they call on the earl to express their sympathy, and Philip insisted a written expression and arrangement of flowers would do well enough.

When the earl and his entourage had arrived to retrieve Charlotte's body from the duke's icehouse, he had not been receptive to Audrey's theories about what might have occurred at the old quarry. At first, she'd thought it only grief and shock that deafened him to her account; however, the following day, when the local magistrate, Lord Webber, had arrived at Fournier House to speak to Audrey, he insisted the death appeared accidental and that the inquest would arrive at that same conclusion.

Audrey had wanted a chance to see the earl again, to make a plea to at least consider his wife had been in trouble in the woods, but Philip put his foot down.

"If he doesn't know Marsden is here yet, he soon will," Philip muttered in answer to Cassie's question.

Lord Bainbury would be furious. He wanted to mark the death down as accidental, caused by misadventure, but of course, the gossip was already spreading through the country-side, and surely into London, that Charlotte had followed in the previous countess's footsteps and had ended her own life.

"I don't understand why he is so eager to move on," she murmured. "Why would he not want to know what happened out there?"

Unless he is hiding something. Audrey knew better than to say that, though. Making such an accusation, even in the privacy of Philip's study, would be going too far. Jumping to conclusions before Mr. Marsden had even begun his investigation would be foolish.

"The man has lost his wife," Philip said. He moved toward a sideboard and poured himself a finger of brandy. "His *third* wife, might I add. Who knows what is going on inside his head? Leave him be, Audrey."

She peered at him, curious. He was not one of Lord Bain-bury's friends or even acquaintances. After Philip swooped in and stole his betrothed, the earl and duke had kept their chilly distance, an ever-present friction between them. It was strange to hear him sound sorry for Bainbury now.

Philip's moods had been changeable this summer. The arrest, the scandal, then his months-long malaise were likely the reasons why. She could not discount the messy ending of his affair with Lord St. John. Augustus, the son and heir of the Marquess of Wimbly, had been meeting with Philip regularly in a set of leased rooms in a shabby part of Seven Dials. The marquess's discovery that they were lovers had driven him to concoct a scheme to punish his son and incriminate Philip, and unfortunately for Belladora Lovejoy, Lord Wimbly had seen her as an expendable pawn.

Countless times Audrey had thought about Lord Wimbly's choices, how deep and severe his fury and fear must have been for him to cause so much strife. How vacant of any compassion or morals he must have been. As he had only been found guilty in the planning of the murder, he had not been hanged. Instead, he'd been stripped of his title and estates and shipped off to Australia as a prisoner. Lady Wimbly and Lord St. John, now stripped of their titles as well, had decamped to Devonshire to reside in the care of her sister and would never return to London. They were utterly, irrevocably disgraced.

"Cassie, was there something you wanted?" Philip asked as his sister ambled toward the windows.

She certainly seemed to have brightened with the idea of the Bow Street Runner's impending arrival. It was the first thing she'd shown an interest in for some time.

"I only wondered if Audrey wanted to take a ride with me. I'm incurably bored," she said with a little sigh.

"I'm afraid I'm going out with Officer Marsden soon, to show him the quarry. Perhaps after?"

"That is not necessary. I will show him to the quarry," Philip said, biting off the words as if they were gristle.

She ought to have expected his suggestion, but still, annoyance stirred in her chest. Audrey maintained a hopefully serene expression. "He would also like to see where I saw Charlotte running through the trees."

He had not specifically said as much but she imagined he would.

"Tell me where, and I will show him."

"I will come with you and show him myself."

She and Philip locked eyes. While he cared deeply about perceptions, it was only after some scandal or near scandal that those perceptions seemed to rule him. About a year before the arrest, he'd had a floundering and uncontrolled habit of visiting opium dens. He'd put Audrey through hell, disappearing for days on end at times. At last, something had made him see the light, and afterward, he'd spent months being stringent, overcorrecting his lack of restraint. She had the feeling that was what he was doing now, too.

"Excellent, I will have my horse saddled as well," Cassie said with a happy leap. She then made way for the door.

"Cassandra—" Philip started, but she only quickened her step and left before her brother could say more.

He speared Audrey with a look that said, *You are responsible for this.* She left the study without reply. Sometimes, leaving Philip to his dark moods was the better choice. Besides, she needed to exchange her walking dress for a riding habit. It seemed Cassie would get her wish after all: an introduction to Officer Hugh Marsden.

CHAPTER

FOUR

Aweight, like lead ballast, filled his gut the moment he turned his hired horse up the manicured drive toward Fournier House. The manor stood at the crest of a knoll, its many windows and gables and chimneys spearing the sky. Flowering vines climbed the exterior, blocking out whole stretches of stone. The place was regal but not ostentatious. Even though it was massive in scale, it was somehow still understated. How a piece of architecture could convey power and wealth, but also taste and refinement, made no sense, but Fournier House managed.

Two great columns topped by massive stone spheres stood together as a gateway to where the drive ended in a circle. Instead of a fountain, as had been at Greely Park, the circular drive was centered by a lily pond bordered by a low stone wall. A few toy sail boats bobbed among the lily pads, and Hugh had the disconcerting image of Audrey and the duke sitting out here, launching them together, laughing as the wind filled the little sails and set them racing. He scowled at his own imagination as he dismounted and cut his eyes away from the toy boats.

Two liveried footmen approached to take his horse.

However, before they could reach for the reins, the Duke of Fournier exited the front door.

"Never mind that, thank you," he said to them. "The officer will need his mount."

"Your Grace." Hugh made the obligatory bob of his head. The duke came to a stop in front of Hugh, his expression barely masking his exasperation.

"Officer Marsden," he replied. "The ladies are waiting for us at the stables."

Hugh knew better than to show his hand by wearing any expression other than one of detachment and disinterest, even if he questioned what lady, other than the duchess, would be joining them.

He followed the duke, leading his horse by its traces, toward the side of the manor. The duke moved with haste, the tails of his green frock coat whipping, the spurs on the heels of his riding boots spinning. Fournier was not pleased to see him. For some reason, Hugh took pleasure in that. He also thought he knew why.

"Her Grace did not inform you that she had written to Bow Street." He watched the duke's back to see his reaction. Sure enough, his spine straightened.

"That does not signify," he replied after a moment. "I will show you to the quarry, officer. You can gather whatever it is you need for your investigation."

An investigation the duke clearly did not support.

"Indeed," was all Hugh replied as a quadrangular stone and timber stable came into view.

Three horses were waiting in the stable yard and standing beside them were two young women. Hugh's eyes went immediately to Audrey. *The duchess.* He should not be thinking of her by her given name, but he kept slipping. He'd done so verbally at Greely Park, too, and the flash of her eyes had scolded him.

The duchess now wore a riding habit, which was more suitable and sturdier for their task. The lady next to her was younger, with the duke's own fair coloring. She watched Hugh's approach with widening eyes and an expanding smile. He exhaled in preparation for what would no doubt be one of the most irritating rides he would ever take.

"Officer Hugh Marsden," the duke said, his voice loud and clipped in impatience. "May I introduce my sister, Lady Cassandra Sinclair. She has insisted on giving us the gift of her presence."

The young woman made a face at her older brother's sarcastic cut before bobbing a curtsey toward Hugh.

"My lady," he said in greeting.

"Don't mind the duke, Officer Marsden, he's almost as dull as the countryside," she said lightly, accepting the hand of a groomsman and mounting her sidesaddle.

He tried not to grin, but Audrey caught him at it.

"Your Grace," he said. She half-grinned before darting a look at the duke. Fournier had taken the reins of his mount and was speaking to the groomsman.

"The duke insisted," she said softly to Hugh.

"I understand." Riding out into the parkland alone, just the two of them, would have inspired gossip and speculation, and the duke would not have invited that. It was also possible he simply did not want his wife alone with another man.

The duchess mounted her own horse without the help of a groomsman. She did not ride sidesaddle either. The skirt of her riding habit was voluminous enough to accommodate, though her raised hem did show a peek of white stocking at the lip of her boots.

Hugh swiftly mounted, and a moment later, he was following the duke and duchess across a rolling stretch of lawn, toward a line of mature whitebeams. Lady Cassandra pulled her mount, a shiny sable, next to his roan.

"Is it very dangerous, being a Bow Street Runner?" she asked, forgoing pleasantries all together. It was something Hugh appreciated.

"The criminals I apprehend are, for the most part, not so dangerous as they are dim-witted."

She laughed, the sound a bit too bright for the task they were undertaking. He was relieved that he would not be finding a body at the bottom of the quarry, but then, that also limited him in his investigation.

"Audrey refuses to tell me anything specific about last April," the duke's sister went on, animated now. "I've asked and asked, but she has been so vague. The only thing she has parted with is that she was shot and fell into the Thames—something she made me swear to hold my tongue about—and that you rescued her."

Hugh's muscles tightened at the memory. The roan snuffled and pranced, feeling the change in its rider's mood. He'd watched, helpless, as Miss Lovejoy's murderer had shot Audrey, the duchess then toppling backward, into the soupy Thames. Thankfully, the gunshot had been a minor wound, but her dress and cloak were so heavy, she would have drowned had Hugh not been there to jump into the river and pull her onto the dock.

"I am glad I was there," he said, watching the duchess's straight back as she and the duke rode together into the stand of whitebeams. A path, wide and groomed, opened up before them. They followed it, the humid air cooling a little in the shade of the trees.

"I see you are just as reticent as my dear sister-in-law," Cassandra said gaily, and loud enough for Audrey and the duke to hear. "It does you credit, sir, not to boast of your heroics."

"I am hardly heroic," he replied, growing uncomfortable with her praise.

"Yes, society does have a different opinion of you altogether, doesn't it?"

"*Cassie.*" Audrey slowed her mount and turned in her saddle. She speared the young woman with a warning glare. "Leave Mr. Marsden in peace."

Cassandra pinned her lips together and sent Hugh an apologetic glance.

"It's all right," he told her. "No harm done. She only speaks the truth. Society does hold a low opinion of me."

"Surely, saving the Duchess of Fournier's life and proving the duke's innocence has gained you some clemency?" she replied, all too pleased to be forgiven and to launch back into the topic at hand.

The duke turned in his saddle. "Cassie, we'll speak no more of it. Forgive her, Marsden, my sister makes her debut next season and clearly does not yet know what is and is not proper conversation." He clucked to his horse and turned forward, only to then turn again, his frustration brimming. "Honestly, Cassie, for one who has lived with our tyrant of an aunt these last two years, I cannot see how you have not learned to curb your tongue."

The young lady sighed emphatically, and Hugh caught her rolling her eyes. "I blame my curiosity and loose tongue on my perpetual boredom this summer."

"May I remind you that you've been given opportunities to take your leave and find entertainment elsewhere? And that you have continually rejected them?" the duke retorted as he continued onward.

Cassandra made a face at the duke's back, and Hugh smothered a grin. She was certainly lively.

"I wish you good luck on your Season, my lady," he said.

Then a bit softer, "Perhaps you will find a match who does not mind *im*proper conversation."

Cassandra sighed dramatically, drawing a curious glance from the duchess. The thick boughs of the trees had thinned here, letting in golden late afternoon light. It shone on the dappled gray coat of her mare and glinted in the duchess's eyes.

"I am afraid there will be little variety of beaus and conversation to be found in London," Cassandra replied. "I cannot say I am hopeful. In fact, I'm not sure the Season is worth it."

"Cassie, you've been anticipating your Season since you were a little girl," Audrey said, sounding astonished. "I cannot believe you to be so indifferent."

Cassandra gave another apathetic sigh. "Perhaps if it were a love match, like yours and my brother's."

Again, Hugh stiffened in his saddle. He knew the truth: their match had been one of convention, not love. Apparently, they played out the farce well enough for even the duke's sister to believe it.

"When he's not so grumpy, he can be rather charming. Wouldn't you agree, Audrey?"

Charming? He'd come across to Hugh as an arrogant prat the few times he had met him. Perhaps it was just their first meeting that had colored his impression of the duke—covered in blood, incoherent, in the presence of a mutilated opera singer. Hugh supposed that might also be the reason why the duke was so standoffish with him. He'd seen him at his worst.

Audrey and Fournier rode side by side ahead, and at Cassandra's question, they each turned to look at the other. A grin touched both of their mouths. Hugh saw it then: their partnership.

He cleared his throat and ignored the shifting ballast in his gut. "Where is this quarry? How much further?"

The duchess faced forward. "A few minutes more."

"What does it produce?" he asked, wanting to divert the conversation from talk of love matches and marriage.

"Nothing anymore," the duke said. "The quarry was closed during my grandfather's tenure as duke. A lode of citrine was discovered when he was a young man and he thought to mine it. Diversify his holdings. However, the lode was not as large as projected, and neither was the demand for the gemstones."

"There is still some citrine, though," Cassandra said. "I've found whole nuggets of it in the ground around the quarry, right on the surface. The color is so beautiful, like liquid sunshine. I have several pieces lining the windows of my room."

Hugh bit back an amused grin. The duke's sister was spirited. Audrey, however, seemed uncharacteristically subdued. *Reticent*, Cassandra had called it. It was the duke's presence, he realized. It gave Hugh pause. Was she always like this when around him? Hugh wouldn't know; the time he had spent with Audrey had been free of the duke. The duchess Hugh knew spoke her mind. She was direct and stubborn.

"Up ahead," Audrey called, and a moment later, Hugh understood what she had meant when claiming Charlotte could not have accidentally come upon the cliff and fallen.

An acre or two of trees had been cleared around an open quarry pit. In the decades since its closure, grass, shrubs, and some young trees had sprung up, but the edge of the quarry was visible from a distance.

Hugh dismounted and looped his reins over the branch of a young oak. The duke and duchess also dismounted, but Cassandra stayed in her saddle. In silence, Hugh approached the ledge. He noticed then that it was unnaturally quiet. There was no birdsong, and the open sky above explained why. Dark clouds had rushed in while they had been riding through the forest path.

The bottom of the quarry pit was at least sixty, maybe

seventy, feet below. The duke's grandfather had done a lot of work, cutting away whole slabs of earth. The laborers he'd employed had left great blocks of stone and loose rubble to gather moss and weeds, and years upon years of leaf fodder had accumulated.

Audrey appeared in his periphery. She approached the ledge carefully, peering over the edge with hesitation. "She was there."

Below, Hugh saw the blood. It had spilled over a few of the larger chunks of scree. He knew what Audrey had seen, could picture it perfectly, and wished she could have been spared. If what she suspected was true, and someone else had been here, watching the duchess discover Lady Bainbury so soon after her death... He looked around the quarry and tried to figure where someone might have hidden. The trees were thinner here, which would have made the act of hiding more difficult to achieve.

"Over there," he said, pointing to where a stone hut covered in vines and half obscured by thorny brush sat about twenty yards from the quarry ledge. "What is that structure?"

Fournier removed his hat and wiped his brow. "One of the old quarry out buildings, I'm sure."

Hugh wanted to have a look inside, but first, he needed to descend into the open pit. There might not be a body, but he was almost positive the duke's men would not have done a meticulous search of the area when they came to fetch the countess.

He removed his tailcoat, gloves, and hat and dropped them unceremoniously onto the ground.

Audrey peered at him. "What are you doing?"

He had spied a route, though steep, down the side of the ledge, to the base of the quarry, and headed toward it now. "I'll be right back."

"Wait." She stepped forward. Then, untied the ribbons on her bonnet.

"Audrey," the duke said as both he and Hugh realized her intention. "You are not going down there. It is too dangerous."

The duchess Hugh remembered now returned. She removed her hat and handed it to Cassandra. The duke's sister took it, her eyes wide with amusement.

"I will be fine, Philip." She met Hugh at the edge, calmly dismissing her husband's order. Hugh swallowed a grin.

"I'll go first. Watch your step," he advised, and then began his descent.

The open pit had been cut away in blocks, leaving jutting ledges and crags. There were a few spots on the cliff wall that were sheer drops, but here, Hugh could find footing on his way down. It looked as though others had traversed it before too.

He paused to look up and check Audrey's progress. She was moving more slowly, needing to hold her skirts aside so she could see where to place her booted feet on the sloping ledge. Her other gloved hand braced the wall of the open pit. Fournier and Cassandra had come to the edge of the summit.

"What are you hoping to prove, Audrey?" the duke asked.

One of her boots slipped, scattering rubble. Hugh tensed, prepared to reach for her, but she steadied herself.

"I don't mean to prove anything," she replied, continuing her descent. "I want to see if Charlotte left anything behind."

Ah. Hugh understood now. She wanted an object to hold. Something to feed her a clue.

"That is thoughtful of you, dear sister, but do be careful," Cassandra called, oblivious to Audrey's gift.

Hugh kept moving, toward the base. The side of the open pit was an impressive display of mantle, showing layers of sediment. A few trees had grown out of it, their trunks curved to reach toward the sun. Vines, both bare and leafy, trailed down from the summit ledge as well. This place had been forgotten, and nature had slowly started to reclaim it.

He arrived at the base and turned to help Audrey, reaching out a hand in case she needed it. The last step down was steep. However, she sat onto the boulder step and pushed herself off easily, landing on deft feet. Hugh eyed the path back up but decided not to worry about scaling it just yet.

The ground was soft as Hugh walked toward the rocks splashed with the telling blood.

"Many quarries transform into lakes over time," he said, his eyes pinned onto the quarry floor.

"This one drains rather quickly." She stepped over the scree alongside him. "What are you looking for?"

"Evidence. Once you left to summon help, the other person might have climbed down here—if in fact there was another person."

"You doubt me."

"No. I doubt what you think you know."

"That is one and the same."

"I need evidence. We can go no further without it." It was as simple as that. Audrey nodded tightly, and Hugh continued to search the ground. He crouched by the bloodied rock, the color of it rusty and fading.

He spotted a few depressions of bootheels in the soft ground, but they could have belonged to the men who'd come to fetch the countess's body. He looked up, toward the summit. It loomed over them. A fall onto these rocks would have brought immediate death—at least he hoped it had. Hugh's stomach knotted at the thought of anyone suffering after a fall from such a height.

"There is nothing to be found down there," the duke called.

Hugh hated to admit that Fournier was probably right. As he straightened his legs, Audrey crouched on the other side of the same bloodied rock. She ran her palm over the tufts of grass that grew between the rubble. Then stood. Hugh watched as she slid her hand into the small pocket of her riding jacket.

"We should ascend," she said, walking quickly from the spot.

She'd found something. Hugh would have placed a hefty wager on it.

He followed her to the ledge path and motioned for her to climb first. She assessed the bottommost boulder, as if trying to decide how to scale it to begin her ascent.

"I'll give you a boost," he finally said, then crouched and laced his fingers, giving her a step for her to place her foot. As she did, he murmured, "What did you just put in your pocket?"

He lifted her up, and Audrey sat down hard onto the boulder. She glared at him, now at his eye level as he stood.

"Absolutely nothing," she whispered, turning to get onto her knees and then, onto her feet.

Hugh pushed himself up onto the boulder behind her. "Liar," he whispered.

She placed her hands onto the ledge, wedged in her foot, and shot a look over her shoulder. Hugh stood behind her on the boulder, eyebrow arched in challenge.

"Keep climbing, duchess," he said softly.

She whipped her head forward, facing the ledge again, and Hugh put every last ounce of his willpower into not observing the backside of her figure, or seeking a glimpse of her ankles, as she climbed the path ahead of him. He was warm and perspiring, even without his coat, when they reached the summit. The duke helped Audrey onto the ground above, his ire evident.

"That was absurd," Fournier said.

"Nonsense," she replied, brushing off her skirt and retrieving her hat from Cassandra. "It was rather invigorating, even if it yielded nothing."

Hugh picked up his coat, gloves, and hat, and took a quick look around the stone hut he'd spied earlier. Roots and vines had taken over, and only a few old, rusted tools were left, along with a withered table and some wooden buckets. Still, from this vantage point, he found he could peer through one of the open frame windows, out toward the quarry ledge, and be obscured by some thorny brush.

The duke eyed the slate sky. "Let us make haste. The weather is turning."

Audrey seemed all too eager to comply, and Hugh figured it was due to whatever she had slipped into her pocket.

They rode about five minutes from the quarry, until Audrey pulled her mount to a stop.

"Here," she said. "This was where Charlotte was when I saw her running. I was up there, at the top of that field." She pointed through the gap in a stone wall, into a sloping field of lush green grass and wildflowers.

Ahead, a narrow footpath wove through the trees, roughly following the stone wall.

"What lies in that direction?" he asked.

"Haverfield," the duke replied. "Lord Edgerton's estate."

Hugh turned toward Audrey. "Your former home?"

She hitched her chin, as if in defiance of the very thought of it. "Yes. About two miles through the woods."

"What would she have been doing coming from there?"

"Fournier Downs stretches over thirty thousand acres," Fournier said, impatience thinning his tone. "This land borders several properties and intersects with multiple walking paths. She might not have been coming from Haverfield specifically."

The duke's displeasure was nearly as palpable as the coming storm. Hugh drew a deep breath to keep from biting back with some equally arrogant retort. Instead, he pinned the duke with a prolonged glare before taking a second look toward the top of the field where Audrey claimed to have been. From such a distance, Lady Bainbury should have been able to hear the duchess hailing her. However, if she'd been running, her own rapid breaths might have been too loud in her ears. Fear could have also narrowed her focus.

The first drops of rain pelted Hugh's cheek. They turned back toward the house then, riding at a faster clip than before. Though they went through the woods and the boughs blocked much of the rain, they were still soaked through by the time they returned to the stable yard.

Audrey dismounted and shook out her skirts.

"Mr. Marsden, you must come in and dry off," she said, breathless. "I'll call for tea."

Hugh's muscles clenched at the thought of sitting down to tea with the duke and duchess. "I've already taken up too much of your time. I'll make my way back into town."

Basil had secured rooms at an inn and tavern where the inquest for Lady Bainbury would be held the following day. Apparently, the back room at the inn was the designated place for death inquests. Made for good business, Hugh supposed. After the inquest, those in attendance would be likely driven to discuss their findings over a pint.

"My best in your investigation, officer," Cassandra said, then turned toward the manor.

Hugh bobbed his head but stayed upon his horse, his trousers thoroughly soaked.

"Thank you for your assistance, Your Grace," he called to the duke, who was attending to his mount with care rather than turning it over to a groom; it was the mark of a true horseman. He grudgingly acknowledged Hugh with a nod and then led his horse toward a stall.

Hugh eyed the duchess, who had removed her hat again. She met his testing stare with one of her own.

"You said you would stay clear of my investigation," he reminded her, his attention slipping to her jacket pocket.

"You want to know what it shows me," she replied. "You know you do."

He groaned, sopping wet and frustrated. The insolent woman was correct.

"If it is anything of import, find me," he snapped, and then dug his heels into his horse's side and rode onward, away from Fournier House.

CHAPTER
FIVE

Not for the first time, Audrey wished she had applied herself to her art lessons when she'd been younger. Her older sister, Millie, had been more than competent at her landscapes and had seemed to thoroughly enjoy the hours she would spend at the easel. Several of her pieces had been pleasing enough to their mother to even be framed and hung on the walls of various rooms in Haverfield. Even James had possessed artistic talent, though nothing so formal as painting. Her brother had carved works of art with his knife, which she recalled him keeping in his pocket at all times. He'd whittle a plain stick into a writhing snake, an ugly knob of wood into a miniature horse or toadstool or hunting hound—whatever struck his fancy.

Once, he'd returned from school with a whole nautilus shell, the exterior polished to a glimmering pearl and carefully etched with a woodland scene. Audrey had thought it was his most beautiful creation yet when he set it into the palm of her hand and told her it was hers to keep. She still had it, the small shell one of her most precious treasures.

As she sat in the breakfast room at Fournier House the

morning after their ride to the quarry, Audrey's fingers itched to at least try to sketch what she had seen the night before when she'd held the object she'd found and pocketed. Though, not as discreetly as she'd believed. Mr. Marsden had seen her. The man was too sharp-eyed—or perhaps she was too clumsy.

With her riding glove on, the button—round, brown, and thick, certainly from a man's coat—had not passed its energy into her. Even as they climbed back out of the open quarry pit, she allowed that the button might belong to one of the footmen or stable hands who'd come to collect Charlotte's body. There had been scattered boot prints in the damp floor of the quarry and in working to lift the countess, a thread might have snapped, a loose button set free.

But later that evening, when Audrey had been able to steal some time alone in her bedroom, she'd taken the button into her palm and allowed the object's memories to unfurl before her eyes.

It was like seeing a different reality playing on the backs of her eyelids. Indeed, the most recent one was of herself, finding the object. Pushing backward through the memories, she viewed the men in the open pit through an unsettling vantage point; it had been as though Audrey herself was lying upon the ground, watching them as they fetched her body. Audrey pushed further back, and even though by then the button's energy was fading along with the clarity of images, she was rewarded: Charlotte, throwing up her arms in defense as the owner of the button rushed toward her at the edge of the quarry. A struggle where Charlotte battered at her assailant and tried to fight. And then, the blurred confusion of a fall that ended in utter stillness.

Audrey tried to see more, but the images faded to murk, then pitch. An object only retained so much energy, and she could never anticipate how much or how little. Sometimes, the well of energy was deep, and other times, shallow. There was no rhyme or reason.

She wished she could draw what she'd seen, even if there had been nothing definitive of the person who had been wearing the article of clothing the button had been on. After breakfast, Audrey called for her brougham. Thankfully, she hadn't yet seen Philip, and she hoped to be gone from Fournier House before he left for The Hare and Crown, Low Heath's posting-inn, where the inquest was being held at noon. Ladies weren't permitted at death inquests, but men of import in the surrounding area were. Philip, as duke and veritable owner of the village, was one such man.

Now, riding toward town, she held the button in her hand, observing the dormant object. Someone had pushed Charlotte from the quarry ledge. There was no doubt anymore in Audrey's mind. Finding the person could be as easy as finding the owner of a coat missing one of its buttons. But where to begin looking?

Mr. Marsden—*Hugh* as she had started to think of him, especially since he'd blundered and called her by her given name—had asked her to stay out of it. Well, how could she? He knew what she could do. He wanted to know what the button had shown her, too. As she rode toward the inn, she told herself she was only going to meet with him and share what she'd gleaned. But then, she considered the inquest itself. By law, Charlotte's remains were to be laid out for inspection and observation, to view any injury or signs of foul play. So, considering it was nearly noon, that meant her body was likely at the inn. Perhaps some other objects that had been on her person at the time of the accident would be as well.

She closed her eyes. Not *accident*. Audrey knew better, even if no one else did.

Seeing Charlotte's body again was not something she looked forward to. In fact, the notion sent shivers through her,

her breath coming short and rapid. At their last tea, Charlotte had been speaking of the first dinner ball she would be hosting upon her return to London for the Little Season. She had been animated, full of life. To see her body, her soul now having flown from it, would not be an easy thing. But if it gave Audrey even the slightest advantage in finding out who had pushed her, she would do it.

The Hare and Crown in Low Heath was a stop along the post road, not just for passenger coaches but for the Royal Mail, and so the establishment was usually bustling. However today, more carriages than usual surrounded the inn and tavern. A death inquest would attract curious onlookers, even if they were not officially taking part in the proceedings.

At Audrey's earlier instruction, Kinson, her driver, pulled the carriage around the Hare and Crown, to the stable yard. She had not wanted to enter through the front door when she'd only been planning to seek out Hugh Marsden. Now that she had a new destination in mind, she wanted to remain unseen even more so.

She waited as Kinson descended from the driver's box and opened the door.

In London, Audrey had her ever-reliable driver Carrigan. Here, her driver was less amiable and, she sensed, more judgmental. Kinson had been the driver at Fournier House for two decades, and Audrey had the impression he was not fond of the most recent duchess. Perhaps he objected to her ties to Haverfield—cold and aloof, Lady Edgerton and the baron were not well liked in the area. Often, she wondered if she was just as cold and aloof as her mother. Audrey didn't smile readily or converse easily; she was reserved, rather than outgoing. Having Cassandra with them this summer had only highlighted how staid Audrey was in comparison. She'd never been as bubbly, coy, or jovial as Cassie and so many other women were.

However, as Kinson helped her down from the conveyance, she knew pretending to be someone other than who she was would be a sham. Audrey didn't have the patience or the wherewithal for it.

"You may return to Fournier House to fetch the duke," she said.

Philip was fond of riding, but the outing yesterday had exhausted him. His malaise from earlier in the summer had weakened him a great deal, and he was only getting his strength back now. Instead of riding to Low Heath, Audrey was certain he would call for a carriage.

"Your Grace, if I may, it would be more suitable if I stay—"

"It isn't necessary, Kinson. The duke will be expecting you, and I have business here in the meanwhile."

Honey-coated words would simply never be her method. Besides, the longer she stood outside speaking to her driver, the greater the chance that someone might see her and waylay her.

Audrey went inside through a back door, one reserved for patrons seeking the outhouse, or a waitress wanting a few minutes in the fresh air, sitting on one of the stools propped nearby.

Inside, a hallway led to the back storeroom. According to Philip, who'd heard it from his valet, Charlotte's body had been transferred from the Fournier icehouse to Lord Bainbury's own icehouse, and it had now been transferred just that morning to the inn for the inquest. If not for Audrey's theories regarding the manner of death, the local magistrate, Lord Webber, would have most likely never contacted the county coroner to come hold the inquest in the first place. How her body had been handled, cleaned, or scoured for any telling evidence concerned her as she approached the storeroom door. But there was nothing to be done about that now.

Pulse quickening, she glanced over her shoulder, to be sure

she had gone unobserved, and twisted the doorknob. She peeked inside the room and let out a breath when she saw it was, indeed, empty. Well. Not entirely. Audrey closed the door, her eyes pinned on the white-sheeted figure of her dear friend.

Charlotte had always been similar to Audrey in temperament; she wasn't given to moods or flights of fancy, and though she smiled and laughed more than Audrey did, she did not giggle—ever. While Audrey was more serious and reserved, Charlotte had been the one to more easily form acquaintances. With Charlotte, Audrey always felt like she belonged. Like she'd found a sort of kindred spirit. Like Audrey had been with Philip, Charlotte had been far too practical to hold out for a love match. Though, Audrey had always felt a bit guilty for causing the earl to go searching for a new betrothed in the first place.

Somehow, seeing her now, a corpse beneath a plain cotton sheet, felt more dramatic than seeing her at the bottom of the quarry. This was just so *final*.

Audrey approached the table where she'd been laid out. When she peeled the top of the sheet back with trembling fingers, she was relieved to see the body was clothed. She wore a simple square-collared white linen chemise. Her hair had been washed free of blood. Crudely done sutures were visible beginning at her hairline and traveling back, toward the rear of her skull. Bruising on her left cheek, temple, and jawline made Audrey wonder, with a clench of her stomach, if that was the side on which she had made impact with the rocks on the quarry floor.

A burst of muted conversation from the front tavern room reached her, and Audrey quickly peeled down the sheet a little lower. Her arms were bare, showing bruising on the left side as well. However, at Charlotte's right wrist was a set of deep scratches and some more bruising. With a dawning suspicion, Audrey hovered her fingers over the marks. They seemed to adhere to the shape of her fingers. Someone had gripped Charlotte's wrist so tightly that it had caused injury.

Audrey stepped closer to the table, and her toe collided with something on the floor. A small leather satchel. It had no business in a storeroom full of food stuffs, crockery, and barrels. It likely had to do with Charlotte. She crouched and opened the satchel to find a folded day dress and a pair of lady's boots. Without taking the items out of the satchel, she could see that the dress was soiled with dirt and blood. It was the white dress Charlotte had been wearing at the time of her death.

Fabric was notoriously difficult to read. It could be done, of course, so with eyes closed, Audrey gathered the crumpled cambric into her hands and allowed the energy inside her mind. Perhaps it was the sheer terror Charlotte had felt while running through the wood and fighting off her attacker that imbued the cambric with such clear energy, but Audrey took in the memories with both relief and dread. Pushing past the more recent handling of the gown by the earl's servants, Audrey also plunged past the event of her fall—the button had shown her enough of that. Instead, she waded into the murkier memories of the minutes before that. Nudging backward through memories was like sinking her head under the surface of bathwater and then coming up for air. With every gasp of oxygen, the energy showed her something different.

As Audrey parted the surface one last time, it was to a misty, practically opaque, memory. Charlotte stood within a room of stone walls; the floor was littered with dry leaves and dirt. Ahead of her was an arched doorway. Beyond that, only trees. The room was bare, with numerous arched window casements, absent of shutters. The energy was giving its last gasps when a figure passed by one of the window casements. A woman wearing a simple straw chip hat, trimmed with a wide, yellow silk ribbon. And then, darkness descended.

Audrey opened her eyes and stared at the cambric crumpled in her hands, willing her mind to sear the memory of the woman in the straw chip hat—what little she could see of her —into her brain. She would attempt to sketch it when she returned home.

Voices boomed in the corridor. Then, the heavy tramping of feet. Audrey stuffed the clothing into the satchel and stood to hastily pull the sheet back over her friend's body. She'd barely taken a step away from the table and clasped her hands behind her back when the door to the storeroom opened. Lord Webber, the magistrate, another man Audrey did not recognize, and Hugh Marsden were the first three to enter. Their eyes landed on her as more men filed in, each one's eyes alighting on Audrey with surprise and shock, Philip and her uncle, Lord Edgerton, included. Only Hugh cocked an eyebrow with clear amusement at her misfortune.

"Oh good," Audrey said brightly, her heart thumping wildly. "I'm not too late for the inquest, I see."

CHAPTER
SIX

H ugh crossed his arms as the Duke of Fournier parted through the room of tightly packed shoulders to reach the duchess's side.

"What is the meaning of this?" the coroner, a man named Wilkes, asked.

Audrey, her chin hitched, replied, "I think it only right that I be included in this inquest, as I am, in fact, the person who discovered Lady Bainbury after her death."

It wasn't a wholly unreasonable request. However, Hugh was almost certain the duchess had not let herself into the storeroom in advance of the rest of their party to simply await the inquest. She had surely been doing a bit of her own *investigating*. By the rumpled state of the sheet covering the body, he presumed she'd already peeled it aside to have a look at the countess. His eyes went to a leather bag on the floor next to the table. The top was open. She'd been poking around in that, too, he suspected.

"You are a woman," the local magistrate, Lord Webber, said, rather needlessly.

"Such keen observation, my lord," she replied lightly, her voice sweeter than she'd ever deemed Hugh worthy of.

Lord Edgerton cleared his throat, his niece's sarcasm not lost on him. Hugh had just made the baron's acquaintance at the front of the tavern, the introduction made by Fournier. As expected, Edgerton had dismissed Hugh with a sniff.

"I have witness evidence to give in the events surrounding Lady Bainbury's death," the duchess pressed.

"Women are not permitted at death inquests, Your Grace," Dr. Wilkes said, with a short, polite bow. "However, I will accept written testimony should you wish to give it."

Fournier slipped his hand around Audrey's elbow. "My dear, why don't I see you to the carriage."

Audrey patted the duke's hand, still smiling serenely. It began to frighten Hugh some. She was certainly showing too much tooth.

"I can see myself out, darling, thank you. If you'll just walk me to the door?"

There was a great shuffling of legs as the jury formed a gap to allow the duchess and duke through. The storeroom wasn't large enough for a jury of twelve men. There was something indecent about cramming the dozen of them into this back room to observe the dead body of a countess. In the few moments of disorder, Hugh observed the duchess whispering something into the duke's ear. Fournier's brows tensed. Then, a look of vexed exasperation crossed his face as he opened the storeroom door and all but shoved her into the hall. Whatever she'd imparted, the duke was not pleased.

"Quite irregular," Lord Webber said once the door was shut again.

Fournier met Hugh's eyes briefly before rejoining the jury around the table. In the tavern, the coroner had laid out the rules of the inquest. Wilkes had made it clear that Hugh was not one of the twelve jurors—he was not an impartial witness, as he had been hired by Lady Prescott to investigate. He was welcome to observe, however. Though a man of middling age, height, and appearance, Hugh sensed in Wilkes a sharp intellect. Unlike the local magistrate, he gave every indication that he took his duties seriously. That, at least, Hugh could appreciate.

"Let us begin, gentlemen," Wilkes said now, unwilling to linger on the duchess's unexpected presence. "We are gathered to determine the cause of death for Lady Charlotte Marie Bainbury, the Countess of Bainbury. Upon inspection of the deceased's remains, I can conclude that the method of death is consistent with a fall from a significant height. Several fractured bones, massive contusions, and a ruptured cranium are all sufficient evidence."

Wilkes drew back the sheet, revealing only her neck and head. The men shifted their footing. Hugh had seen his share of corpses, but when they were that of women or children, he never failed to feel a weightier pang of remorse. There was no avoiding the twist of his stomach at the sight of this woman's heavily bruised face and misshapen skull.

"Now, we are left to determine the cause of the fall," Wilkes continued. "Whether it be accidental, misadventure, self-inflicted, or murder. We can all agree to rule out any natural causes of death."

"Lord Bainbury believes it to be misadventure," Lord Webber imparted. "He says that his wife enjoyed taking walks in the parkland surrounding their estate. She often walked unaccompanied. She most likely slipped and fell."

The earl himself was not present, as he would surely not be an impartial member of the jury. However, it seemed he had the magistrate well in hand.

"Noted," Wilkes said. "I have spoken to his lordship as well, and he cannot account for why her ladyship would have been so far afield from their own parkland. He suggests she lost her way or was perhaps taking a woodland route to visit Her Grace, the Duchess of Fournier."

"If she commonly took walks on the footpaths surrounding her estate, I find it difficult to believe she would have lost her way," Hugh said.

"Lady Bainbury visited Fournier Downs often, however never on foot," the duke added before Wilkes could admonish Hugh for speaking, rather than just observing. "She sent no card ahead on the day of her death to indicate she would be paying a call."

Surely, the coroner would see Lord Bainbury's suggestions were weak and insipid. Among the jury, there were a handful of men who looked to be farmers and common laborers, and one man who might have been gentry. None of them had any personal stake in naming the cause of death. They resided on Fournier Downs lands, not Bainbury's smaller estate, which Hugh had learned since his arrival did not encompass any formal village such as this.

Lord Edgerton again cleared his throat. "As unseemly as the topic is, we must take into account the possibility that her ladyship intentionally put her life to an end."

"Do you have any evidence to reflect that theory, my lord?" Wilkes asked.

"Her melancholy was well known," the baron replied.

The duke canted his head, wearing an expression of doubt. "Melancholy? This is the first I am hearing of such a disposition."

Lord Edgerton regarded Fournier with a smug arch of his brow. "Forgive me, Your Grace, but perhaps such common knowledge failed to penetrate the noble walls of Fournier House."

The baron shared a conspiratorial glance with a few of the other gathered men. From their answering smirks, Hugh immediately understood that the baron shared an alliance with the commoners that the duke did not. He seemed the sort to visit the tavern on a regular basis, buying rounds of ale.

The duke regarded the baron with cool dislike, and then the man Hugh considered as possible gentry stepped forward. Though he was handsome and appeared youthful, the lines surrounding his eyes betrayed his age. Probably in his fourth decade, though with no graying hair to be seen. His clothing was of good quality, if not fashionable. His hands were ungloved but clean, with no callouses to speak of. He wore wire rim glasses, a high, starched collar and a cravat tied in a tall Napoleon style.

"As Lady Bainbury's physician, I would like to provide evidence that could, ah, possibly, correspond to the baron's suggestion," he said.

"Doctor Ryder, if I remember correctly from our introduction?" Wilkes said.

"That's correct," the doctor said with a timid nod.

The coroner waved his hand. "Go on."

"Yes, as I said, I am Lady Bainbury's physician and, though I hesitate to offer what are private dealings between myself and the lady, I can confirm that the countess was indeed melancholy after suffering two miscarriages this last year."

"When did these occur?" the coroner asked without delay or surprise.

"Ah, yes, well, I do have the exact dates in my notes in my office, but if I recall, the first was in September, and the second was early March."

Doctor Ryder didn't exude confidence, which Hugh thought a little odd. His own good friend, Grant Thornton, the fourth son of the Marquess of Lindstrom, and thus left to make his way in the world, had become a physician as well—much to his father's discontent and the ton's ridicule. Thornton was anything but wavering.

"And when did you observe her melancholy?" Wilkes asked.

"We met regularly. Often weekly. I would prescribe a tincture to help her, as she was quite distressed in not being able to provide a child for the earl."

Hugh recalled something the duchess said when he'd met her at Greely Park. "The earl and countess wed how long ago? Nearly three years?"

Doctor Ryder, Lord Edgerton, and several others exchanged quizzical looks, while Wilkes speared him with a look of warning. As it was a question, rather than a comment, he remained patient.

Fournier replied, "Just under three years, yes. They married a few months after the duchess and I."

Hugh gritted his molars, understanding why Fournier would recall the time so clearly. Audrey had been betrothed to Bainbury first; the poor woman laid out on the table now had, in a way, taken her place. "And you say only just this last year the countess became distraught over not bearing a child?" That seemed oddly...belated.

"Who is to say she was not distraught beforehand?" Lord Edgerton replied. "Perhaps she has been unable to carry a child to term since they wed."

"That is speculation, my lord, whereas we must deal in fact," Wilkes replied, earning a sneer from the baron. "Doctor, have you any knowledge of any previous miscarriages? She had a physician in London as well, I presume."

"Yes. Doctor Lewis. She did not mention any previous, ah, delicate conditions."

Wilkes paced next to the table, silent for a few moments as if deliberating upon the information that the doctor provided. From his time as a foot patrolman, Hugh knew some melancholy women threw themselves into the Thames or consumed an overdose of laudanum to put themselves out of misery. However, Lord Edgerton's claim, along with Doctor Ryder's feeble suggestion, didn't convince him that the countess would take such drastic measures.

Wilkes came to a stop at the head of the table. "Does anyone have any further evidence to present?"

Hugh glanced at the duke. Audrey had testimony; as she was not permitted to give it herself, it was the duke's responsibility to share it. Lords Webber and Edgerton also turned to Fournier. There was no question the magistrate had shared Audrey's claims with the baron; he'd likely already spread the tale far and wide.

Fournier appeared pained as he took a breath and stepped forward. "Her Grace was riding on Fournier Downs parkland Tuesday afternoon. She saw Lady Bainbury running through the woods a distance from where Her Grace was with her horse. My wife called out to her, but the countess appeared frantic and did not respond. Her Grace followed in the direction the countess was taking and came upon her body in the old citrine quarry pit."

Hugh cleared his throat, annoyed by the duke's omission of one key piece of information. "I have heard this testimony from the duchess as well and would like to add that Her Grace also heard a woman's scream shortly before she found the countess at the quarry pit."

Fournier narrowed his eyes on Hugh but confirmed the additional information with a terse nod.

"So then, the last person to see the victim while she was alive was Her Grace, the Duchess of Fournier. Her Grace is also the person to have found the body," Wilkes summarized.

Though these were just facts, hearing them lined up next to one another and the tone of Wilkes' voice put Hugh on alert.

"That is correct," the duke replied.

"Was the duchess riding with an attendant? A companion, perhaps?"

"No. She was alone, as she usually is when riding." The duke looked unperturbed, clearly not catching on to Wilkes' line of questioning.

"And what would you say was the duchess's relationship with the deceased?"

"They were very good friends."

"No tensions between them? No animosity?"

Fournier's icy glare finally cut toward the coroner. "None. I do not care for whatever it is you are insinuating."

Wilkes held up a hand, palm forward. "No disrespect is intended, Your Grace, I am simply reviewing all facts and possibilities, as my duty requires."

"The fact is," Hugh said, risking a reprimand from the coroner, "the only reason you were summoned, Dr. Wilkes, is because the duchess petitioned Lord Webber for an inquest. He was ready to forgo the cost of a coroner and certify the death as accidental."

Webber glared at Hugh, his fleshy chin cutting into the starched points of his collar, but it would take more than a county magistrate to cow him.

"Her Grace's testimony casts serious doubt onto the theories of death by accident or misadventure," Hugh went on.

"Officer Marsden, I am in agreement, however I will ask you to allow me to conduct this inquest as I see fit," Wilkes said.

Hugh nodded in assent, unsurprised and undeterred by the set down. If anything, it gave him hope.

"Now, if we can—" Wilkes began.

"May we view the body as a whole?" the duke interrupted.

The request was met with more uncomfortable foot shuffling. The gathered men exchanged curious glances as the duke held his chin high. The man hardly looked as if he'd like to see the body as a whole; in fact, his coloring was a little peaky.

Wilkes only hesitated a moment. "Yes, of course. That is only proper for an inquest." He then retracted the length of the sheet covering the countess. She wore a simple cap-sleeved chemise, which reached to just below the knee.

"Is this really necessary?" Lord Edgerton asked, looking away from the body. "It is unseemly."

"Death is often such," Wilkes replied, brushing off the baron with admirable restraint. Hugh wasn't sure he could have been so tactful. "Your Grace, did you have a particular question in mind?"

Fournier cast a quick glance toward the countess's bared arms. Bruises discolored the length of the left arm, while the right only had a few around the wrist, along with some scratches.

"How do you find the bruising, Dr. Wilkes? Consistent with a fall into the quarry?" the duke asked.

Hugh clamped down on his inner cheek to keep a grin from forming. The duchess had whispered something into the duke's ear upon leaving the storeroom. She'd put him up to this.

"Yes, I was coming to that," Wilkes said, taking a prolonged look at the duke. Then, "Observe the scratches and the bruises around her right wrist."

Hugh did, and then realized why Audrey had wanted them pointed out during the inquest.

"They aren't consistent with a fall from the quarry," Hugh said.

"Correct," Wilkes said, with another blasé glance at Hugh. "They appear to have been inflicted very soon *before* death."

"Those scratches," one of the farmers said, speaking up for the first time. "Are they from some scrub brush? Thorns?"

"Possibly," Wilkes replied. But then, he placed his own fingers along the four gouged lines on her wrist and demonstrated what Hugh thought: that they were more in line with a person's fingernails.

By all accounts, it looked as if someone had grabbed the countess's wrist, and in the struggle, left behind evidence.

The jurors glanced toward the magistrate. Conflict darkened his expression. His acquaintance with the earl was well known, and Hugh knew he was not the only man standing here wondering if Lord Webber had obscured some pertinent knowledge.

"I suppose it would be in order for me to raise some questions with Bainbury," he muttered after a few moments.

"Very good. I will join you," Wilkes replied. He brought the sheet higher, covering the body. "I do not believe we have enough information at this point to conclusively determine the cause of death. Are we in agreement? Please make your opinions known."

Nods and murmurs of assent followed, though Lord Edgerton grumbled, "What now? Are we to meet again another day? The poor woman requires a burial."

"She will receive one, my lord, in due time. Thank you for attending gentlemen." Wilkes took a small bow toward the grouping of men, dismissing them. He then said, "Your Grace, Officer Marsden, might I have a word?"

Hugh anticipated a scathing reprimand from the coroner—for a simple, unobtrusive observer, he had been rather loquacious.

Wilkes waited until the room cleared before relaxing his shoulders somewhat. After a protracted moment, he said, "Your Grace, I do not believe your wife is a murderess."

"What a relief," Fournier replied dryly.

"Her witness testimony worries me. It could appear to the wrong party that she knows more than she does."

The duke remained stone-faced, but Hugh suspected Wilkes was saying something Fournier had already considered. Besides the killer himself, Audrey likely knew more than anyone. She'd also found something at the quarry. What had it shown her?

"I would like to request the use of your icehouse to store the deceased for the time being," Wilkes added. "Your estate's proximity to Low Heath would be more convenient for the proceedings."

Hugh also assumed the coroner did not want to relinquish the countess into the hands of a possible suspect.

"Very well," Fournier replied. He gave a sad glance toward the body. It was a sorry thought indeed, storing the remains of an acquaintance.

Wilkes nodded, the bob of his head solemn and respectful. Fournier cut Hugh a cool glance, then left the storeroom.

Wilkes visibly relaxed even further now that all the titled men were gone. It was only the two of them; two blue collar working men who dealt with death and justice on a regular basis. Wilkes crossed his arms and arched a brow.

Hugh gestured toward the sheeted body with his hat. "You know she was pushed."

"I do not believe she was alone at the quarry when she fell."

Hugh grinned. Wilkes knew what he was about, he'd give him that much. "You're joining Lord Webber for his interview with Bainbury. I wanted to interview the earl myself. Perhaps we could confer after the fact and see if there are any discrepancies."

Wilkes wagged a finger. "You have a horse in this race, Marsden. Lady Prescott is paying you to declare this death anything but suicide, isn't that correct?"

"She is paying me to deliver the truth surrounding her daughter's death. I've promised nothing more than that."

The coroner seemed to accept his reply, but he still peered at Hugh with a calculating gaze. "You arrested Fournier in the spring for murder, and from what I have heard, helped secure his exoneration as well. Rumor has it you and the duchess herself hunted down the true killer."

Hugh wondered what other rumors the coroner had heard, but he appreciated the succinct phrasing.

"Her Grace has a keen mind," Hugh allowed.

"I hear she was shot."

Hugh grimaced. "She could have been a bit more careful."

Where the devil had Wilkes heard that? He supposed, as it had happened in the light of day at the wharf, onlookers must have started passing around the story.

The coroner stood straighter and lowered his arms to his side. "I don't want her involved in this investigation."

Good luck with that, Hugh wanted to say. Instead, he simply replied, "She isn't. She is merely a witness."

Wilkes's facial expressions were aggravatingly serene; Hugh couldn't tell what he was thinking. Most people did not have that mastery, and as a Bow Street officer dealing with liars on a regular basis, Hugh was thankful for it.

"I've taken lodgings here for the time being," Wilkes said. "I am sure we will meet to discuss our findings?"

Hugh nodded, grateful. The man wanted answers just as much as he did.

He left the storeroom, a knot of tension in his shoulders. No sooner had he started toward the front of the tavern with a vision of a tankard of ale to wet his parched throat, a knobby-boned runt leaped into the hall, nearly tripping him.

"Christ, Sir, what were you doing? Hiding in the woodwork?"

The boy grinned, pleased with his ability to startle. "Got this for ya." He handed over a small square of paper, folded in half but not sealed. Hugh plucked it from Sir's fingers—which were cleaner than usual, he noticed. He must have submitted to Basil's entreaties and bathed.

Hugh opened the paper and read two words: *Your room.*

A swell of agitation and something entirely dangerous flooded his stomach and chest. Hugh crumpled the note in his fist and met Sir's circumspect gaze.

"Whistle twice if there is trouble headed toward my room."

The lad gave a sharp nod, and Hugh headed for the stairs.

CHAPTER
SEVEN

A udrey did not dare pace the small room above the tavern. Too close to the window and she might be seen by someone outside; too close to the door, and someone might spy her shadow at the gap between the floor and the foot of the door. What she was doing was absurd, of course. If someone were to find her in Hugh Marsden's room, it would not just be herself to suffer the consequences. But she had to speak to him. Had to tell him all she knew, and Low Heath was too small to give the two of them any privacy at all.

Philip must have already been on his way to the village when Kinson had started back for Fournier House. Surely, he had directed the driver back to Low Heath, and had expected Audrey to wait in the carriage after she was all but tossed out of the inquest. When Philip did not find her there, he might search for her. Or he might assume she'd set out on foot for Fournier House; he knew she was self-sufficient in that regard. He'd take the carriage home, expecting to see her along the route, or find her when he arrived. Her absence would worry him; so, Audrey knew she only had a handful of minutes once the principal officer arrived.

The scrubby street boy that she recalled from the spring had come along with Hugh to Hertfordshire; the lad, Sir, had simply appeared at her side as she left the storeroom. "Got anything for me to do, duchess?" he'd asked by way of greeting.

The idea had come to her in a flash. Reckless. Stupid. And she'd berated herself for the next thirty minutes while she waited in Hugh's room. The boy had likely read the note—if he could read—but Audrey did not think he was a threat at all. He seemed devoted to Hugh Marsden. Audrey had touched door-knobs down the narrow, twisting upstairs corridor until she'd found the one that gave up the image of Hugh closing it that very morning. Picking the lock had been easy; it was a skill she'd refined while at Shadewell Sanatorium, and she kept extra hair pins in her reticule at all times now, just in case. There was something about locked doors that made Audrey tense; she never wanted to find herself locked in somewhere again, without a tool to employ for an escape. Of course, it wasn't lost on her that she had used her pins lately to break in to rooms, rather than out of them.

However, with circumstances so dire, she determined the risk was acceptable. Charlotte had been killed; Audrey could not sit back and trust that the men downstairs would do right by her. Well...*most* of the men at least.

She had settled herself into a cane-back chair next to the slim bed, though her legs were restless to move. Her skin prickled with suppressed nerves. Hugh's traveling case was tucked under the bed; his shaving kit lay on a bureau alongside some little jars. His bedding was meticulously made. As the floorboards in the corridor creaked and footsteps approached the door, Audrey tensed.

The doorknob twisted, and Hugh came inside, closing the door quickly behind him. Audrey sprang from the chair as his eyes clapped onto her.

She held up a hand. "I know what you're going to say."

He clenched his jaw. "Then you should listen to my imaginary voice in your head and leave. *Immediately*."

His tone was soft, but Audrey didn't know if it was out of caution or anger.

"You wanted to know what I found at the quarry," she reminded him. "And what I saw."

"You did not need to come to my room to inform me."

"Then tell me, Mr. Marsden, where else could we go to discuss it without being seen?" she asked, getting annoyed. And a little hurt by *his* annoyance.

He groaned. Then stepped further into the room and shrugged out of his jacket. "Very well. Tell me what you saw— both instances. I know you were in that storeroom downstairs *touching* things."

She gaped at him. "You make it sound lewd!"

He hushed her with a pointed glare, then tossed his jacket onto the bed. It was overly warm in the room, what with one small window and a lack of any air currents. He stood in his waistcoat and shirtsleeves, hands on his hips, waiting for her to speak.

Audrey averted her eyes and explained the vision she gleaned from the coat button, and then, the images that had come to her when she held Charlotte's dress. One blurry-faced man in a coat and hat; one woman in a straw chip hat.

"The button isn't much in itself," she said, pulling it from her reticule and holding it out to Hugh. He hesitated, then stepped forward and took it from her palm. "But it belongs to the man who struggled with Charlotte at the quarry. I know my visions count for nothing with the law, but her bruised wrist, those scratches...they are evidence, are they not?"

Hugh inspected the button, turning it over in his hand. "The coroner agrees the death is suspicious in nature. He's going to investigate further."

Relief spiraled through her. Audrey let out a gust of air and even allowed a small smile. "Oh, thank goodness. That's excellent." When Hugh lifted his eyes from the button and he was still glowering, Audrey pulled back. "You aren't happy? But now you can investigate, unhindered."

"Happy?" He tossed the button onto the bed; it landed atop his jacket. "Not entirely, no. I want to find whoever this man was in your vision. I want justice for Lady Bainbury. But I don't like that your witness testimony might agitate him."

Audrey wasn't particularly fond of that either. "But what more could this person possibly think I know? I've already given my account. I didn't see anyone." When Hugh gave her a withering look, she shrugged. "Well, no one, *officially*. And the woman in the hat was barely visible. I can try to sketch her, but I don't know what good it will do."

Hugh scrubbed a hand over his jaw and turned away. He walked across the room, farther away from her, and Audrey took a deeper breath of air. His masculine scent of musky oakmoss lingered.

"Lady Bainbury was inside a stone structure, you say?" he asked, repeating what she'd explained from her vision.

"Yes. It was in the woods, and it can't be too far from where I first saw her, running. It looked like a shell of an old stone cottage."

"On Fournier Downs parkland?"

She shook her head. "I don't know. Perhaps. I could search for it—"

"*No*." Hugh paced back toward her. His dark eyes were expressive enough; he needn't have said anything more to make his opinion clear. But he went on after a calming breath. "You've promised to stay out of this investigation."

She squirmed and wished she could take back the vow. "If I could only find the cottage and touch it, I might be able to learn something more useful."

"I don't want you going into those woods alone," he said, his voice deeper than before.

Audrey bristled. "I would not be so dense as to go alone. I'm sure I can convince Cassie to come with me."

"And several footmen," he grumbled.

She rolled her eyes. But she understood his worry; she'd been rash when she'd gone in search for Mr. Fellows's boat at the London docks. She'd put herself into direct danger to find evidence that would clear Philip's name. However, tramping through the woods surrounding her own property did not seem equal to snooping around a suspected killer's houseboat.

"Why don't you like Lord Edgerton?" Hugh asked, rolling his shoulders to release tension from them.

She peered at him, taken aback by the question. "What makes you think I don't like him?"

"The two of you didn't share even a glance back there in the storeroom." Hugh crossed his arms. "And he and the duke were frosty toward one another, to say the least."

It wasn't difficult to imagine that. In his insecurity, Lord Edgerton chose to mock Philip; and Philip, in his disdain for the baron, attempted to overlook his very existence. Had the duke not been married to his niece, perhaps Lord Edgerton would act as many others and try to ingratiate himself into Philip's social circle. However, her uncle's discomfort with Audrey and her ability was too formidable—and Philip's animosity too apparent.

She turned toward a framed landscape on the wall, the colors drab, the composition uninspired. "We've never been close."

"He is friends with Bainbury, I take it."

"Yes."

He had more questions; Audrey could sense him working to pace them. He'd once told her she was too brash, too obvious in her questioning technique, and now, she could feel his own patient technique being put into play.

"It was he who arranged for your betrothal to Bainbury?" He came closer to the landscape, pretending to observe it too.

She turned toward him. "What does this have to do with Charlotte?"

Hugh forgot the painting and met her stare. "I'm not yet sure. Maybe nothing."

"Then why do you want to know?"

"Does the baron know what you can do?"

Audrey inhaled a short breath. Hugh Marsden was certainly adept at side stepping at a dizzying rate.

"Yes," she answered, refusing to show herself as discomposed. "My mother and sister do as well."

This seemed to surprise him. His brow jumped briefly before smoothing out again. "What is their opinion of it?"

"To hold an opinion of it would mean to acknowledge it, and they refuse to do that. So, I'm afraid I can only speculate that they think me...strange."

Hugh did not know about her stay at Shadewell. The ton believed she had taken a tour of the Continent and then been visiting with her great aunt in Scotland for the two dreadful years she was confined to the institution. She'd missed her first Season because of it, and her mother and uncle had made some excuse about her poor health and the need to stay in Scotland a bit longer.

They likely had not felt much guilt about the lie, since it was, in some way, based in truth. The sanatorium was *nearly* in Scotland, and her health *had* been poor—though not until after her committal. While she had endeavored to bury the memories from those few years there, some persisted. Not all of them were horrible, however. She had found a place for herself at Shadewell at least, in the library with others like her—patients who were of sound mind but had been sent away for one reason or another. They were superficial friendships, really. Nothing that had lasted once she'd been discharged.

After her release, Audrey had spent a few months at Haverfield before the Little Season in September. By October, her uncle had arranged the betrothal with Bainbury. It was more than clear her mother and Lord Edgerton did not wish to subject Audrey to a proper Season and risk her oddity becoming known. It was absurd, as by then she knew better than to tell anyone. She'd made a drastic mistake in thinking that her ability was something special, something that she could share with those closest to her.

Until she'd met Hugh Marsden, she had sealed up that part of herself and vowed to ignore it forevermore.

He tensed one eye, something he did when contemplating, as if he could somehow peer at the thought a bit closer. "If Lord Edgerton is aware of your ability, I worry he suspects you know more than you are saying."

Audrey was surprised at herself for not yet thinking of that. She'd become so accustomed to her family's dismissal that she'd resolved to dismiss them as well. Still, Hugh's suggestion didn't concern her.

"Even if he does, he won't acknowledge it. He can barely bring himself to acknowledge *me*. If not for my status as duchess, they would be happy to forget I existed at all."

She didn't mean to sound self-pitying; she didn't mourn the loss of her blood ties in the least.

Hugh glanced back at the painting, but then, finding it as mediocre as Audrey had, shifted his attention toward the bed beside them. She was suddenly aware of their proximity and the impropriety of her barging into his room and lying in wait for him, for a moment alone. It flustered her, and the continued silence from Hugh, his closeness, and the way he seemed to be inspecting the striped pattern of the bed's top blanket did not help. The need to fill the silence bubbled up and could be the only reason why she heard herself asking the inane question, "How have you been?"

He looked up, as if rising to the surface of some thought. Whatever he'd been thinking in that stretch of silence, it had not been related to Audrey or their current position in his room above a tavern.

"Busy," he replied. "And yourself?"

Did he really wonder, or was he only being polite?

"Not very busy at all. The country is dreadfully dull."

Hugh's mouth twitched. "That's what Sir says."

The street boy. "You brought him with you."

"And Basil, my valet. It seems he was worried about my ability to dress myself properly."

Audrey bit back a grin. "And Sir?"

His countenance darkened a degree. "The lad is clever. He's proven useful."

He spoke blithely, but there was nothing cavalier about bringing a street boy along with him to a case in the country-side. She suspected Hugh cared more than he was comfortable admitting to.

"I heard that the duke was unwell earlier this summer."

It didn't surprise her that he'd heard the rumor. Low Heath was a small village, and many of its residents had relatives employed at Fournier House. Not to mention that gossiping about the lords and ladies provided much entertainment.

"He's recovered now," she said, curious as to what, exactly, he had heard.

Greer told Audrey that the understaff suspected a case of

malaria, which was absurd considering Philip had been to no part of Africa or India to contract the disease. However, she wondered if Greer had simply been sparing her the truth of the staff's whispers. Philip's malaise bore all the hallmarks of a venereal disease and well Audrey knew it. After learning of his affair with St. John, which had, he admitted, lasted several months, she suspected he'd contracted something unsavory. Once more, she was grateful their marriage did not include any of the traditional obligations.

"Did Doctor Ryder attend to him?" Hugh asked next.

"Yes. That's right, I saw him in the storeroom. He was among the jury."

Hugh paced away from her, opening the narrow path between the bedstead and the plaster wall. "Did you know of Lady Bainbury's losses this last year?" he asked. When Audrey frowned, making her confusion plain, he explained. "Two babes. Miscarriages, both."

Her stomach plummeted, and her chest ached for her friend. Poor Charlotte. She had not confided in her about the events. Hadn't even hinted that she wanted a child. Then again, Audrey, also childless after nearly three years of marriage, understood that speaking about the topic with anyone wasn't easy. It had been yet another circumstance Charlotte believed they had in common.

"That is awful," she murmured, distracted by the new revelation. She thought back on her meetings with Charlotte over the summer and tried to recall if she'd given any indication but could come up with nothing. "I would have thought, out of all her friends, she would have shared something like that with me."

"You were that close?" Hugh asked. She frowned at the question.

"Close enough." He was astute enough to put together why

Charlotte and Audrey might be able to bond over such a subject. She didn't need to say explicitly. It wasn't a proper subject for them to discuss. Then again, none of this was proper.

"I should go," she said, realizing with a start how long she had been sequestered here, in Hugh's room. Philip had long since left for home.

Hugh nodded tightly, then stepped to the door and peered into the hallway.

"It's clear. Sir will be at the bottom of the stairs. He'll let you know if you should wait."

Audrey stepped toward the door, ready to leave and yet also hesitant. "What will you do now?"

"Arrange an interview with Bainbury. I'd like to speak to the countess's maid as well."

Audrey wished she could do the same, but it was out of the realm of possibility for her. "I'll let you know what I find in the woods."

She reached for the doorknob, but before she could open the door, Hugh placed his palm onto the wood panel just above her hand, to hold it closed. Her pulse knocked in her neck. He stood so close, his sleeve brushed against hers.

"Be careful out there, duchess."

She glanced up at him, and his dark eyes seared hers. Then, he stepped back, dropping his hand, and allowing her to open the door. Audrey swept into the hallway and did not take in a full breath until she was back outside in the sunlight, starting home on foot toward Fournier House.

CHAPTER
EIGHT

The sun was slipping behind the treetops by the time Hugh made it to the earl's estate. He'd taken a curricle, hired from the stables at Low Heath, and dropped Sir off about a quarter mile from the entrance to Bainbury's drive. The manor—a blocky Tudor manse reminiscent of an overgrown hunting lodge—was situated down a long, straight drive off the main road, about a half hour from Low Heath.

Sir had taken to his task with great aplomb, leaping onto the dirt road and saluting Hugh with a finger to the side of his nose before Hugh snapped the reins and carried onward. The lad had agreed to show up at the servant's entrance at Bainbury Manor and apply as stable or house help. There was no telling if he'd be accepted or not, but Sir had a way that would loosen the jaws of even the most taciturn people, and Hugh didn't doubt he would unearth some valuable nugget regarding Lady Bainbury.

The scratches and bruising along her wrist left him with no doubt that she had been, in some way, helped along into the grave. That Bainbury would attempt to brush off his wife's death as accidental, and not seek answers or justice for her mistreatment, stoked Hugh's temper. The earl either wanted to avoid scandal or avoid blame.

When women were killed, husbands were, by and large, the culprits. This Hugh knew from countless cases in London. He would not dismiss the earl as a suspect simply because of his privilege of peerage.

The horse's shod hooves and the curricle wheels sent clouds of dust into the air as Hugh drove along the stately path to the manor. The landscaping was simpler here than at Fournier Downs; more trees lined the property, casting shadows, fewer gardens adorned the lawns, and the heavy, humid air weighed like a dreary pall.

It was troubling to think, if not for the duke's timely interference, Audrey would have been mistress of this manor instead. The concept made him feel ill, especially when he wondered if Charlotte's fate would have become hers. Bainbury had now lost three wives. The circumstances surrounding his second wife's death, a suicide by a bullet to the head, had intrigued him enough to glance at the files in the Bow Street records room before leaving for Hertfordshire. Suicides rarely needed investigations, and this one had been no different.

He rolled his shoulders as a surge of heat and frustration attempted, yet again, to settle in his chest and stomach. Audrey's visit to his room had left him agitated, and Sir's sly, sideways glances after helping the duchess escape the inn and tavern, unnoticed, had not helped.

"It was not what it appeared to be," was all he'd said to the boy, who'd scrubbed the tip of his nose and looked away as if doubtful.

What had the woman been thinking, sneaking into his room? It had been entirely too brash and heedless, though it shouldn't have surprised him. It was exactly the way she'd conducted her "investigation" in London back in the spring. While he understood why she'd wanted to speak to him alone, there was certainly another way to go about it rather than ensconcing herself into his private bedchamber while the duke and coroner and magistrate were all gathered downstairs.

Finding her there had created a firestorm right in the center of his sternum. He'd half wanted to toss her out on her ear. The other, impractical half had wanted their private conference to stretch out longer than it had—and that was a problem.

"Not a word of this to Basil," he'd warned Sir after assuring the lad that the duchess had merely wished to speak to him on an urgent matter.

"Me gob's a steel trap, Mister Hugh," he'd replied.

Hugh brought his curricle to a stop in front of the manor's main entrance and two footmen saw to his mount and conveyance. A barrel-chested butler met Hugh at the door.

"His lordship is not receiving callers, sir. This house is in mourning."

"I am aware, my condolences. My name is Principal Officer Hugh Marsden of Bow Street and I'm—"

"Ah. You are the Runner whom Lady Prescott hired, are you?" The butler's well-practiced sneer deepened.

"That is correct," he replied, anticipating the butler's next retort.

"The Earl of Bainbury has instructed me to turn you away should you blacken his doorstep."

"Of course he has." Hugh sighed. It was always such a shame when things became unpleasant. "I will return tomorrow, and the next day, and the day after that, until he admits me. If he does not, I will have no choice but to proceed in my investigation with his lordship as my central suspect in the murder of Lady Bainbury."

"Murder? Preposterous!" the butler seethed.

"The inquest has been suspended as foul play is now alleged. Have the magistrate and Coroner Wilkes arrived yet for their interview with the earl?"

The butler's nostrils flared. His jowls somehow even managed to appear offended. "They have not."

"Luckily for the earl, I have preceded them. He might want to be prepared for the news they bring. As well as the questions."

It was a bit heavy handed, but Hugh was hoping the butler's wish to protect his employer won out. It did.

"Wait here."

Hugh stayed in the foyer, a footman planted next to the front door to watch him with a reptilian-like gaze. The young man barely blinked as the butler shuffled off to alert Bainbury. Only an indistinct raised voice distracted the footman from his marble-like cast. A moment later the butler reappeared, his poise slightly rattled.

"This way, Runner."

Hugh did not bother to correct him. While there were numerous foot patrolmen and horse patrol officers in London, he was one of several principal officers at Bow Street. Being called a *Runner* grated on Hugh's pride—it was where he'd started, as a foot patrol, but he'd worked his way up the ranks at Bow Street and had earned his designation.

However, he knew he'd gained entry at Bainbury Manor by the skin of his teeth and wouldn't push his luck. The butler turned into a study. It held shelves of books, a leather couch, and a pair of club chairs before a hearth; an ornate desk, large windows, glass doors overlooking a terrace; and austere hunting portraits on the wood paneled walls. It was the sort of masculine room one found in all the homes of the peerage. Hugh's own father, the Viscount Neatham, had possessed one just like it, both in London and in Sussex. Though on a smaller scale, even Hugh's own study at his Bedford Street residence resembled it.

The Earl of Bainbury stood at the glass door, open to the terrace, his hands clasped behind his back. He was waiting for Hugh with a formidable scowl in place. The earl was well into his fiftieth decade, though there was a hard, almost preserved youth, about him. His strong jaw was currently clenched, his sharp blue eyes spearing Hugh without remorse.

"What do you want?" he demanded.

"My lord, thank you for seeing me."

"I was not given much choice in the matter, was I?" He strode away from the window and cut his eyes from his unwanted visitor.

The earl stood an inch or two shorter than Hugh, but that in no way diminished him.

"As you already know, I have been engaged by Lady Prescott to investigate Lady Bainbury's untimely death."

Bainbury reached his desk and gripped the lip. "The woman had no right."

"She is her ladyship's mother," Hugh reminded him gently.

"Charlotte was my *wife*," he argued.

Hugh took the opening offered up to him. "Which leads me to question, my lord, why you would be so hasty in your determination on what happened at the quarry. Are you not curious as to how your wife came to be found on Fournier Downs land, at the bottom of an old, open pit quarry?"

The earl's grip on the edge of his desk tightened, his knuckles turning first red, then white. "Your questions are impertinent."

"That is the general nature of my work, my lord." Hugh disregarded the earl's answering glare. "Ask no questions, receive no answers. You've asked no questions, while Lady Prescott has."

Bainbury released the desk and surged forward. "You dare suggest that I am somehow to blame? You, a man of such low birth and scandal that he is relegated to the laboring class, have no right to even speak to me."

He'd gambled that riling the earl would prove useful, and so far, Bainbury had not let him down. Poking and prodding at an open wound almost always produced results. That the earl knew of Hugh's "low birth" didn't perturb him. Most of the ton did. After his duel with the current Lord Neatham, in which Hugh's shot burrowed into the viscount's arm and rendered it useless, he was written off as a blackguard. Not just because of the duel, of course, but the reason for it: Neatham had formally accused Hugh of ruining Miss Eloisa Neatham, Hugh's own half-sister. It made his skin crawl and his stomach twist that so many believed the lies, even now, but he'd long since given up caring what the ton thought of him.

"You wanted Lady Bainbury's death classified as misadventure to perhaps dampen the rumors that yet another one of your wives had committed suicide," Hugh stated, deliberately brash. "However, the coroner has concluded that it is highly unlikely the manner of death is either misadventure or suicide. On the contrary, there is evidence she was pushed."

Bainbury turned his back on Hugh in favor of a decanter on his desk. He poured himself a whisky, tossed it back, and slammed the glass onto the desk.

"Or perhaps you knew it was murder and decided suicide would surely be the lighter scandal to weather."

The earl did something unexpected then: he laughed. The grating sound broke through the study like glass cracking.

"And you would suggest I chased my own wife through the wood and pushed her into Fournier's quarry? *Fool.*"

The earl was far too arrogant and proud to have done the deed himself. The Earl of Bainbury, dashing between trees with murderous intent? He could have more easily poisoned the countess at dinner or smothered her in her sleep. Not to mention the ugly button Hugh kept in his trouser pocket, found by the duchess—the earl's valet would have rather dug his own grave and buried himself alive than allow his master to leave the house wearing a coat adorned with such unfashionable and humble buttons.

"Where were you at the time of her death?" he asked anyway.

"Here, of course. And the rest of my household staff can verify that."

"When did Lady Bainbury leave the house?"

"I don't know," he said impatiently. "One o'clock? Two? She often took jaunts into the parkland. I did not keep a record of her daily activities."

"Indeed," Hugh murmured. He didn't act like a grieving widower at all. "I'd like to speak to her maid."

Bainbury waved a hand in dismissive approval.

"Doctor Ryder revealed the countess was melancholy over not being able to carry to term twice this last year. Did you observe the same?"

The earl's mask of fury slipped, if just for a moment, at the mention of Charlotte's miscarriages. He poured himself another drink. "She was saddened, of course, but as I told her time and again, there was no need to bless the marriage with a child. My first wife gave me three children, all of them grown. I have my heir and spare. Anything more is extraneous."

The earl's heartless reply revealed the true depth of his regard for his wife. It was shallower than even Hugh had imagined. That Charlotte might have wanted a child for herself did

not even seem to cross the man's mind. It made Hugh wonder...
why marry for a third time?

As he'd just stated, he had his heir and spare. Even though
the earl held on to vestiges of his good looks—his strong
jawline, sharp blue eyes, and athletic build—he was past his
prime. Clearly, he did not hold much, if any, affection for his
third wife. A man of his status could have simply taken a
mistress or two. Why bother to legshackle himself? Unless he
needed the one thing Charlotte had brought to the marriage: a
dowry. Were his coffers so low? Had he made some bad invest-
ments or gambled away a good portion of his fortune? Three
years on, and her dowry might have run dry. His debts could
have grown. Perhaps he needed to marry again—secure
another dowry? Hugh's mind jumped from thought to thought
as he stared down the earl.

"What is that rabid look in your eye, Runner?" Bainbury
demanded.

The state of the earl's finances intrigued him, as did the
circumstances surrounding his second marriage. He did not
know how long that union had lasted, but he did recall the
second countess had been far younger, much like Charlotte.
With an attractive dowry? Most likely. He would get nowhere
asking Bainbury his probing questions. The lady's maid, or
other members of the staff, might be more receptive.

"Three years ago, you were betrothed to Miss Audrey Haver-
hill," Hugh said instead. "She jilted you in favor of the duke."

The gleam of fury Hugh received now outshone all the
others the earl had tossed his way so far. "What does this have
to do with Charlotte's death?"

"Is your wounded pride the reason you've dismissed Her
Grace's witness testimony? Your wife might have been in
danger. Her Grace saw her running. Heard her scream. Why be
so defiant in believing the duchess?"

With vehemence, the earl stepped closer to Hugh. "It is because I know she sees things that do not exist."

Hugh went still as alarm clanged through him. What could he possibly mean by that? Surely, he couldn't know of her ability. "Explain," he said, his voice clipped.

"Lord Edgerton wanted to be rid of her, you see. He confided in me that she...told tall tales for entertainment."

Hugh fixed his glare on the earl. "Are you accusing the duchess of being a liar?"

"I am simply saying that there are things about her that have been buried to protect Edgerton and his family."

"What things?" Hugh despised himself for pressing on, but he wanted to know what the earl had been made privy to.

Bainbury scoffed. "You think I would tell you? A scoundrel Runner?"

"Then I have no choice but to treat her testimony as truth." Hugh started toward the door, finished with the earl. It was safer to leave now too. The fire in his chest over Bainbury's comments about Audrey had grown too hot, too quickly.

"She was gone for two years," the earl said to Hugh's back. He stopped abruptly and turned. Bainbury wore a mean grin as if finding pleasure in revealing this. "The excuse was that she was traveling the Continent and then had a prolonged stay with an aunt in Scotland. Before I accepted Edgerton's proposal for a marriage to the chit, I had a man look into things. There is no aunt in Scotland. There is no record of Her Grace's travels abroad."

A pit opened in the bottom of Hugh's stomach. "Where was she then?"

"Edgerton increased her dowry so that I would not need to know that answer." The earl sneered. "The Duchess of Fournier is not a reliable witness. If she continues to press the matter, I will have no choice but to publicly raise the question of where she was for those two, long, mysterious years."

Hugh barely held his temper in check as he took slow, even steps toward the earl. He stopped an arm's length away, his stare unyielding. "You would find that course of action ill-advised. She is a duchess. You are nothing in comparison."

A new glint in the earl's eye chilled some of Hugh's stoked temper. He was suddenly aware that in his anger, he'd let his own mask slip.

"And you, Marsden, are no better than the dirt on the bottom of my boot." Bainbury snorted a laugh. "This interview is over. Another will not be permitted. Get out."

Hugh departed the study, gritting his molars and wishing he could have reined in his displeasure at hearing the earl speak of Audrey in such poor terms. In a high dudgeon, he found his way belowstairs and ripped through his interviews with the staff.

The countess had been fatigued the last few weeks, her lady's maid, Miss Dorothy Gates, provided. The cook agreed that her ladyship had not been eating as much, and two footmen claimed to have seen her weeping in the hallways of the manor on two separate occasions. It certainly sounded to Hugh as if Dr. Ryder's observation about melancholy was correct. Miss Gates retrieved the small glass bottle of laudanum the doctor had given the countess. Tasting a small drop on his fingertip, he concluded it was just as the doctor said—a tincture of opium.

From the staff, he learned the countess had left for her regular constitutional walk in the surrounding parkland just past noon. Miss Gates said she usually walked alone, and that day was no different.

As he conducted his interviews, a stone lodged in Hugh's gut. The countess had been undoubtedly despondent. He could see where the staff and even the earl might simply assume she had ended her own life.

Finally, he took aside Miss Gates and spoke to her privately.

"You would know her ladyship better than anyone. You would bear witness to things other servants would not. Did she and the earl often argue?"

She pressed her lips thin and hesitated.

"Miss Gates, it could be imperative to discovering what happened to the countess," Hugh said, as gently as his riled temper would allow.

She shook her head, her brow puckering with confusion. "No. Honest. They barely acknowledged one another."

A thought came to Hugh, and he put it toward the young maid as delicately as he could. "Was it possible the countess was seeing someone outside the confines of their marriage?"

Her confused expression fled instantly, and she shook her head, certain. "She hardly left the manor, sir. There were no gentlemen visitors either."

That did not necessarily mean the countess hadn't taken up with a particularly handsome footman or stable hand employed on the premises. But he didn't press the issue. He'd spied Sir in the kitchen, spooning up a bowl of porridge with gusto. The lad winked at Hugh when no one was looking, and he presumed he had successfully landed himself a position at the manor. He would gather up information and deliver it to Hugh within twenty-four hours.

"One last question, Miss Gates," he said as the maid shifted her footing, restless.

"The countess's fatigue, her lack of appetite, and weeping... might there have been a more personal reason for her symptoms? Something more delicate?"

The maid knew what he was asking. Her perceptive eyes glanced over his shoulder, toward the commotion in the kitchen. She lowered her voice as a blush tinged her cheeks. "She was no more than two months gone."

Hugh nodded, understanding perfectly well. The countess had been with child.

He was willing to wager everything he possessed that it had played a role in her death.

CHAPTER
NINE

Audrey wanted to go into the woods in search of the stone cottage as soon as she arrived home from Low Heath. However, when Philip opened the front door instead of a footman, his expression stony, she'd resolved to wait until the next day.

"If you believe your appearance at the inquest will not make its way back to London..." he'd said once they'd been enclosed in his bedchamber. Graciously, he'd left the rest of his sentence unfinished. He'd certainly been about to call her a fool.

What with his own reputation in such a precarious state, and Cassie's first Season to think about, Audrey knew London society was his primary concern these days. His sister's happiness meant the world to him, and he wanted only the best, most advantageous match for her. Having a duke for an elder brother would all but ensure she found one, but the finer men of the ton would steer clear of even the largest of dowries if there was any unresolved scandal attached. And unfortunately, the men who would present themselves despite it might only view the dowry as prize enough, thinking little of Cassandra herself.

It had taken most of the evening to convince Philip that no harm had been done, however she wasn't fond of lying and had, in the end, confessed to meeting with Hugh Marsden to inform him of some visions she'd had. Philip deplored that the Bow Street officer knew of Audrey's ability—not to mention his own deepest secret. And when he'd finally worked it out of her *where* she had met with Mr. Marsden, he'd been nearly apoplectic with rage.

"You put yourself in that blackguard's bedchamber? Have you lost your mind?"

Audrey shushed him, knowing it was too late. The footmen in the corridor outside Philip's bedroom had certainly heard.

"The cad could have taken liberties!" he'd hissed, heeding her advice to lower his voice.

"He would never! You do him a disservice suggesting that. Mr. Marsden is trustworthy. He is a gentleman."

She had not divulged her own bewildering feelings for the man. They did not signify. They *could* not.

Philip had calmed eventually, and with reluctance, he related what the coroner found at the inquest, including that Charlotte's body was again resting in their icehouse. The copper-domed structure, the interior of which comprised of three inner chambers and a center well stocked with blocks of ice, was embedded into a hillside a short walk from the kitchen entrance at Fournier House. Meats, dairy, root vegetables, and many more of the house's food stores were kept there to maintain freshness. Audrey hated to think of Charlotte being treated as storage, but admitted it was necessary while the investigation continued. She then told Philip about the button she'd found and what it had shown her. At the mention of a stone cottage, Philip had frowned.

"An abandoned property on Bainbury's land?" he'd suggested.

"Do you know of any closer by?" she asked, but he had not.

The following morning, Philip announced he was meeting with his steward to discuss the hiring of an engineer to implement an irrigation ditch on a nearby farm. He'd seemed to have forgotten all about the stone cottage, which suited her perfectly. She changed into a walking dress and sturdy boots, chose one of her muslin bonnets, and told Greer she was off for a ride.

She did not expect to see anyone on the path toward the section of wood that she, Philip, Hugh, and Cassie had traveled a few days before, but she soon came up behind Cassie, whose mount was walking at a leisurely pace.

"What are you doing out here?" Audrey called. Her sister-in-law gave a short scream and twisted in her saddle, her eyes large with fright.

Audrey apologized for giving her a scare, but also bit back a chuckle. "I did not think Fortuna and I stealthy enough to be able to sneak up behind you so quietly."

Cassie breathed out and laughed at herself. "I suppose my mind was wandering, and I wasn't paying much attention."

"Are you going anywhere in particular?"

Cassie looked ahead and behind them on the path. "No, just out riding. What about you? What is your destination?"

Audrey recalled Hugh's request that she not comb through the wood and parkland on her own. She didn't truly want anyone's company, but it would at least put the Bow Street officer at ease. And in return she would not need to endure more of his ire.

"I am looking for something," Audrey said. "A stone cottage."

Her sister-in-law's eyes narrowed, and she frowned. "Whatever for?"

The harsh snap of Cassie's tone surprised her and gave Audrey an inkling. "Do you know of it?"

"There are quite a few ruins out in these woods. Why would you wish to find one?" she asked, again fervently, as if alarmed. Perhaps she, like Hugh, thought it unwise to go too deeply into the wood. But then again, she was out here, riding alone too.

Audrey quickly whipped up a falsehood and was astonished that she did not feel much guilt for it. "Something was said about it at the inquest, I hear. A theory that Charlotte had been there before she ran this way."

The excuse was vague, and should Cassie ask Philip, he would not be able to verify it, but for the moment Audrey did not concern herself.

Cassie's frown deepened. She peered up the path, the boughs of the trees casting heavy shade. "How strange," she murmured. "It might be the witch's hut."

"The what?" she asked, astonished.

Cassie grinned at the shocked look Audrey must have been wearing. "Not a real witch's hut, of course. That's just what we called it when we were young. Michael and Tobias would tease that they would leave me out there for the wicked witch if I pestered them too much."

The night before, the duke had displayed confusion when she'd related the vision she'd had. "Philip didn't seem to know of a ruined stone cottage."

"He wouldn't," Cassie said with a snort of laughter. "He never liked exploring. He'd have rather stayed in the library. I don't think he ever came with us."

Audrey was suddenly happy she'd come across her sister-in-law now. "Do you remember how to get there?"

"I suppose... Yes, I could show you," she said, giving her horse a nudge to continue along the path.

Audrey followed, grateful. Now that they weren't accompanied by men, Cassie had chosen to ride astride as well.

"Did they say why she was at this cottage?" Cassie asked after a few moments, and Audrey's stomach sank at the need to carry on with the fib.

"No," she replied simply. Then, before Cassie could ask anything more, she cleared her throat and changed the topic. "I fear I have been a terrible chaperone and hostess to you this summer, Cassie. To find you riding alone, aimlessly, only highlights how few diversions there are here for you. We still have a few weeks left of summer. Won't you consider joining Michael and Genie at Greenbriar before she enters her confinement? There are several families nearby, and Philip is more than well now."

Cassie shook her head decisively. "There is really no need. I've enjoyed the solitude."

A lengthy pause ensued as they entered the forest path. Audrey wasn't sure she believed her. Cassie was too much of a social creature to be contained to the quiet countryside. She spent the month of May with Michael and Genie in London, on Grosvenor Square, and Genie wrote at length at how Cassie had hardly ever been at home. Routs, dinners, dances, and all manner of entertainments occupied her to the point where Genie—tiring easily due to her pregnancy—had needed to hire another chaperone for the young woman. Miss Frances Stinton, a well-respected spinster who had chaperoned many a young debutante, had even expressed trouble keeping up with Cassie.

Her bubbly chattering with Hugh Marsden the other day had demonstrated her usual attitude. Perhaps he had simply been the most intriguing person Cassie had met so far this summer, and why shouldn't he have been? He was handsome and masculine and so very different than the dandies and rakes and nabobs filling her usual circle to the brim.

She frowned as the forest path thickened and the humid air cooled with the shadows. Was it mere novelty that drew Audrey to Hugh as well? It seemed a shallow thing. But no, she wasn't drawn to him. She was merely...affected by him. And who wouldn't be, for all the reasons she'd just considered?

"I am excited to have a nephew or niece, aren't you?" Cassie asked after a few more minutes of riding in silence.

Audrey was grateful for yet another change of subject. "I am. Genie and Michael will be wonderful parents."

Her other sister-in-law was kind, charming, and sincere. With her soft, summery beauty, Genie was the perfect English rose. Michael had been swept off his feet the first time he laid eyes on her, and their engagement had been almost immediate. Theirs was a true love match, Audrey knew, and she often felt like a fraud when she and Philip were within the same room as Michael and Genie. Not that she didn't love Philip—she did. He was her most ardent friend and confidant. She would rather have that as a basis for marriage than the usual transactional union between two estates.

"I am happy for them," Cassie went on, her tone oddly wistful. "Genie is more than ready to be a mother. She's perfectly poised for such an enormous addition to her world." She sighed, but then brightened and turned to Audrey as if an afterthought. "As are you, if only you and my brother would grace us with the future duke."

Audrey's stomach constricted at the teasing jest. It was not wholly unexpected. With Michael and Genie about to be blessed with a child, she and Philip had anticipated a new round of murmurs and gossip to make its way around the ton, questioning when the duchess herself would produce an heir. The blame, of course, would come to rest upon her shoulders. It was something she and Philip had discussed and agreed would simply need to be endured.

That didn't mean it didn't prick at her, even coming from Cassie, who she knew meant no insult. It would be best to state it once and for all, and perhaps Cassie would inform Genie, who would then tell Michael.

"As much as I wish I could give you more nieces and nephews to spoil, Philip and I have come to terms with the fact that it isn't meant to be."

Cassie slowed her mount. "Oh, Audrey, I'm so sorry. I spoke carelessly just now. I suspected you were having trouble conceiving and it was heartless of me to mention it so blithely."

"Please, do not berate yourself." She urged Cassie to keep riding. They were headed toward the gated field where she had seen Charlotte running. "Philip and I have made our peace with it, truly."

At least, they had at first. Seeing Genie and Michael prepare for their little one had brought a strange yearning into Audrey's chest; she hadn't dared discuss it with Philip and wondered if he felt it at all.

"Well, I will not cease hoping, sister," Cassie said before turning her head to dash away a tear. Grateful they were doing something active rather than sitting down to tea with no option but to face each other, Audrey gave her horse a small nudge with her heels.

They rode past the gated field and carried on through more stretches of woodland. Cassie pulled ahead, increasing her horse's gait.

"Are you sure you know where you're going?" Audrey called.

"Of course!" Cassie called back, a touch too loudly. "It's not far. It's been years, but I could never forget!"

Her voice carried, and Audrey wondered at her enthusiasm. Perhaps she was simply trying to outpace herself from the awkward topic of babies.

The humid air still felt cool along the forest path, but her mount was working up a lather. Through the canopy, a gray sky threatened more rain. It wasn't until the trees thinned into a small, overgrown clearing, and Cassie slowed, that Audrey noticed the lack of birds trilling and crickets humming. Rain was imminent.

Practically consumed by shrub brush, weeds, and vines, the stone cottage sat in the middle of the clearing. It looked forlorn, forgotten by the rest of the world, and left to crumble. Hunks of stone were missing from the exterior in places, and the thatched roof had moldered and all but disintegrated.

Cassie slowed her mount to a halt. "Here it is," she said, still overly eager. "It looks like its aged a hundred years since I last saw it!"

She dismounted, and Audrey quickly did the same. They looped their reins over an old hitching post.

"Is this Fournier Downs land?" Audrey asked, eyeing the cottage's gaping arched entrance and the window embrasures, all open to the elements.

"I'm not sure," Cassie said, walking through the tall grass. Meadowsweet and clover had crept in, and purple harebells flowered. Some of the vines wrapping the cottage were lush with ivy and others were brittle and long dead. "It could be, or it might belong to Haverfield. Michael would know."

Audrey had certainly never come this way from Haverfield before. She would not have forgotten such a fine playhouse for children. It must have been abandoned long ago to have decayed to its current state. She approached the entrance, wanting to touch the stones. A glance over her shoulder showed Cassie searching the clearing. With her companion occupied, Audrey quickly removed her riding glove and laid her palm on the rough stone. She closed her eyes, and immediately, the image of the weed- and flower-strewn clearing billowed into her vision. The same overcast afternoon; the tree limbs and leaves hanging heavy and torpid with no breeze, just the promise of a storm.

Audrey gave a push, backward through the stone's energy, but before anything could consolidate into a vision, a scream rent the air.

She dropped her hand and whipped around. "Cassie!"

She was gone.

Another scream sent her heart lurching up into her throat.

Audrey dropped her glove and ran around the corner of the cottage, terrified at what she'd find. Her sister-in-law, being set upon by an attacker or a wild animal? With relief, she found Cassie standing in another patch of overgrown grass and shrub brush. But her relief was short-lived. For Cassie, with her hands clasped over her mouth, was staring down at something in the grass.

On trembling legs, Audrey approached. In shock, her mind pieced together what she was seeing: a woman, splayed on the ground, face down. She wore a light green jacket, a plain gray cotton dress, and serviceable boots. The yellow ribbons attached to a straw chip hat were still tied around her chin, but a blood stain flowered over the pale straw weave. That hat...it was the same one from Audrey's vision. The woman passing by the cottage's window. This was she.

"My God!" Cassie gasped. Audrey took her arm and pulled her away from the body. For the woman was certainly dead.

"You must fetch help, immediately," Audrey said, and when Cassie refused to look away from the woman's prone figure, gave her a little shake. "Cassandra. This woman has been killed. We need to fetch Philip and Officer Marsden, and whoever else you can find. Ride back to Fournier Downs—"

"And leave you here?" she shrieked, at last coming to her senses.

"Someone should stay with the body, and you know your way through these woods far better than I."

"But what if the killer is still about?" Cassie's question was not unwarranted. It was, in fact, quite reasonable. However, as shaken as Audrey was, she wanted the opportunity to find some item on the poor woman's person. She wanted to hold it and search it for memories. Before, when finding Charlotte, she'd been too affected to do so.

"The blood on her hat is dark, not bright crimson, indicating it has been some time since the attack," she said, leading Cassie toward their horses. The color of the blood stain, however, did not assure her as much as the horses did; neither appeared spooked in any way. Horses tended to sense dangers that human could not yet see.

"If you ride quickly, you'll be back within a quarter hour, at the most," she told her. "I will be fine, but the sooner Philip and Mr. Marsden arrive, the better. Please, Cassie, ride swiftly!"

The encouragement seemed to be all Cassie needed, for paired with her own shock and fear, she mounted her horse and tore away, back into the woods. As soon as she disappeared, Audrey turned toward the place the body lay. Just as it had been with Charlotte, she did not want to approach; did not want to look upon the lifeless corpse of yet another woman. This, however, was a stranger. Perhaps it would not be as difficult. And this time, she would not allow cowardice or fear to rule her.

Her stomach turned as she came upon the woman again. This time, Audrey noticed more. A basket, not far from where she'd fallen. A few bundles of herbs, the stems tied with twine, had scattered. Crouching next to the woman slowly, pushing back her own discomfort and trepidation, Audrey reached for the hat and tipped up the brim a little. With a start, she pulled back her hand and stumbled as she tried to stand. This woman was not a stranger as she had at first thought. Audrey recognized her and not just by the straw chip hat and yellow ribbons from her previous vision. She was a maid at Haverfield. Her name escaped her at the moment, but she was certain. This woman worked in Lord Edgerton's kitchen.

Two dead women in the woods within one week was too much to be coincidence. This maid's death had to be related to Charlotte's. The cottage connected them. Charlotte had been here shortly before her death. Now this.

Bracing herself, Audrey crouched again next to the body. The victim wore no jewelry, though that was not surprising for a servant. The basket on the ground had been the last thing the woman carried. Audrey stooped and with her one ungloved hand—she would have to find the one she'd dropped later—grasped the handle. She opened her mind to the energy, though with her racing heart, it was difficult to control the images that barreled forward. They were as quick as her lashing heartbeats —the woman, coming upon the cottage, then pitching forward, toward the ground; earlier, coming through the woods; pushing back further, Audrey saw the familiar sight of the kitchen at Haverfield.

Something cold struck her on the forehead, and Audrey gasped as she released the basket. The clearing, as it was now, came into view as she stumbled back again. A few more cold splashes against her cheeks and nose convinced her it was only the dark clouds, finally opening. Rain came down quickly. Her pulse hammered. She would be soaked through if she stayed outdoors. The only option was the stone cottage and its patchy, dilapidated roof.

As Audrey ran toward the entrance, her horse nickered and bucked. Perhaps it was the sudden rain that spooked him, but the animal's agitation made the small hairs upon her arms prickle and stand on end. Audrey started toward her horse, intending to calm him—but stopped at a dash of motion in her peripheral vision. Something had moved in the trees beyond the clearing.

Turning again, Audrey bounded into the cottage. The single room held an old hearth, a shabby loft, and creeping vines along the floor and inner walls. Rain puddled in spots on the stone floor. As she pressed up against a wall, away from the doorway, she cursed under her breath. How could she have been so stupid? She should have left with Cassie, not taken the opportunity to peer into the woman's memories. Trapped in the damp and dim old ruin, all she'd done was back herself into a corner.

CHAPTER
TEN

On his second visit to Fournier House, Hugh determined he liked the place even less than before. It grated on him—the manicured lawns, the vibrant green grass, the stately oaks spaced just so to provide shade but not dominate the landscape. The flowering vines and climbing roses clinging to the exterior of the manor made his back teeth ache. Why did it have to be so bloody perfect? So refined and yet wild and untamed at the same time? At least at Bainbury's estate he had not admired the architecture or grounds or anyone within its walls. He hadn't coveted any of it.

No, Hugh did not want Fournier House. He wouldn't know what to do with a place like this. He wouldn't know his purpose.

He was just in a black mood, still riled from his interview with Bainbury the afternoon before. The man had worked his way under Hugh's skin much too easily with all his talk about the duchess's unaccountable two-year disappearance. The earl's thinly veiled threats against her had been dangling bait, and like a heedless puppy, Hugh had snapped it up. Then, of course, the revelation that Lady Bainbury had likely been with child had plagued his thoughts for the rest of the evening. If she had miscarried yet again, perhaps she had decided a leap from the quarry ledge was an acceptable end to her anguish.

He'd taken supper with Basil at the inn, glowering into his stew, ignoring his valet who had been complaining about the sorry state of the clothespress in Hugh's room. A splintered shelf had pulled a thread loose on a shirt or some such, and Basil did not think it could be easily repaired—the shirt, not the shelf, he clarified. Hugh had tried to feign concern, but really, he could only mull over why Charlotte, who had been dejected at the loss of two other pregnancies earlier that year, would be so melancholy about this new chance at motherhood.

When the coroner, Wilkes, had entered the tavern for a bowl of stew and a plate of kidney pie, Hugh had nearly called the man over to discuss his findings. But he'd hesitated, wanting more time to ruminate. He'd gotten nowhere for the rest of the evening, so, that morning, he'd left a wax-sealed letter for the coroner with the innkeeper to meet him at Fournier's icehouse at one o'clock to discuss a possible autopsy. Hugh needed to know if she had still been *enceinte* at the time of her death. Gut instinct nearly shouted that if she was, it played a role in her murder.

As before, when he pulled his curricle into the circular drive of crushed rock, he eyed the lily pond and the toy boats listing on the surface of the water. There was no breeze, the humidity too severe and the threat of rain imminent. Two footmen in the ducal livery colors of pale blue and gold braid came to attend to the curricle and its matching pair, but Hugh had no more than stepped aside when a commotion near the stables drew his attention.

At first, he could not reconcile what he was seeing: a horse and rider charging toward the complex, the hem of her dress carelessly hiked to her white-stockinged knees, her hair unpinned. It was Cassandra, the duke's sister, and she was shouting for help. He charged toward the stables while a hundred different possibilities streamed through his mind, all involving the duchess. When Cassandra's frantic eyes lit on Hugh, her expression told him he'd been right.

"She's dead!"

Hugh juddered to a stop, his stomach lurching.

"I don't know what happened! She's dead. In the wood! A...a woman. I don't know her."

His heart restarted as he comprehended her panicked words. A woman. Not Audrey.

"Where is the duchess?"

"She stayed behind. She said someone should remain with the poor woman, but I didn't want to leave her alone."

The stable master and a few grooms, all of whom had come running at the tumult, told Hugh they'd saddle him a mount. Hugh waved them off.

"No time. Lady Cassandra, if you'll allow my impertinence, we'll ride together. Take me to the duchess."

She nodded quickly and held out her hand. At any other time, in any other situation, he would have paused the few minutes for a mount to be readied for him, but at that moment, he would rather start running on foot than hang about, waiting. The duke's sister seemed to understand and allowed him to settle into the saddle behind her.

"Fetch His Grace and send for the coroner in Low Heath," Hugh instructed the stable master.

"Tell my brother it's the ruined cottage beyond the western meadow!" Cassandra shouted as she dug in her heels and turned the horse back toward the field and trees beyond.

"Here, take the reins," she said a moment later as the brooding sky finally split apart, and rain began to fall in sheets. "I will guide you."

Grateful to have the reins in his grip rather than the young woman's dainty waist, he followed her direction and plunged into the wooded path, the same one they'd taken the other day.

"What can you tell me?" he asked.

"We rode to the abandoned stone cottage."

Hugh gritted his teeth. The cottage from Audrey's vision. She'd found it.

"She was lying in the grass when we got there," Cassandra added.

"Who?"

"I don't know!" Cassandra cried, breathless, her voice shaking from the rough gallop. Rain spattered the boughs above, but all Hugh could think about what the duchess, staying behind with the body like a bloody fool! For the opportunity to hold some object belonging to the woman, most likely.

Hugh slapped the reins and the mount carried them faster. The jarring of their bodies was uncomfortable, but Cassandra was slight, and the circumstances were too dire to think about any impropriety.

Gusts of wind swayed the tree branches and the horse's hooves splattered along the mired path, sending clods of mud into the air around them. The duke's sister pointed the way, and as the path narrowed to nothing more than a deer trail, Hugh was forced to slow. His heart pounded, his irritation steaming him from the inside out. All that heat chilled, however, when a dappled gray mare came trotting toward them.

"It's Fortuna, Audrey's mount!" Cassandra said. Hugh recognized it, and though he hated to stop, he leaned out to take the horse's traces. The animal was spooked, it eyes wild. He hushed it as he dismounted.

"How far ahead is this cottage?"

"Not far. The clearing is up there. But why has her horse run off?"

Hugh didn't answer. Instead, he instructed her to ride back to meet with the duke and the others.

"Are you certain?" She glanced behind them with trepidation. The path was dim, the rainstorm having sucked much of the light from the wood.

He patted her mount's neck and covered her hand with his. "They won't be far behind now. I cannot risk your safety if there is trouble at the cottage."

Not to mention his only desire was to focus on the duchess's safety. He could not see to that if the duke's sister was with him.

She nodded and, soaked to the bone, her hair limp and ruined by the rain, she turned her horse and once again, began riding back the way they'd come.

Hugh mounted the dappled gray and rode onward, coming to a stop when he finally saw the unkempt dell ahead. It had probably been a quarter hour at the most since they had left the stables, but it felt like time without end. He dismounted at the stone hitching post and fed the reins through the brass ring. The rain had lightened, though a stormy breeze still swayed the tops of the trees. All was silent, and the stone cottage, wrapped in vines and blanketed by grass and weeds, looked to be slumbering.

There was no sign of Audrey. His skin prickled. He did not see a body, but the grasses were high, and it could have been hidden within. Hugh withdrew his flintlock pistol, hopeful the rain would not dampen the primer and powder. Slowly, he crept toward the cottage. The open doorway and windows gaped black and fathomless, the door and shutters having long since shed. The place had been left to rot; half of the roof had collapsed.

Dread settled into his bones as he climbed a pair of stone

slab steps and set his foot on the threshold. No longer breathing, he cocked his flintlock and entered the cottage. A blur of motion to his left preceded a blow to his chin by one thousandth of a second, but Hugh didn't lose his footing. He shoved his assailant backward just as a springtime scent of jasmine and musk shuttled into his senses. With a surge of relief, Hugh released the primer on his flintlock as he grappled with a pair of arms battering him. One hand, still in possession of a stone, repeatedly slammed into his shoulder.

"Stop!" he shouted, inhaling her familiar, heady scent again. He pinned her arms to her sides and pushed her against the stone wall. "Audrey, stop."

She went utterly still, her wild eyes staring, shocked into comprehension. And then her arms were around him, gripping him in a desperate embrace. "Oh, thank God, Hugh," she gasped. "Thank God, it's you."

The stone dropped, clattering onto the floor and her hand fisted into his jacket. She was soaked and shivering, and a dam within him fractured. Hugh gathered her closer, cupping the back of her drenched, unpinned hair. He closed his eyes, breathing her in, marveling at the firm press of her body against his.

"Are you injured?" he managed to say, his good sense slowly stirring.

"No, but there was someone out there," she replied, still shaking. It wasn't cold, so he imagined it was shock working its way through her.

He peeled her arms from him and stood back to look at her. "When? How long ago?"

"I...I've been hiding in here ten minutes. Maybe fifteen. I saw movement in the woods and heard sticks snapping. I thought you were him—*oh*." She touched his jaw, and for a moment he didn't understand why. But a throb of pain made itself known, and he remembered her striking him with the stone.

"I'm sorry," she said.

"Don't be. It was quick thinking." He covered her hand, still at his jaw attempting to wipe away blood, and squeezed.

"Fool woman, what were you thinking staying here?" Before she could answer, he released her and stepped away. Raising his flintlock again, he narrowed his eyes on her. "Don't move. I'm searching the clearing."

"Where is Cassie?" she asked as he went to the doorway and peered out. The rain was misting now, but the winds were still just as strong.

"She went back to meet the duke and whoever else can come," he answered, then glared at her again. "*Stay*."

"I am not a dog," she objected.

Hugh grimaced and stepped out. The clearing was still empty, but Audrey's horse had calmed and was standing at the hitching post, munching on wet grass. He was nearly certain whoever she'd heard was long gone. They had been given plenty of time to enter the hut and attack Audrey. His ire stoked at the knowledge. It was what he'd feared—that he would enter the ruined cottage and find her sprawled upon the floor, dead.

The tall trunks and limbs swayed and tossed, but no one was hiding within the trees. Hugh lowered his pistol and tucked it away. The body Cassandra spoke of was in a patch of tall grass. It was indeed a woman, and by the look of her clothing, she was of the working class.

"It is the woman from my vision. The one the button showed me."

Hugh spun around and swore under his breath. Audrey had, as expected, not stayed put in the cottage. He swallowed a reprimand and instead, removed his jacket. "Hold it over your head."

She did, though he wasn't sure what use it would do. They were both drenched.

"Are you certain?" he asked. She nodded.

"I recognize her. She was a maid at Haverfield."

"How far is the estate?" he asked, glancing into the trees again. A bare bit of dirt between two trees ahead drew his attention. He got closer and saw it was another foot path. "She must have come through here."

"The path might lead to one of the lower pastures," Audrey said. He glanced back at her. Her wan coloring concerned him. She'd had a shock and had spent the last quarter hour believing she would need to fight off a murderer. Hugh only wanted to gather her to him again and hold her, but that moment in the cottage could not be repeated.

He focused on the new victim. "You stayed behind to touch one of her belongings," he guessed.

"Her basket."

"Anything?"

She shook her head. "She was struck from behind. She didn't see her attacker."

He searched the ground again, from where the body lay prone to the head of the footpath. While not well worn, the path saw plenty of foot travel. People came this way, to the cottage often. But why?

A whistle sounded through the clearing, and then a jangle of tack chased it. The Duke of Fournier shot into the dell on a regal stallion, though at the moment he himself looked ragged. He wore no hat or gloves and was not at all prepared for riding.

"Audrey!" The duke caught sight of her and immediately dismounted. He rushed to her, sparing Hugh not even a glance.

"I'm fine," she told him, but the duke still inspected her closely. He saw the body in the grass and with an arm around Audrey, led her away from it.

Two more riders, both stable hands, joined them in the clearing, and then Cassandra too. She let out a cry and jumped from her horse, to embrace Audrey.

"What the devil are you doing out here?" Fournier asked the duchess.

"Cassie and I went for a ride and—"

"We discussed this. You were to stay out of it!"

Hugh suspected it was only panic driving his anger, but he still grew warm with annoyance.

"A woman has been killed, and there is a body to see to, Your Grace," Hugh said, raising his voice before the duke could speak again. Fournier now speared Hugh with his full attention. There was suspicion and displeasure in his mien, but Hugh didn't have the wherewithal for it.

"If you will escort the duchess and Lady Cassandra back to the manor, your men and I will follow with the victim. Coroner Wilkes should be arriving soon."

The duke looked like he wanted to argue but held his tongue and led the women toward the horses. Audrey's eyes skated over Hugh's briefly as she passed. A few drops of rain slid under his loosened cravat and chilled the back of his neck.

"You there," he shouted to the two stable hands, hovering a far step away from the body. "Shore yourselves up and let's get this over with."

CHAPTER

ELEVEN

T he shivers had reduced in their violence, but Audrey couldn't shake them entirely. Philip had railed at her the entire ride back to Fournier Downs, his voice competing with the whipping wind, the rustle of the tree branches, and the labored breathing of the horses. Cassie tried to defend their outing, saying they were only searching for the cottage mentioned at the inquest. Philip had growled, "Is that so?" knowing full well nothing about a cottage had been mentioned at the inquest.

When they finally returned to the manor, Cassie bid them an early goodnight before being whisked to her bedchamber. It was no wonder. The poor girl had been grievously distressed to find a dead body, and then, riding back and forth along the woodland path in a tumultuous rainstorm had exacerbated her misery.

In her own bedchamber, Audrey had let Greer strip her of her sopping dress and boots and then submerged herself into the copper tub full of hot water and soap. Her boudoir was also attached to the sitting room in Philip's own collection of rooms, and she could hear him angrily knocking about in there. A light rap on the connecting door didn't necessarily surprise Audrey as she was toweling off, but she also did not know if she had any energy left to defend herself.

"Just a moment," she called, then nodded to Greer who took her leave. Audrey wrapped herself into a velvet banyan and called for him to enter.

He was in trousers and shirtsleeves and had forgone any finishing touches like a neckcloth and waistcoat. His golden-brown hair had been toweled off, but it was still darker than usual. His relaxed shoulders and rueful expression put Audrey at ease.

"Forgive me my temper," he said, coming across the boudoir's sapphire Aubusson carpet and extending a glass of whisky. Audrey accepted the peace offering and sipped the spirits, hoping it would warm her.

She hated arguing with Philip. It was so rare an occurrence that she was simply not accustomed to it. She supposed if they bickered all the time, she would become immune to his displeasure being directed toward her.

"Only if you will forgive me. I should have brought a footman or two with us—"

"Or your husband," he interjected with an arched brow.

"Or my husband," she added with a wry grin.

"I understand you are eager for answers," he said. "And your ability to see things the rest of us cannot leads you to feel like you must do certain things alone. But Audrey, you need to place more value on your own safety."

She sipped her whisky in silence. Philip sighed and ambled away, toward a pale oak dressing table where Greer kept her silver and mother-of-pearl brush and comb, and small cases of hair pins and jewelry.

"Come," he said, taking up the brush. "Your hair is a mass of tangles. Are you housing a bird's nest in there?"

She scowled at him but laughed, appreciative of his attempt to lighten the mood.

"Greer will brush my hair."

"I am just as capable, thank you." He motioned for her to sit on the velvet settee and with an indulgent sigh, she acquiesced. He began to tease out the damp knots, which were nowhere near as abundant as he had claimed.

"We should discuss what we will say to the coroner. He has arrived, I'm told," Philip said.

"We will tell him the truth," Audrey replied, curious about his comment. "Cassie and I came upon a body in the woods, and we sent for help."

Philip paused in his efforts. "It is not as simple as that. The coroner is an astute man, and he will not like that you have now found *two* bodies in the woodland surrounding our estate."

Unease trickled through her. She had not yet considered that fact, but he was correct. It did appear rather unlikely.

"I have no other excuse except to say it happened by chance both times. And it's not even an excuse, it's the truth."

"I know it is, darling."

"So does Mr. Marsden. He will vouch for me."

Philip paused again in his brushing. He did not care for the officer, she presumed.

"Were you meeting him there?"

Audrey pulled forward and turned on the stool to stare up at her husband. "No. Philip—"

He held up a hand. "I am not blind to the way he looks at you, and others will not be either. This is a very public situation. There will already be enough gossip."

"He does not *look* at me in any particular way, and I did not ask him to meet me," she said, growing angrier by the moment. Was Philip accusing her of planning a *tryst* in the woods with Hugh? While investigating her dead friend's potential murder?

She stood, impatient to be dressed, and for him to leave.

"Very well, I believe you," he sighed. "I just worry, that is all. He is...unsuitable for you."

She speared him with another direct, cutting glare. "There is nothing at all between Mr. Marsden and I, not like that. And anyhow, isn't that a shade hypocritical of you to decide?"

He'd taken a lover for months and hidden it from her. They had always agreed that should they stray beyond the confines of their untraditional marriage they would discuss it first.

Philip grimaced. "I was at least clandestine with St. John."

She gaped at him, incredulous. "You call *that* clandestine? You were arrested for murder!"

"That is beyond the point. Marsden is mired in scandal with that business with Neatham and his sister."

She bit her tongue and went to the boudoir door, swinging it open. "Greer. I'd like to dress now."

"Audrey—"

"You are wrong about him. Mr. Marsden is a perfect gentleman and has made no overtures toward me. In fact, I am quite sure he thinks me a nuisance. He despises all things connected with the ton as well, so your worries are unfounded. Now, I need to dress if you don't mind."

Her maid entered the boudoir with hesitation, likely having heard much, if not all, of their argument. Philip heaved a vexed sigh, placed the brush back onto the stand, and left. Audrey finished her whisky in a single toss, and Greer hurriedly dressed her. Hugh *had* been a perfect gentleman. Nothing untoward had occurred. If anything, she had been the one who was too forward in the stone cottage when she'd thrown herself into his arms and nearly sobbed with relief. He'd simply held her in return. The security of his arms, his own sigh of relief at finding her unharmed, had not been an overture in the least. Only a display of concern.

Audrey turned her thoughts to more important things. Hugh and the stable hands had certainly transported the dead woman's body back to Fournier House, then interred it into the icehouse, alongside Charlotte. Philip, Hugh, and the coroner could all be discussing important developments without her as she primped in her boudoir. Audrey finally told Greer to just pin up her hair.

She met with Verly at the bottom of the stairs and was informed that His Grace was in the study. As she approached, voices could be heard behind the door, one of which made her pulse skip. Audrey pushed back her shoulders, annoyed with herself, and entered.

She made an effort to find Philip first. He stood holding a glass of whisky at the hearth, the fire newly stoked. After so many days of hot, humid weather, Audrey had been longing for the brisk weather of autumn, not this damp, bone-deep chill.

A shorter, trim man in clean and pressed if not overly fashionable clothes, rose immediately from one of the club chairs. It was the man from the inquest. And standing behind a second club chair, rubbing a thick towel over his dark head of wet hair, was Hugh Marsden. He'd stripped down to his shirtsleeves and waistcoat, his drenched jacket and hat set up before the hearth's flames to help them dry.

She locked eyes with Hugh but severed the connection quickly, Philip's admonishments still wending their way through her head.

"Dr. Wilkes, may I present my wife, Audrey, the Duchess of Fournier," Philip said. "Darling, this is Dr. Wilkes, the coroner."

The proper introductions having been made, Dr. Wilkes now bowed at the hip. "Your Grace."

She found she could not part her lips to speak. Philip pulled a tartan wool blanket from the back of his study's leather couch and draped it around her shoulders.

"You're still shivering," he said.

"Thank you." She clutched the blanket like a shawl and with reluctance, approached the hearth.

Hugh had a glass of whisky in the hand that was not scrubbing the towel through his hair. He tossed the drink back.

"I have informed the coroner that you came upon the new victim's body with Lady Cassandra," Hugh said, his voice firm and clipped. He was angry, she realized. A departure from the tenderness he'd shown at the clearing. "I've also related that you think you saw a person in the woods immediately following."

"What?" Philip stepped away from Audrey's side. "I have not heard of this. Explain."

Audrey wasn't sure if he was speaking to her or to Hugh until she saw that he held the Bow Street officer in yet another searing glare. Hugh matched it with one of his own, likely in reaction to the duke's imperious command.

"It was after Cassie left to fetch help," Audrey said quickly, stepping in before either one could speak. "I saw movement in the trees. My horse was spooked. I think there was someone there, but I went into the ruined cottage and...well, no one came after me."

Until Hugh arrived and she set upon him with a rock she'd jiggled loose from the wall. He sported a raw scrape and faint bruise on his jaw. Then, of course, they'd embraced. She pinned her bottom lip between her teeth and tried to dispel the memory of how he'd clutched her to him, hushing her, promising her that she was safe.

Belatedly, she realized Dr. Wilkes was speaking. The coroner looked at her, expectantly.

"Can you repeat that?" she asked, feeling even more discombobulated.

"You also believe someone was in the wood near the quarry

when you happened upon the countess's body," Dr. Wilkes said. His voice betrayed no suspicion, but she remembered Philip's comment in her boudoir, about how dubious the coroner might be about her finding two bodies within one week.

"Yes, but that time, I didn't see anyone. It was only a feeling."

The coroner nodded, but she withered at her own statement. She needed fact, not *feeling*. Annoyed with herself, she turned toward the fire.

"Why would you choose to stay?"

The coroner's next question shouldn't have caught her off guard. Hadn't Cassie questioned her? Philip and Hugh, too? She couldn't exactly tell Dr. Wilkes the truth—that she'd wanted a chance to inspect the body and touch one of the dead woman's items to peer into its memories. So, she shrugged a shoulder in what she hoped was a blithe manner and said, "It seemed disrespectful to leave the poor lady all alone."

If the coroner questioned the veracity of her answer, his serious expression gave no indication. "I see."

Hugh, who had been alternately drying his dark hair and sipping another whisky, tossed the towel onto a chair. "Let us all speak plainly. Whatever the motive for these two killings, the duchess has twice now nearly interrupted the man in his deed. He might believe she has seen more than she has. He might even suspect she could identify him."

The hot bath, the whisky, the blanket over her shoulders, none of it had whisked the chill from her limbs. Now, she felt the slide of more ice in her veins.

"Are you suggesting my wife is in some sort of danger, Marsden?"

Hugh's expression remained hard and inscrutable as he met Audrey's eyes, not the duke's. "I do. It is imperative, duchess, that you do not go off on your own again. It would be best if you stayed in at Fournier House for the time being."

She gaped at him, livid, and perfectly aware of his ulterior motive—to keep her out of his investigation. The very investigation *she* brought him to Hertfordshire for! Yes, it was true that she might have been seen by a killer, but fear for her own safety had not cowed her before, and she wouldn't let it now. Her friend had been pushed to her death; a maid from Haverfield had been bludgeoned. If there were any way Audrey could help discover the killer, she would do it. Besides, she had every intention of going to Haverfield the next day to speak to her mother and uncle, and hopefully to question the kitchen staff. Mrs. Landry was still Cook for his lordship, and Audrey knew the older woman had a soft spot in her heart for her.

She smiled sweetly. "I will take your advice into consideration." Her tone was so honeyed that Hugh only clenched his jaw and finished the rest of his whisky before turning to the hearth. He knew her too well to believe she was being sincere.

"What I would like to know is the reason for your visit to Fournier House today, Marsden," the duke said.

The coroner stood up from his club chair, his hands clasped behind his back. "Officer Marsden wished to discuss a new element in the investigation into the countess's death."

"New element?" Audrey echoed, freshly riveted.

He turned his bespectacled eyes toward her. "Your Grace, it is a matter of delicacy and not suitable for such refined company."

She frowned. That was the second time that day a man had decided something was not *suitable* for her. "I assure you, Dr. Wilkes, I am not the delicate flower you have mistaken me to be."

"I must insist, Your Grace—"

"My wife will remain." Although Philip's voice was not baritone, he projected it with definitive ducal grandeur. The coroner immediately assented with a deep nod. "What is this new element?"

Hugh peered at the duke with something curiously like respect, though Audrey was certain the emotion would be difficult for him to reconcile with. She pressed her lips together to stop a grin.

"When I questioned Lady Bainbury's maid, she revealed the countess was expecting a child," Hugh replied.

Audrey's heart plummeted. Her jaw softened. Hugh's dark brown eyes found hers, and she recalled discussing Charlotte's melancholy in his room above the inn just the day before.

Charlotte had been cheery at their last meeting, but not uncommonly so. She hadn't been bursting at the seams with delight as Genie had been when she had finally announced that she would be giving Michael an heir soon. However, if Charlotte had suffered two other miscarriages recently, she might have had some reservations. She would have wanted to be further along before making an announcement.

"What bearing could this have upon the investigation?" Philip asked.

"Isn't it obvious? If Charlotte was expecting a child there is no reason why she would have thrown herself from the quarry," Audrey said.

"Or if she had recently suffered yet another loss, it could have pushed her toward self-destruction. However, first I must verify the countess's state. I have come to perform an autopsy," the coroner stated. Audrey cringed.

"Is that really necessary?" Philip asked, his aversion plain.

"It is, Your Grace. I must gather facts, not suppositions made by servants, even those closest to the countess."

The duke sighed in resignation. "Very well. I take it you will be attending the procedure, Marsden?"

Hugh took his jacket from where he'd draped it over the oval fire screen next to the hearth. The fine wool still looked sopping wet. "I am."

"Wearing that?" Audrey asked.

Hugh inspected his jacket, as if wondering what she found offensive about it.

"It is soaked. *You* are soaked, crown to foot," she explained. "And I assume you are performing the autopsy in the icehouse, Dr. Wilkes?"

The man nodded once in answer. He was brief, direct, and formal, though she found his formality more due to respect than arrogance, which she appreciated.

Audrey turned to her husband and widened her eyes. Philip sighed again.

"Verly," the duke called, and because the butler had been standing just outside the study door, he appeared at once. "Have Officer Marsden turned out in something dry and suitable to a...medical procedure."

"That isn't necessary," Hugh insisted, continuing to don his wet jacket.

"Don't be stubborn," Audrey said.

"That's the pot calling the kettle black," he muttered.

"You'll be frozen within minutes wearing those clothes. The duke surely has something that will fit you."

"I am not wearing the duke's clothes," he bellowed as he grabbed his hat and slapped it onto his head. Drops of water shuttled down his temples.

Audrey covered her mouth to stifle her sudden amusement. Hugh tucked his chin and glared at her, betraying himself with a twitch of his mouth. Only then, did she recall that Philip, Dr. Wilkes, and Verly were still present.

Philip's narrowed gaze wiped the grin from her lips. Verly and Dr. Wilkes wore matching inscrutable expressions.

"Not to worry, Marsden, I'm sure a footman has something more to your measurements. Verly." Philip stepped aside, a clear indication that Hugh was to exit the study and follow the butler.

With one final piercing glare at Audrey, he did just that, his hessians leaving damp marks on the polished floor.

CHAPTER

TWELVE

The rain cleared out by the time Hugh returned to Low Heath. Barely a chair in the tavern was vacant, and the jovial ruckus was almost offensive after the last two hours he'd spent in Fournier's icehouse with Coroner Wilkes. Hugh made his way through the crowded tavern, requesting kidney pie and a tankard of ale to be delivered to his room. The somber task of opening the countess's abdomen to the coroner's educated eye and determining the state of her womb had left an oil slick sensation under Hugh's skin. Paired with intense hunger, the feeling was not especially welcome.

It was not the smell or the sight of human innards that had disturbed him, for Hugh had been witness to dozens of similar scenes before—Miss Lovejoy's mutilated body and Mr. Bernadetto's slashed throat were just two of the more recent ones that came to mind. No, what lodged like a stone in his chest after he'd left Wilkes to the task of closing the necessary incisions, was the confirmation that the small life that had barely taken root within the countess had shared its mother's fate. It was confirmed. As her maid claimed, Lady Bainbury had been with child and roughly two months gone.

He climbed the stairs and made his way to his room with the dark thought that the person who had harmed the countess might have known they were also doing away with the unborn child. That the babe was, in fact, the incentive. Hugh rolled his shoulders as he entered his room, the muscles knotted with tension. He came to a stop and stared at his valet, who stood next to the open clothespress, a hammer in his hand.

"Christ, Basil, what are you doing?"

Basil brought the tool down upon what looked curiously like a new shelf, hammering a nail into place. "I was not going to tolerate more snagged threads."

Hugh closed the door. "So, you decided to repair it?"

"Something had to be done."

"You are entirely too at your leisure," he muttered, removing his damp hat, and tossing it onto the bedstead.

Basil followed the flight of the hat in astonishment, and then whipped his attention back to Hugh and stared, agog. "Pierce my eyes, *what* are you wearing?"

Hugh had anticipated Basil's certain discontent when he'd accepted the clothing from one of the duke's footmen. The broad, fall-fronted trousers were cut from low-quality tweed and were billowy around the thighs; the slightly yellowed, drop-shouldered shirt was a size too large and had been darned at the elbow more than once; and the jacket... Hugh shrugged out of the threadbare sack coat.

"It's a long story, but suffice it to say, I needed to borrow some clothes from one of the duke's footmen. My own will be delivered tomorrow, clean and pressed and meeting your standards, I'm sure."

Basil sniffed. "The duke should pay his servants better if they are reduced to wearing such dreary things on their day off."

Hugh made no comment but thought of Audrey and how

she'd imagined the duke would be willing to lend some of his own clothes. As if Hugh would put on a duke's clothes! And Fournier's at that. Hugh had dressed and met Wilkes in the icehouse without delay and had thankfully not seen the duchess on his way.

Tension coiled in his shoulders again at the thought of her. He'd known she would search for the cottage. She had at least not gone alone, but good God, the woman was a magnet for disaster. She could not have possibly predicted finding yet another slain body; however, the desire to blame her for the misfortune was right there on the tip of his tongue.

He wasn't angry with her exactly, just frustrated beyond reason. Hugh rubbed his bruised and scraped jaw as Basil muttered to himself about having to now launder second-rate garments. He'd be forced to mend them as well because it would be entirely beneath his standards to return them with tears and loose threads, even if they had been there before.

"And what sort of fisticuffs did you get into at the duke's household?" Basil asked, now eyeing his chin.

Hugh dropped his hand and undressed down to his smalls (damp but at least still his own). "Another long story." He did not wish to discuss how he'd subdued the duchess before she could bash in his skull. As impressive as her fight had been, the idea of her huddling in the cottage, fearful of a potential killer closing in on her unwound a tight curl of latent hostility within him.

He also couldn't divest himself of the unexpected and stirring response he'd had to Audrey's embrace. Both of them drenched, breathing heavily, clinging to each other...her figure had fit against his with remarkable perfection. Even now, a pulse of heat fired from the pit of his stomach. The overwhelming need to shield her had left a twisted friction that stretched from the base of his throat, straight to his groin.

He emitted a growl and snatched the folded stack of fresh clothing from his valet's hands. Considering the time of night, Basil had brought forth a nightshirt and banyan. Hugh dressed moments before his tray of pie and ale was delivered.

"There's been another murder," Hugh announced after drawing deeply on the tankard. Basil dropped the hammer onto the floor.

"My goodness. Who is it?"

As Hugh forced himself to eat, he informed Basil of the events of the evening. His valet, after picking up the dropped hammer and finishing with his unnecessary project, digested the news and said, "The person Her Grace saw in the woods had every opportunity to attack her. That he did not indicates he does not wish the duchess harm."

Hugh mulled that over, seeing the value of it. Perhaps he'd been wrong to suggest she was in danger.

"Or perhaps the killer did not attack Audrey because he heard her tell the duke's sister to ride for help," Hugh suggested.

"Addressing the duchess by her given name, are we?" Basil's suggestive tone dripped with sarcasm.

"I don't know why I keep you on." Hugh sat back in his chair and took another slug of his ale. Basil chuckled, but then jumped with a start when a slight figure leaped onto the frame of the open window.

Sir laughed at the valet's show of fright, and Hugh couldn't hold back his own grin. The lad had promised a report within twenty-four hours, and here he was.

"Fiend," Basil muttered. "Is the door too puzzling for you?"

"Aw, come off it, Baz, a spy's gotta be stealthy, ain't that right Mister Hugh?" Sir said, coming to sit on the window embrasure. Hugh held up his tankard in salute. "We're picking up the earl's repaired saddle, but Joe wanted to wet his gullet downstairs 'fore we shoved off."

"What have you learned at Bainbury's?" Hugh asked.

"Nothing much. The lady was sad all the time and wouldn't eat. The servants all liked her well enough, but nobody's sobbing rivers over her or anything, what with her being the third countess to cock up her toes."

Before leaving London, Hugh had pulled the reference file on the previous countess's death. Lady Mary Finborough had married Bainbury just two years prior to her suicide. Exited the world via a bullet to her brain. A maid found her in bed, muff pistol in hand. The file had not included much more than the particulars, but he recalled the lady's family had an estate in Bower's Grange, a half-day's ride from Low Heath.

"Were the earl and countess on friendly terms?" Hugh asked.

Sir shrugged a bony shoulder. "The cook says they took their meals on their own. The toff is hardly ever here, but the lady stayed year-round."

It was possible Bainbury would maintain his husbandly rights and bed his wife from time to time, but he thought it more likely the countess had taken a lover.

"Any scandal about an affair? Was there another man?"

Basil *tsked*. "Come now, the boy is hardly out of short pants."

Sir scowled. "I just haven't gotten meself a new pair yet, is all. And just so you know, I did hear a bit of rum juice: they think the doctor came 'round a time too much."

Doctor Ryder. Hugh recalled he'd claimed to have met with her often to provide her with her medicinal laudanum. Hugh despised the opiate tincture that was prescribed to so many women, and men as well, mostly as a way to reduce nerves. The stuff was nothing more than an acceptable narcotic, and damned addictive at that. Ryder had deemed Charlotte's melancholy severe enough to require it, but perhaps there had been another reason for his visits. Without Bainbury—who had stayed in London for the Season to sit in Parliament while the countess was in Hertfordshire—she would have had no obstacles should she embark on a tryst with the local physician.

"They also don't like the duchess none." Sir's eyes homed in on the half of the kidney pie Hugh hadn't been able to stomach. He picked up the plate and extended it.

"Keep talking," he ordered, "even with your mouth stuffed."

Basil muttered about rapidly diminishing principles, but Sir dug in with gusto. Crumbs fell from his lips as he explained how most of the staff thought she might be "dicked in the nob" after what happened with the duke in the spring, and wished she'd let things alone.

"His heir's about to get legshackled, and this business is causing problems," he added.

"Lord Renfry?" Hugh asked. Bainbury had three children, though the heir was the only one for which Hugh had bothered to find out a name.

"Yup." Sir wiped his mouth. "He's gone up to London to escort the lady and her family here. Supposed to be an engagement bash or some such. Now, o'course, it's all ruined."

"Nothing like an inconvenient death and mourning customs to scupper a good party among the ton," Basil said, his voice rich with sarcasm and condescension.

Hugh held up a hand. "Hold there, Sir—you said Renfry's gone *back* to London? Meaning he'd been here in Hertfordshire before?"

The lad shrugged. "Suppose so. One of the grooms—I don't like him. He's a nervous one. Got a secret, I bet—says Renfry's got a temper and takes it out on the horses. Says he quarreled with him a few weeks back and nearly lost his post."

The boy was good, and though Hugh sometimes had reservations about using him as a courier and informant, he compensated him well enough. Also, he wanted to keep Sir on the straight and narrow; honest work for Hugh left the lad less time to get up to no good with the gangs of the East End.

"All right, good work. Anything more?"

Sir patted his belly after polishing the plate with a few licks of his tongue. "Nope. But cor, I've never ate so good in me life. This country living ain't for just the sheep after all."

Basil plucked the plate from his lap. "The sheep have better manners, I suspect."

Sir tipped his cap to them and scurried out the window, disappearing from view, as good as if he'd dropped straight to the ground below.

"What next?" Basil asked, though Hugh couldn't be certain if it was a rhetorical question born of exasperation, or if it was sincere about his next move in the investigation.

"A visit to Lord Edgerton tomorrow," he replied, settling on the latter. "I'd like to know whose body I transported earlier this afternoon."

THIRTEEN

Audrey couldn't eat more than a slice of toast before setting out for Haverfield. Her stomach churned all night after Hugh and the coroner left. She'd gone to her bedchamber and paced while the autopsy had been underway.

News of the pregnancy had cast yet another layer of darkness over Charlotte's death. The two were related. As was the woman in the straw chip hat. But how? The itch of intuition wouldn't leave her be for the rest of the long night. Finally, at the blue of dawn, Audrey had slept fitfully for a few hours. The crummy bit of half sleep only seemed to make her feel worse as she dressed for the morning's visit to her former home in a somber dress of deep burgundy cambric, paired with a black embroidered spencer and matching gloves.

Greer informed her that the duke had already risen and had left with his steward, and the lightness that descended over Audrey's shoulders made her feel a pinch guilty. She'd been prepared to invite Philip to Haverfield. Hugh's warning that she should not go off by herself had not frightened her, but Philip's discontent after the debacle at the stone cottage had been clear.

Their marriage was the sort that often left them independent of each other, and Audrey thought perhaps an effort to include Philip might go a long way in soothing his recently gloomy moods.

However, he was already gone, so she shook off the guilt and called for the brougham.

Haverfield had been the country seat for four Lord Edgertons since the time of Henry VI. The barony was firmly established and respected, the home itself situated on a hillock with a quaint prospect overlooking a dale with intersecting stone walls and pastures. For anyone else, the estate would surely appeal. But for Audrey, there was a bleakness about it that seemed to seep into her bones whenever she visited. It was not something that happened often. She didn't seek her mother out, and Lady Edgerton did not seek Audrey. It was as though, with her marriage to the duke, the baroness had wiped her hands clean of motherhood. Then again, her mother did manage to see Audrey's older sister, Millie, Lady Redding, from time to time. The thought would at times send pangs through her chest, squeezing her heart in a weak show of jealousy, but they never lasted. All Audrey had to do was remember some of the cruel, cold things her mother had said to her over the years, recall the way she had summoned two matrons from Shadewell to Haverfield to pick her up and trundle her off to the sanatorium like some prisoner, and the envy died.

Millie could have the baroness all to herself.

The hard, cool glaze of indifference had settled once again upon Audrey's shoulders and expression by the time she was led into the drawing room at Haverfield. It was early in the day for callers, so she wasn't surprised to find herself waiting for several minutes while the butler, Gregson, left to summon the baron. The carriage had passed the dowager house along the drive, but her mother would not be found there, Audrey was certain.

That was where her mother *claimed* to reside, even though she was not officially a dowager baroness. The new Lord Edgerton had never wed, and so there would be no new Lady Edgerton. The reason was clear to anyone who cared enough to look. Audrey's mother and uncle were romantically involved. They were discreet about it, as a marriage to his former sister-in-law would be a voidable union, if ever challenged. Polite society would not favor it. It was, surely, one of the reasons Lady Edgerton no longer went to London. She and Audrey's uncle ensconced themselves at Haverfield. For how long they had been carrying on their liaison, however, was the real question. Had it predated the previous Lord Edgerton's death? Audrey didn't want to know.

Sure enough, when her uncle entered the drawing room, Lady Edgerton was with him.

"Goodness, Audrey, we weren't expecting a call, and so early too. Has something happened? Is the duke unwell?" her mother said with more annoyance than alarm.

"The duke is fine, thank you," she replied. "I'm sorry to call so early, but there is something I wished to discuss."

She'd also wanted to arrive before the coroner or Hugh Marsden.

"We were just taking breakfast," her uncle said, then with indifference, "I suppose you could join us."

"Thank you, my lord, but no. I'm not sure this is a discussion to be had over a meal."

Her mother's brow furrowed in concern, and she quickly rang for tea before taking a seat. "Well, then, do sit and be out with it."

The baron grimaced, though Audrey suspected it was in reaction to being told he would not be getting back to his breakfast plate right away. He remained standing behind the baroness, his hands resting upon the back of the chair. Once again, Audrey recoiled at a memory that had been seared into her brain, compliments of a rope of sapphires her mother had insisted she wear to a musicale some years ago, when she'd finally returned from Shadewell. Pressed into Audrey's palms, the necklace had fired off an image of her uncle's near naked form clasping her mother to him. The dowager had screeched about Audrey's clumsy fingers when the sapphires had clattered to the floor. From then on, Audrey had not been able to wear sapphires—or look at her uncle—without the ghost of that memory interjecting itself.

She sat across from her mother and asked, "Are any of Haverfield's maids missing?"

Her mother's lips popped open in surprise. She peered at Audrey as though a grotesque insect had just landed in her soup. "*What?*"

"Our maids? Missing?" Lord Edgerton spluttered. "What is this about?"

Audrey had spent some of her sleepless night deliberating how best to approach the questioning. Which information to give and what to hold back. As her mother and uncle already disapproved of her for the most part, she knew it would only anger or unsettle them if she announced she had stumbled upon yet another dead body.

"A woman was found on Fournier Downs land yesterday afternoon," she explained evenly. Then, after a pause, added, "She was deceased."

The baron released the chair and came around the arm to stand before Audrey. She wasn't keen on him glowering down at her, but she also didn't want to jump to her feet. Poise and calm would benefit the situation more.

"What gives you the notion this woman was one of our maids?"

Audrey lifted her chin. "I believe I recognized her."

As expected, her mother gasped with dismay. "You've *viewed* this dead woman's body?"

"I have."

Withholding that she had been the one to find it continued to be her best strategy.

"I say, this is beyond the pale, you coming here to discuss such a turn of events. Where is Fournier? Why hasn't he come?"

Audrey straightened her back and pressed her shoulders lower. The duke knew the coroner and Hugh were planning to visit; he hadn't deemed it necessary to come himself. She hadn't anticipated her uncle viewing that as odd, though she could see now it was shortsighted of her.

"He is attending to other business," Audrey replied, leaving it vague as to whether it had to do with the dead body or something else.

The baron muttered something low in his throat in response, but it wasn't audible. Nor would she have liked to have heard it anyhow.

"Fetch Mrs. Banks," her mother instructed the footman waiting by the door. No sooner had the servant disappeared on his task to find the housekeeper than Gregson, the butler, replaced him.

"My lord, my lady, Dr. Wilkes and Officer Marsden to see you."

Audrey sighed lightly. They had arrived earlier than expected. Within moments the two men entered the drawing room. While the coroner eyed Audrey with mild surprise, Hugh only pursed his lips and fought the apparent urge to groan.

"Your Grace," Dr. Wilkes said, directing a short bow toward her. Only then did he greet the baron and baroness, a propriety that undoubtedly pricked at both her uncle and mother. While they had schemed to have Millie and Audrey marry higher in society, and Millie's marriage to a viscount was something to be lauded, Audrey's ascension to duchess had seemed to have the adverse effect. Her standing in society was now much higher than theirs, and they acted as if it was an insult.

"I take it you are here to discuss the body my niece has just informed us about?" the baron said by way of greeting.

The coroner and Hugh remained standing. "Indeed, my lord. It is a possibility the deceased was a maid in your employ," Dr. Wilkes said.

The baroness wrung her hands. "This is vexing. Very vexing. I've sent for my housekeeper. Mrs. Banks will tell us if a maid is missing."

"Where was she found on Fournier's land?" the baron asked.

"The woods," Hugh answered, his vague answer seemingly deliberate. It was not a satisfactory answer for the baron.

"He's got thousands of acres, my man. Where specifically? And how was she found?"

Uneasy silence descended. Neither the coroner nor Hugh seemed to want to announce Audrey's involvement, and she was certain it was because of Hugh's warning the evening before. Any gossip that she might have seen the killer would travel like flame on parched grass.

Thankfully, Mrs. Banks arrived just then, breathing heavily, her cheeks reddened from hastening to the drawing room.

"My lady?" she said with a bob. A maid bearing the tea service entered on the housekeeper's heels.

"Are any staff missing this morning, Mrs. Banks?" the baroness asked as the maid attempted to deliver the tray. Audrey's mother waved the maid aside, and the girl went still, tray in hand.

"Yes, my lady," the housekeeper said, her heavy brow lifting in surprise. "Ida Smith. She was absent from her duties last night in the kitchen and is still missing this morn." She looked askance at the coroner and Hugh. "Is Ida in some sort of trouble?"

Ida Smith. Audrey frowned. Having a name to associate with the poor woman gave her death a solemn finality.

Hugh addressed the housekeeper's question. "We'll need someone to come to Fournier House to confirm her identity, but I'm afraid Miss Smith has met a violent end."

Mrs. Banks gasped and covered her lips. The tea tray in the maid's hands shook and rattled, and the girl clumsily set the whole thing down onto the table with a clatter.

The baroness yelped. "Annie, my goodness!"

"I'm sorry, my lady." The maid righted a few toppled cups and a spilled pitcher of milk.

"You should exert more self-control."

"She was simply startled, Mother," Audrey said, annoyed by her lack of care or understanding.

"I'll ask you not to make excuses for my staff," her mother snapped while brushing at her skirt, acting as though the pot of tea had spilled upon it. Audrey pursed her lips and refrained from shaking her head in exasperation.

The maid, Annie, met the duchess's eyes. They flared in what might have been alarm before averting to the carpet. Audrey felt a pang of sympathy for her; her cheeks were bright red from embarrassment. She wore a long-sleeved flowered muslin dress paired with a brown scarf, which she had tucked into her bodice. A dark purple marking reached up her neck from under the tightly crossed panels of her scarf. A burn? Bruise?

"Go on to the kitchen, Annie," Mrs. Banks said with a slightly more maternal tone. The girl swiftly fled.

"A violent end?" the baron repeated Hugh's earlier words. "Are you saying this maid was *murdered*?"

"I am afraid so, my lord," the coroner replied. "Officer Marsden and I will need to speak to your servants."

The baron jerked his head back. "Whatever for?"

"Your servants will have more information about Miss Smith that might prove useful to the investigation," Hugh answered, sounding as if that ought to have been evident. Audrey agreed it should have been. But then, the baron scoffed.

"Yes, yes, I know that. What I meant is why must Marsden be involved? He is here from London at the behest of Lady Prescott, not me. I will not have him badgering my servants."

Her uncle's behavior, speaking of Hugh as if he were not in even the room, smacked of arrogance and superiority. Audrey simmered with a sudden urge to defend him.

"My lord," Dr. Wilkes spoke before Audrey could determine what to say, "the questioning of your servants will conclude much sooner if I am joined by another competent officer of the law."

"Competent," the baron sneered. "No, I will not have it. I was a rather good friend of the fifth Viscount Neatham, you know."

"How lucky for the viscount," Hugh said, not even bothering to mask his sarcasm.

Lord Edgerton glared. "No man who so disrespected Neatham's heir is welcome in my home. I will ask you to leave, Marsden."

Audrey gaped, while Hugh held the baron's glare with equal loathing. A small, barely-there tug at the corner of his lips hinted at amusement, but Audrey couldn't imagine what Hugh could find so diverting.

"Uncle, this is absurd," she said. "You are being rude."

"Do not speak to your uncle that way," her mother said,

lashing out with the same buried anger she'd shown after Annie dropped the tea tray.

She forced the hard glaze of indifference to settle back upon her shoulders. When it was in place, Audrey coolly replied, "I will speak to him however I choose."

The baron curled his upper lip. "You've become quite the little upstart since you married Fournier, haven't you? Turned your back on us."

Audrey stood from the sofa with all the calm grace she could muster. "Can you truly blame me?"

The baron stepped forward wearing a sneer so intense it was nearly comic. "We *saved* you, you ungrateful girl."

Her eyes burned, Dr. Wilkes and Hugh hazy in her peripheral vision. She did not want to look at either of them after this embarrassing display of familial discord, especially with her uncle's veiled reference to when they sent her away to Shadewell to "restore" her mind.

"My lord," her mother whispered, a frantic note on her tone as she peered at their company.

"I will take my leave, as requested," Hugh said, his voice raised as if to divert the baron's attention. "Dr. Wilkes, I'm sure you can cover things here."

Eager to be gone as well, Audrey bid her mother and uncle a lackluster good day and swept from the drawing room.

"Any woman who can unravel a man's patience so quickly and thoroughly deserves applause," Hugh said, catching up to her outside the front entrance. Her driver opened the carriage door as she approached.

"In that case, there should be gales of applause interrupting all our conversations, Mr. Marsden."

"I take offense, as I believe I am an excruciatingly patient man."

Grateful at his attempt to lighten the air, she faced him. "I apologize for my uncle's behavior. He is abrasive at best."

"He's a horse's arse," he replied, eliciting a sharp laugh from Audrey. "But that is no fault of yours. Don't apologize for him, especially after the way he spoke to you back there." Hugh's eyes darkened, and she waited for him to ask what the baron had meant when he claimed to have saved her. But instead, he looked to his curricle and frowned.

"I don't suppose you could give me a lift into Low Heath? Wilkes and I traveled together, and I should leave the curricle for him for when he finishes his interviews."

Audrey hadn't expected such a request, and her surprise must have shown.

"I can ride in the box with the driver," he added, but she instantly shook her head.

"No, don't be absurd. You'll ride with me." She heard how commanding her tone was and was even further flustered. He bit back a grin.

"Of course, Your Grace," he replied with mocking reverence.

She instructed the driver and settled into the carriage, on the forward-facing bench as she generally preferred. Hugh sat across from her, and when the driver shut the door, closing them within, Audrey half-wished she had accepted Hugh's offer for him to ride up front.

His knees were entirely too close to hers. She shifted her own aside.

"You trust Dr. Wilkes will share all he discovers with you?" she asked as disappointment from not being able to talk to the staff set in. Then again, she could have hardly gone into the kitchens herself to ask questions. A duchess entering that part of the house would have caused too much agitation and discomfort for the servants; they certainly wouldn't have spoken plainly around her. No, the coroner would have better luck.

"I do. I find him to be high on intelligence and low on arrogance. And with two murders now, I think he knows there is something larger at play here."

Audrey frowned. "How do you mean?"

"They are connected. I just don't know how yet."

It was the same inexplicable feeling she had had as well. "The baby had something to do with the motive for Charlotte's murder."

Hugh peered at her, letting her statement linger. "Why do you say that?"

"Instinct, I suppose."

He nodded. "Most people have rather good instincts; they just fail to listen to them. In this case, I agree with yours. What else does your instinct say?"

"That it was not Bainbury's child," she replied.

"You think she had taken a lover," he replied.

"I do. As do you, if I'm correct."

"You are." He grinned and she tried to bury her delight at their exchange. But then, when he remained quiet, she narrowed her eyes.

"You aren't going to tell me who you suspect?"

"Why, so you can call on him for questioning and alert him to our suspicions? No."

Audrey hid her further delight at his use of 'our suspicions'.

"You aren't going there right now?" she asked.

"I am not. I'm paying a call on Lord and Lady Finborough."

It took Audrey a moment to place the name. She had not known Bainbury's second wife, but she recalled how, after their daughter's death, the marquess and marchioness had withdrawn from society.

If Hugh was calling on them, he had good reason. The most

obvious one sent gooseflesh up her arms. "You don't believe she committed suicide."

"I know nothing of the sort," he replied. "But I do have questions."

Audrey bit her lip. "I could have Kinson drive you there."

Hugh crossed his arms and pinned her with a knowing look. "And you would, of course, feel compelled to introduce me to the marquess and marchioness."

"It would only be polite." Lord and Lady Finborough would more likely give Hugh an audience if he arrived with a duchess.

He sighed and peered out the window at the passing trees. She was certain he was drawing out his answer just to goad her. Or perhaps he knew just how unceremonious it was for her to accompany him. There was no adequate reason for it, other than to mollify her own curiosity...and to avoid going home. It wasn't that she was avoiding Philip or Cassie, but the prospect of being cooped up in the house all day when she could instead be doing something active to help solve Charlotte's murder, and now Ida Smith's, could not have appealed less.

"Very well." Hugh finally turned away from the window with a teasing grin. "After all, a duchess can do as she pleases."

CHAPTER

FOURTEEN

Upon leaving Kilton House, the country seat of the Marquess of Finborough, Hugh had the disorienting sensation of having been dropped into the middle of a labyrinth. Seated across from him, Audrey worried her lower lip while staring out the window. Silence surrounded them like a bubble as the driver trundled them back toward Low Heath. It appeared they had both been laid low from the interview with the marquess and marchioness.

The duchess's presence had been, Hugh was forced to admit, a benefit when they'd first arrived. As most ton would be, Lord Finborough was not keen on speaking to a Bow Street Runner about his daughter's death four years prior. He'd been immediately suspicious of Hugh's motives, especially after hearing the news about the newest Lady Bainbury's demise. He had not been able to turn out a duchess, however, and when Lady Finborough joined them, she expressed gratitude for Audrey's visit. Unlike her husband, Lady Finborough was not skeptical of their interest in their daughter's death.

"At last, perhaps someone will listen to us."

"How do you mean?" Hugh asked.

"Our doubts, of course," the marchioness answered. "Mary did not die by her own hand. I did not believe it, and neither did his lordship."

They explained that Mary had been happy, practically radiant the last time they saw her, about a week before her death. She had taken her mother aside and told her that, although it was still early on, she might have some happy news to announce very soon.

"She was with child," Audrey deduced, her astonishment plain. Hugh had felt the same connecting strike ringing through him.

Shows of emotion were not the way of the ton, but the marchioness's tears could not be hindered. Lord Finborough had scowled at Hugh as if he held the officer responsible while Audrey gently asked if Bainbury had known of his wife's condition.

"He wouldn't listen to us, practically gave us the cut direct," the marquess said.

"Suicide carries a taint," Hugh had said. "Perhaps he wanted to distance himself from it as quickly and thoroughly as possible."

"The earl did not care. Mary's death would be gossip for as long as the mourning period lasted, but he knew there would be other young misses waiting to land an earl," Lady Finborough had replied. Hugh saw her reasoning—as shameful as suicide was, a man's title could withstand just about anything.

The carriage ride to Kilton House had lasted just over an hour, and Hugh began to wonder if the return would be undertaken in complete silence. It would not be such a bad thing; he needed time to think about the possible connecting threads the questions around Mary's death now introduced. He could see Audrey's mind was at work as well.

"They were both with child when they died," she whispered

at last. The carriage rocked along the road, the stifling heat working up a sweat under his clothes. He loosened his cravat despite the impropriety and Basil's certain chastisement.

"Who would not want those babies born?" she asked.

"Bainbury told me he didn't need more children, considering he already has his heir and spares," he replied. "But another child would not have posed any threat to him or his heir. He had no motive to not want them born."

"And even if they were not his, he would claim them," Audrey agreed.

"Certainly. It is the honorable practice."

For a true gentleman, declaring that a child born to their wife was not theirs by blood was a dishonorable act. The same could be said about lords and their by-blows, although the rules of morality there were a little more muddled. While most gentleman would not formally recognize a child sired outside the bond of marriage, it was the honorable thing to care for them monetarily. What had made Lord Neatham so much the eccentric was the act of bringing his by-blow into his own home, raising him alongside his legitimate children, and allowing his short-lived mistress to remain as nanny. And when Hugh's mother had no longer been needed as nanny, she'd been given a tidy set of rooms attached to the carriage house and an annual living.

To say that Viscountess Neatham had been bitter about such an arrangement would be an understatement. Though to Hugh, the viscountess and her opinions had little mattered. She'd barely been involved with her own children, and she and the viscount had been all but strangers.

"Perhaps Bainbury grew enraged when he learned Charlotte had a lover. Mary might have had one as well." Audrey didn't put any true feeling into the speculation, and Hugh thought that illustrated the problem perfectly.

"No, he would not have cared, not if the earl's disinterest in Mary matched the disinterest he displayed when speaking of Charlotte," he replied. "Passion is what drives a man to kill his wife. Anger. Hatred. Love. They are all there together on the edge of a very thin sword."

He met her eyes and found they were peering at him with scrutiny. "You have come across many cases like that in your time at Bow Street?"

"Unfortunately."

When a woman was killed, nine times out of ten, the killer was her husband or father or brother. And more than half of those cases were the result of a man losing his temper, taking things too far. He would be brought into custody a blubbering mess of anguish and regret.

"Do you enjoy your job, Mr. Marsden?"

The question took him by surprise. He shifted on the brocade cushion. "I don't think I enjoy it as much as I value it."

"Value?"

It would be difficult to put into words without exposing too much of himself. However, Hugh had nothing to be ashamed of.

"You are aware of my history, and the rather complicated position I hold in society. I am lucky Sir Gabriel took me on as a Runner after the debacle with the current Viscount Neatham."

"You refer to the duel," she said.

Hugh didn't like speaking of the duel. Invariably, it always led to the question of why his half-brother, Bartholomew, challenged him to pistols at dawn in the first place. And that was not something Hugh discussed, ever.

"I do," he said, then swiftly continued, "Sir Gabriel gave me a chance to remake myself, and that is something I am thankful for."

A slow grin spread across her lips, and Hugh wondered if he'd said something amusing.

"If I had been born a man, I think I would have liked to have been a Runner. From what I have seen, it is an exciting job."

Hugh was grateful she had not pressed for more information on Neatham and the duel. She had to be curious; the woman was insufferably inquisitive. Her restraint impressed him.

"If you had been born a man, you would now be Lord Edgerton, and I'm afraid the Runners' ranks are alarmingly low on barons."

The duchess laughed, a bright and stirring chime that gave him the oddest sense of victory. But the mention of the baron also reminded him of what Bainbury revealed, about Lord Edgerton and the baroness trying to hush up some possible scandal regarding Audrey. Her two-year absence in which she had not been on the Continent or in Scotland. Where else could she have been? For all the dispassion he'd shown his dead wives, Bainbury had seemed to light up with fervor when speaking of the duchess. It unsettled Hugh.

"Speaking of the baron," he began. Audrey's smile slipped, as if she knew what he was going to say. "What did he mean at Haverfield, when he said they'd saved you?"

The baron had practically seethed the words. He'd made no attempt to hide his bitterness over his niece's lofty title and her dismissal of them once she married the duke.

Audrey fidgeted with the delicate lace trimming of her gloves. "Just that they tried to better my circumstances with the betrothal to Bainbury, and I rejected it in favor of the duke. They were greatly ashamed."

Hugh had interviewed plenty of men and women over the years. He knew when someone was skirting the question at hand.

"The betrothal to Bainbury was a way to save you? From what?"

The duchess stopped fidgeting and clasped her hands together in her lap.

"It has something to do with your ability," he mused.

"Mr. Marsden, please."

Pressing on with questions when someone did not wish to answer them was simply part of Hugh's job. But he reminded himself that Audrey was not a suspect. She'd done nothing wrong. Her dark blue eyes turned glassy as she held his gaze, then drifted to her clasped hands.

"You've trusted me with the truth before." He cocked his head to try to look her in the eye. "You can do so again."

She shook her head. "I do trust you, but this... I'm sorry, I can't. Not yet."

Hugh straightened and sat back against the squab. *Not yet?* Those two simple words should not have pleased him as much as they did.

"I understand," he said. Whatever it was, it had caused her pain. It might be best if he didn't know just yet. He needed to focus on the murders and not who had hurt the duchess, or why.

They rode on in comfortable silence, broken only by topics not connected to the deaths. Audrey told him about Cassandra, whose summer at Fournier Downs was not going according to plan and how patient she had been at their lack of diversions. There was supposed to be a house party and they were to have attended one as well. But the duke's illness had thwarted it all.

When Audrey described some of the duke's symptoms, Hugh nodded and commented that he was glad to hear Fournier was recovered. However, it did not escape him that the symptoms sounded very much like those of a venereal disease. It wasn't uncommon of course; Thornton had once told him more than half his patients had one disease or another. Husbands passed things on to their unsuspecting wives with little thought or guilt. Though perhaps Audrey and the duke's marital arrangement protected her from such things. Hugh shifted his jaw. One could hope.

As they passed a signpost announcing that Low Heath was just a quarter mile ahead, Hugh reached back and knocked upon the wall of the carriage. The driver slowed, and Audrey frowned.

"I will walk from here," he announced. Arriving at the posting-inn in the duke's carriage was sure to draw attention, and if Hugh was going to investigate properly, he didn't want to be seen as the duke or duchess's lapdog.

Audrey nodded tightly. "Yes, of course."

He opened the door, but paused, holding it there for a moment. "Thank you for your help with the marquess and marchioness."

Her astonishment wiped away whatever feelings she'd had on his abandoning the coach. "Oh. You're most welcome. I'm sure I didn't do much more than listen to what they were so eager to tell us."

It was partially true. Once overcoming their skepticism, Lord and Lady Finborough had seemed to exhale with long-held opinions and hurts. Still, he and the duchess had conducted the interview relatively smoothly. It had felt natural, even.

"Good afternoon, Your Grace," he murmured before leaping to the dusty lane. He shut the door and from within, Audrey called to the driver to continue home. He watched the pale blue carriage disappear down the lane, and then he set out on foot.

By the time the first structures in town came into view, he was covered in road dust and sweat. He doffed his hat and wiped his brow with the kerchief Basil insisted he keep tucked into his breast pocket. Wasn't the countryside supposed to be full of cool breezes? Unlike polite society, he was accustomed to spending the doldrums of summer in town, where the air turned practically toxic with heat, humidity, and vapors rising off the Thames and through sewer grates as the city slowly boiled. The air here was certainly fresher and better fragranced, but he couldn't help but long for another quick storm to snap the humidity.

Ahead, a row of brick homes curved on a slight descending hill toward the village proper. Hung on a post outside one of these homes was a shingle for Dr. Joseph Ryder. Hugh slowed. The doctor would not be expecting him, and catching a suspect by surprise was usually the best method for extracting useful information. Though Hugh could not quite see the timid doctor shoving a woman to her death, or bashing in another's skull, the fact that Bainbury's household chattered about him visiting too often, and that it might have been a ruse for an ongoing assignation, was intriguing enough to want another talk with the doctor.

He stepped up to the front door and brought down the brass knocker. A moment later, an older woman wearing a pinafore, her white hair tucked up under a mob cap, opened the door. Doctor Ryder's nurse.

"Is the doctor in?"

"Have you an appointment?" she returned. When he answered that he did not, she stepped aside and gestured to the foyer. "Wait here."

Less than a minute later, she returned to lead him to Doctor Ryder's office. Hugh entered as the man was tying his cravat. The doctor flinched, his hands falling from his neckcloth.

"Officer. Forgive me, I wasn't expecting a call."

"I was passing by and thought to stop in."

The doctor dismissed the nurse, then gestured to a chair, but Hugh remained standing. The doctor's half-finished neck-cloth drooped, revealing a patch of reddened skin. A port wine stain, not a bruise or other injury. No wonder he wore his cravat to his chin, Hugh thought as a half-formed memory nudged at him. A doctor with a large birthmark on his neck...why did that ring so familiar to Hugh?

He glanced around the cluttered office. Stacks of books on shelves appeared disorganized, interspersed with trinkets; papers riddled the desk and spilled over onto a well-worn cushioned chair.

"How can I be of service?" the doctor asked after a protracted moment of quiet. "Are you feeling unwell?"

"I'm perfectly healthy as far as I'm aware, but thank you." Hugh peeled his eyes from a hand-stitched sampler bearing a proverb: *A cheerful heart is good medicine.* It looked like something a young child had done, and Hugh wondered if the doctor had a wife and children.

"No, I've come to ask you a few questions about Lady Bainbury—the previous."

Doctor Ryder's brows furrowed behind the rims of his spectacles. "You refer to Lady Mary Bainbury?"

"That is correct. Were you her physician as well?"

He seemed to recall his forgotten neckcloth and set about finishing the knot. "Yes, I was." He turned toward his desk and away from Hugh. "I don't see how that is relevant to this investigation."

"I've just come from Kilton House and a meeting with Lord and Lady Finborough," Hugh said. "Were you aware that the previous countess was with child when she died?"

He watched the doctor closely, and in doing so, saw him falter again with his half-formed cravat. The slightest fumble, but it was there, nonetheless.

"I...yes," he said with a slight sigh. "Yes, I did."

"Did Bainbury know?"

Doctor Ryder let out another exhale and gave up on the

knot. He sat heavily into his wooden swiveling chair behind his disorderly desk. "No. The countess said she wished to tell him as soon as the danger of losing the baby was greatly reduced, but then after her death... Well, I decided it would be added pain if I revealed it to the earl. What would be the point?"

Hugh only nodded. "And what about Charlotte?"

The doctor blinked owlishly. "What do you mean?"

"Did you know she was with child?"

He rolled back his chair and leaped to his feet. "What? No, I... How do you know this?"

Unless the doctor had spent time in his youth at Drury Lane or some other theatre, Hugh was inclined to believe his shocked reaction. The thought of the theater put Hugh in mind of London. If Ryder trained there, Thornton might know of him.

"Wilkes performed an autopsy to determine it."

The doctor sunk back into his chair, bracing his hands upon his desk. "I did not know. She...she was not forthcoming about her condition. Perhaps even she did not know?"

Hugh shook his head. "She knew."

Doctor Ryder rubbed his chin. "I hope it gave her some happiness before... Well, it was what she wanted: a bit of joy in her life. She had that, for a short while, at least."

"Do you mean to say the countess did not have joy in other parts of her life?" Hugh asked. "With the earl?"

The doctor shifted in his chair, sitting forward before standing up. "I do not like to speak out of turn, but it was my suspicion that she was not content in her marriage. The bloom had come off the rose, so to speak."

"And drops of laudanum would help her how, exactly?"

Doctor Ryder puffed out his chest, though it remained rather emaciated, even with the padding of his waistcoat and jacket. "When taken sparingly, laudanum calms and restores. Trust me, officer, I know the temptation many have to consume more than the recommended amount. Because of that, I made sure the countess only had a small vial—a quarter dram—in her possession. I would replace it every week."

That would account for his frequent visits to Bainbury Manor. So frequent that the countess came to look forward to them? Or to perhaps equate the doctor with the effects of the drug he prescribed?

Taking in Joseph Ryder once again, Hugh could contemplate how Charlotte might have found herself enamored. Though late in his fourth decade, he was physically fit and handsome in a studious and philosophical sort of way. He wore no gold band on his left ring finger. But the sampler...

"Do you have children, doctor?"

He pulled back at the unrelated question. *Good.* Hugh wanted to keep him flustered.

"Why, yes, in fact, I do. A daughter," he answered, a hesitant grin forming. "She is employed at Haverfield." His doting grin expanded. "Just a maid at the moment, of course, but Annie has dreams of being housekeeper at an estate someday."

Hugh perked up. *Annie.* The maid who nearly dropped the tea service tray and got a scolding from the baroness? As the doctor had not made mention of another body being found the day before, Hugh determined that gossip had yet to reach the village.

"I visited Lord Edgerton this morning," Hugh said. "I believe I saw your Annie delivering tea."

The doctor's pride showed in his smile. He in no way appeared concerned that Hugh had been at Haverfield speaking to the baron. Though he could not put the doctor entirely out of his mind as a suspect, and something about the port wine stain on his neck still pricked the back of Hugh's mind, just out of reach, Ryder seemed a little too oblivious of any violence done to a maid at his daughter's place of employment.

"Thank you for your time, doctor. I'll see myself out."

He'd write to Thornton; he might know more about the curious half-memory of a birthmarked doctor that Hugh's mind currently grappled with.

He paused before leaving the office. "One more thing. Lady Mary...was she melancholy as well?"

Doctor Ryder's brow crinkled. "Melancholy? Mary? No." A small grin touched his mouth before flattening out. "She had a sunny disposition. Everyone was drawn to her. She was..." After a moment of searching for the right word, he gave up and ended with, "Well, no matter. Thank you for stopping in, officer."

Hugh left the office, curious as to how the doctor might have finished his sentence. How would he have described Mary further? Certainly not suicidal.

He made his way to the inn, with every step sinking deeper into a muddle. One he could not have anticipated when the duchess's letter had arrived for him in London.

CHAPTER FIFTEEN

S cented water dripped from a sponge as Audrey washed herself that evening. A network of pipes had been installed into Fournier House the previous year, to carry heated water up into her and Philip's individual bathing chambers. After returning from the outing with Hugh earlier, then indulging Cassie by sitting for her in the rose garden while she sketched Audrey's likeness, and then enduring an awkward dinner with Philip and her sister-in-law, in which no one dared broach the events of the day before, Audrey had only wanted a good, long soak to ruminate on her visit to Kilton House.

She had left the marquess's estate with a heavy heart; Lord and Lady Finborough's despair over their daughter's death had not dulled in the handful of years since. Audrey could only imagine the pain they had endured after hearing Mary had taken her own life in such a violent manner. If Mary had been exultant with the knowledge that she was carrying a baby, it made little sense that she would do such a thing.

The mystery over the second Lady Bainbury's death wasn't the only thing weighing Audrey down as she returned to Fournier Downs. Hugh's questions about her uncle's outburst had twisted her up inside. He knew she was keeping a secret from him, and how she wished he would simply let it go. It was none of his business anyhow! It was her past, her pain. And yet, she sensed he would not be easy until she confided in him. Either that, or until he was able to pick apart the secret for himself. She let the sponge drop back into the water with a splash and reclined, closing her eyes as the lavender-scented steam curled around her.

Yes, she had confided in him before, and it hadn't been anything like she'd feared. He'd been skeptical of her ability at first, but he'd quickly trusted her. Believed her. But if he learned she had been locked away in an asylum for two years, it would change the way he saw her. Thought of her. Maybe he wouldn't trust her any longer. Audrey rocked her head side to side. What a fool she was! What did it matter what he thought of her? And why, *why* did she wish to confide in him? It was madness.

Greer entered the boudoir carrying her nightdress and robe.

"More hot water, Your Grace?" she asked, setting the things down and approaching the dials to pipe in more water. She had already freshened it once before.

"No, I should be getting out. Any longer in and I'll shrivel."

Her lady's maid wrapped her in toweling and dressed her for the night. Audrey declined the robe—it was far too hot for it. Even with all the windows open, there was barely a cool breeze coming in.

"Greer," Audrey asked while she lingered in the threshold between the bedchamber and boudoir, "do you know anything about Ida Smith?"

The staff knew about the second murder, of course, what with the woman's remains being installed in the icehouse for the time being. The inquest was being held the following morning, Philip had said near the end of dinner, then, spearing

Audrey a look, added, "I expect you to remain in the house while it is being held."

Her maid used a long hook to pull the plug in the copper tub and began to tidy the boudoir. Greer's usual placid expression pinched with concern between her brows now.

"I have heard a few things about her, yes."

Audrey waited with an expectant tuck of her chin.

"It's well known that she was a midwife before turning to service," Greer went on.

At this, Audrey straightened. "Midwife?"

Her maid nodded before collecting the laundry and toweling in a basket. Why would Charlotte have been meeting with a midwife when she already had Dr. Ryder for a physician? Titled women did not summon midwives to assist in their births. If Charlotte and Miss Smith had been meeting in such a secluded place, it was not for anything aboveboard. And why would Miss Smith return to the cottage a few days later?

"She has a good reputation, Your Grace. *Had* a good reputation," Greer corrected herself with another frown. She pressed her lips together, as if contemplating saying something more, but the connecting door to Philip's sitting room opened, and Greer made a hasty exit. Given the time of night, she might assume the duke was paying a marital visit. Then again, Greer was highly observant, and Audrey imagined she knew the truth behind the ruse they had taken to operating once or twice a week. In fact, it would not be so great a surprise if the entire staff knew that the two of them simply lounged about the bedchamber for a half hour or so before Philip bid his wife a good night.

In the beginning, they would have great fun with it, moaning loudly and jumping upon the bed to make as much noise as possible before devolving into fits of giggles. On their wedding night, Philip had even insisted on making a shallow slice on his forearm and dripping some blood onto the sheets as evidence of claiming her maidenhead. Whether or not Greer believed it, Audrey couldn't say.

Now, as soon as Greer had gone, Philip sat on the edge of Audrey's bed and held her gaze. He raised one brow in his chastising manner.

"You will be relieved to know I was not alone once today," she preempted.

"I'm not sure *relieved* is the word I would choose, but I am thankful you at least took that warning seriously." He toed the heels of his slippers and removed them before settling back onto the bed pillows, then crossing his ankles upon the coverlet.

Audrey joined him, tucking her legs underneath her, and leaning against the bolster pillows while waiting for him to continue.

"Dr. Wilkes and Officer Marsden had the interview well in hand with Lord Edgerton. You did not need to insert yourself."

"But—"

"And do not try telling me you were only there to visit with your mother. It would be the weakest, most inane lie you could ever attempt. The woman is a viper."

"And she's only gotten worse," she said, then told him the insensitive things she had said to the serving maid who'd nearly dropped the tea tray when hearing Ida Smith had been killed.

"We got into a little spat after, and my uncle accused me— once again—of being too high in the instep now." She scrunched her nose and grimaced.

"I find an endless amount of enjoyment in thinking about how inferior he must feel."

Audrey nudged his shoulder. "You're terrible."

He crossed his arms and grinned. "Thank you. Shall we

rattle the bedstead a little? I've been quite cross with you lately, and that often leads to violent lovemaking."

She glowered at him playfully, careful not to betray the surprising twist in her belly when her mind leaped to Hugh Marsden. Spending more time in his presence was complicating things.

Audrey sighed and stretched out her legs next to his. "I'm not in the mood, darling."

Philip chuckled. "Very well, sedate and routine it is. Even if I am cross with you."

"For going to Haverfield?"

"For going to Kilton House." He speared her with another look. She cringed. Of course he would have found out. This staff was his after all. Excluding Greer, they were loyal to him above her.

"You'll be interested to know what we learned from Lord and Lady Finborough."

"I do not care what you learned, Audrey. We are supposed to be having a respite; instead, we are embroiled in another murder investigation."

She pushed herself up and stared at him, incredulous. "It cannot be helped! My friend has been murdered. I cannot stand idly by if there is something I can do to aid the investigation."

"Did you use your ability today? Did it assist you in whatever it was you learned at Kilton House?"

He knew what her answer would be. Philip only wanted to make a point, and when she sealed her lips, he practically gloated.

"No, but I was able to help the interview along," she said, and it was true. Hugh had even commended her for it. Her ability had nothing to do with it, just her title. Her position.

Suddenly, the praise he'd paid her earlier, thanking her for her help with the marquess and marchioness, rang hollow, when before it had not.

"Let Marsden and the coroner do their jobs." Philip no longer sounded perturbed. In fact, his tone had softened to something almost placating. As if he could sense the sinking sensation in the pit of her stomach. "And darling...the less time you spend in Marsden's company, the easier you will feel."

Hadn't she just been thinking the same thing? Still, when Philip left her room after a few more minutes of awkward silence, she wondered if distance would be enough of a remedy.

"THIS IS UTTER TRIPE," Cassie moaned.

She sat at the writing desk in the morning room, angrily scratching out what she had just written on the paper at her elbow. She was slumped most unladylike in the chair, her arm resting atop the desk, her head in her palm as she cast aside the quill pen and crumpled the paper.

Audrey, reclining only slightly more decorously on a chaise, lowered the novel she'd been attempting to read for the last hour. She couldn't even recall what had happened in the previous chapter. The inquest for Ida Smith was currently underway in the icehouse and she was near to bursting with curiosity about what was being said. Three footmen had been put on guard outside the doors to the stone-fronted earthen cave, to hinder anyone from entering, so she had decided to keep her distance.

"How can it be tripe? It is a letter to Genie, not a love sonnet," she said to her sister-in-law.

Cassie pulled a fresh sheet of paper from the desk drawer—the third she had needed thus far. "I have nothing to write. I cannot relate what has been happening here—Philip has forbidden it for fear that it would upset Genie in her delicate condition—and so all I have been able to comment on is the weather and Mrs. Babson's scrumptious puddings."

Audrey sighed and closed her book. Once again, she felt a pang of regret for Cassie's wasted summer. The poor girl was deliriously bored, moping about, staying indoors within her bedchamber for too many hours each day. Audrey wished she had accepted the offer to join Genie and Michael in Kent or assented to Audrey summoning her previous chaperone, Miss Frances Stinton, for her to attend one of the house parties she'd been invited to. But each time, Cassie had turned her down. No, she wanted to stay here for now, she would claim. And yet she did not act as if she did. The only time Audrey saw any spark of interest in her was when Hugh had come to Fournier Downs. The old Cassie had returned, however briefly.

"Just inquire as to how Genie is feeling and tell her that Philip is doing much better. Perhaps you could write a line or two about which modiste she would recommend when you arrive in London next month."

Cassie rubbed her temple, and after a frustrated flutter of her hands, corked the inkwell and set down her pen. She pushed back the chair. "I'll write later, I think."

The doors to a brick portico were open, letting in the chirp of birdsong, a happy sound that was entirely at odds with Cassie's demeanor. Audrey sat up and set her feet on the floor.

"We haven't spoken much about the other day," she said. According to Greer, Cassie had spent the whole day abed after finding Ida Smith's body at the cottage. "It was a horrible thing to see."

Cassie wrapped her arms around the ribboned waist of her day dress but kept her eyes on the carpet. "I confess I was most undone by it. I'm sure that is what is bringing me low today."

Audrey nodded, but as her sister-in-law excused herself, she questioned if Cassie had spoken genuinely, or if she had just been latching onto the excuse Audrey had provided. Then, she chastised herself for doubting Philip's sister. She was becoming far too skeptical and suspicious.

Greer entered the morning room only moments after Cassie departed. "Your Grace, may I ask a few minutes of your time?"

The unusual request drew a frown to Audrey's face. Greer began to apologize for the interruption, and Audrey wiped the expression. "Of course you can, Greer. Is something wrong?"

The maid looked over her shoulder as if to be sure no one else was entering on her heels and stepped closer to the duchess. She lowered her voice. "There is someone here to speak to you."

Audrey's interest sharpened, but before she could ask who was calling, the maid continued, "It needs to stay mum, Your Grace, as it's to do with the inquiry. She is waiting for you in the potting shed behind the glasshouse."

Utterly baffled and intrigued, she nodded and assured Greer she would go as casually as possible.

"Thank you, Your Grace. I think this will help," she said, holding Audrey's eyes an extra moment as though to impart weight to the statement.

Excitement rippled through her as she left the main house a minute later, choosing to exit through the ballroom door. No one would witness her leave through there, seeing how the room had been shut up all summer. Outdoors, she made her way around the corner of the west wing, offering a gardener a smile as she passed him. Her limbs trembled a little as she saw the small brick potting shed. Flowering ivy clung to the exterior, almost obscuring the windows. Audrey pulled open the door, and the cool and dim interior took her by surprise. Her first thought was that she should come into the potting shed more often on such hot and humid days. Her second thought was for the woman she spied, tucked behind a stand of wooden shelves.

"Hello?" Audrey said tentatively. "My maid said you wished to speak to me?"

The woman emerged, and Audrey exhaled, recognizing her. "Dorothy? Is that you?"

"Yes, Your Grace," she replied, bobbing a curtsey.

This was Charlotte's lady's maid. Audrey stepped closer, more curious than before. "Dorothy, what is this about?"

She was probably a little older than Audrey, with a plain, round face and a starched white complexion. Dorothy had always been pleasant, and Charlotte had often commended her for her talents with a hot curling iron. With Charlotte's naturally curled hair, the hot iron would smooth out her ringlets. Audrey nearly smiled, thinking of her friend's frequent exasperation with her wild red curls.

However, Dorothy looked far too drawn and worried for Audrey to grin.

"I can't stay quiet any longer, Your Grace, but I didn't know to whom to speak. His lordship doesn't want us talking to the Runner or the coroner fellow, so I thought you might be able to pass along what I have to say? I don't trust anyone else, Your Grace...I'm frightened."

The maid certainly appeared to be, and with gooseflesh prickling her skin, Audrey checked the windows to be sure they were not about to be interrupted by the gardener or anyone else.

"Please, Dorothy, go on. I give you my word, I will inform Officer Marsden and not tell anyone I spoke with you."

She nodded and took a shaky breath. "My mistress, she was with child."

"Yes, I've been made aware of that," Audrey said, wondering

if that was all. There was nothing especially frightening about it.

"She didn't...she didn't want to keep the baby," Dorothy said, nearly whispering.

Audrey held her breath, stunned. "Do you mean..." How to say it? *Purge* was the first word that leaped to her mind, but she couldn't bring herself to utter it.

Dorothy nodded grimly. "I was to arrange a meeting with Miss Ida. She's known to help women like my mistress. There are certain herbs and berries, you see, and..."

Recalling the bundles of herbs that had been near the dropped basket, Audrey's lips parted. She nodded, understanding. But it didn't make any sense. "Charlotte wanted a child, I thought. After the miscarriages, she was distraught."

Dorothy nodded vigorously. "I thought so too. She often confided that she wanted a purpose, a distraction from the earl. She knew he wanted nothing to do with a *brat*, as he called them, but she didn't care. The baby would be hers." The maid's eyes grew glassy. She scrunched her nose against the sting of tears. "So, when she wanted to meet with Ida, I was taken by surprise. But I did as she asked, of course, and arranged for the meeting. It wasn't my place to say anything contrary."

A foreboding thought entered Audrey's mind. "The meeting was to take place at the stone cottage in the woods."

Dorothy nodded. Audrey closed her eyes and again saw Ida Smith's body, lying in the tall grass and wildflowers, a basket and bundles of herbs spilled nearby. But that was days after her meeting with Charlotte. Days after Charlotte's death. What had Ida been doing there again?

"Was the meeting set for the day Charlotte died?"

Again, Dorothy nodded, but this time she could not stopper her tears. They streaked down her blotchy cheeks, though she swiftly wiped them away.

"She went alone then?" Audrey asked.

"Yes, Your Grace. There are several paths through the woods leading to the cottage. Some come from Low Heath, others from neighboring properties. It is—*was*—Ida's usual meeting spot."

Understanding shed through Audrey, buoying her. A piece of the puzzle had come together, though there was much she still did not understand. But now she knew what Charlotte had been doing in the woods that day. She'd been running from the direction of the cottage, which meant whoever was chasing her had likely discovered the meeting. Was that why Ida had then been killed? Had she seen Charlotte's attacker?

Again, Audrey recalled the murky tail end of the vision that Charlotte's dress had provided: Charlotte, standing within the stone ruin, and the hazy image of who she now knew was Ida Smith passing before the window. The man in the brown sack coat and hat had to have been there as well.

"I don't mean to sound insensitive or a gossip, Dorothy, but...do you have any reason to believe your mistress was conducting an affair?"

The maid pressed her lips thin as she sniffled and wiped her cheeks dry. "I think she might have been, yes, but she was guarded about it. I never saw her with anyone beyond family and the staff, and some lady friends, like yourself. And the doctor, of course."

"Could he have been her lover?"

She frowned. "Doctor Ryder's visits were so swift, and I was with my mistress for most of them. I don't think it's possible."

"Perhaps one of the staff?" Audrey pressed.

Loyalty among the serving class was thick and taken seriously; she knew she was asking much of the maid to point a finger toward a man with whom she worked alongside. But she shook her head decisively. "No. I do not think so, Your Grace."

Slightly deflated, Audrey nodded. "Thank you. This could very well make all the difference in the investigation."

The maid bobbed another curtsey and started for the shed door. But Audrey held up a hand.

"One more thing: Did you suspect that the previous Lady Bainbury, Mary, also had a lover?"

The question was met with a blank expression. "I'm sorry, Your Grace, but I wasn't lady's maid then. You might ask Annie though."

"Annie?" The name rang familiar, though she couldn't place it.

"Annie Ryder. She works at Haverfield now, but she was lady's maid to the previous countess."

Audrey masked her surprise. "Ryder? Is she related to the doctor?"

Dorothy nodded, and after Audrey murmured her thanks, the maid departed. She left the shed as well, making sure to stop and say hello to the gardener, to distract him from spying the maid on her clandestine retreat.

As she continued along the gravel path circling the perimeter of the house, she recalled the maid serving tea at Haverfield. Annie had been her name. The same woman who'd been lady's maid to a countess? It was quite the demotion. Perhaps there was something behind it, but for now, she needed to find Hugh and inform him of everything Dorothy had said. She checked the tall case clock in the main hall. Nearly noon. The inquest for Ida Smith would likely be finishing up. Audrey turned for the icehouse.

CHAPTER
SIXTEEN

The same jury of men filled the Duke of Fournier's icehouse for Ida Smith's death inquest, with one exception: this time, a representative from Lord Bainbury's household had agreed to appear.

Lord Renfry, the future Earl of Bainbury, stood among those gathered around the sheeted figure of the slain Haverfield servant. He must have gained his tall stature from his mother, the first late Countess of Bainbury, but he did inherit the earl's strong jaw and striking looks. He stood stiffly, his attention darting from the sheeted figure of Ida Smith to the one on a cot set out of the way, behind the circle of men.

Like a few of the others present, Renfry had pinned flower buds to his lapel in the hopes of offsetting any potential unsavory odors. The cold air trapped within the thick earthen walls of the icehouse did have a slightly pungent aroma, though Hugh thought it only to be onion, parsnip, and other root vegetables. Ida Smith's body was too new to be emanating foul smells, however Lady Bainbury's might be reaching its keeping point. It had been a week since her death, and almost as soon as the jury was gathered, Lord Edgerton decried the situation.

"The woman needs to be buried," he bellowed. "This is outrageous. You've had days to determine the manner of death. What are you waiting for?"

"Answers, my lord," Wilkes replied in his unruffled manner, which only seemed to ruffle the baron further.

Hugh cut in before he could make another outburst. "Fournier's icehouse is preserving the remains well enough. Perhaps Lord Renfry would like to view the body and make his goodbyes to his stepmother?"

The young lord clapped his eyes upon Hugh's with alarm and revulsion. "That is unnecessary."

He was a few years shy of thirty, Hugh would estimate. He'd arrived the previous day with his betrothed and her family, as expected, though instead of celebrating their upcoming nuptials, they had the somber event of a funeral to attend.

"The two of you were not close, my lord?" Wilkes asked, perhaps hearing the same lack of affection that Hugh had.

"Close in age, perhaps," he replied bitterly. Ah, so Bainbury's heir was not keen on his father's penchant for marrying younger women. Women younger than Renfry, even.

"Did you object to the age of the lady, or the lady herself?" Hugh asked.

Renfry adopted a competent version of his father's sneer. "What I object to, is being asked these ridiculous questions. We are here to discuss this other woman's death, are we not?"

"As we have not yet reached a conclusion in the countess's death inquest, my lord, all questions are pertinent," Wilkes said. "We can, of course, interview you separately after this inquest, if you prefer."

Renfry clenched his jaw as he looked around the grouping of men, as if seeking support from them. Neither Fournier, Edgerton, Dr. Ryder, nor the others gave it, though the baron rolled his eyes in impatience.

"Very well," Renfry ground out. "I did not object to Charlotte herself. I've made it clear to my father from the beginning that his decision to marry women half his age—first with my mother's replacement and then with this newest—was undignified and unnecessary. It is the marriage I objected to. Does that answer your question, officer?"

Hugh suppressed the urge to grin; the young man's statement had breathed new life into the investigation, and he did not even appear to comprehend it.

"Indeed, it does," Hugh replied, crossing a look with Wilkes. The coroner cleared his throat.

"Let us begin," he said, and leaving behind the topic of Renfry's distaste for his stepmothers, launched into the particulars of Ida Smith's demise.

Peeling back the sheet to her clavicle, Wilkes pointed out the evident injury to the woman's skull and concluded a violent blow to the back of the head was the cause of death. The duke gave testimony, discussing how and where the duchess and Lady Cassandra Sinclair had found the body.

"One moment now," Lord Edgerton said, agitated yet again. In fact, Hugh was beginning to think the man existed in a perpetual state of agitation.

"The duchess, once again, finds a dead body? Just...stumbles across it in the woodland of Fournier Downs?"

"That is correct," Fournier replied, his impatience evident.

The baron guffawed. "I say, isn't that a bit bizarre?"

Hugh found that he would like nothing more than to plant a facer into the baron's nose, and the scowl Fournier was wearing suggested he was currently having that same desire.

"Extraordinarily rare," Wilkes said before Hugh or the duke could speak. "However, the facts remain as they are, as we currently know them. Officer Marsden, can you provide us with more details from the discovery of the body?"

The coroner's skipping onward, dismissing whatever the baron might have wished to say next, was not lost on Lord Edgerton, who glowered.

Hugh quickly divulged his arrival at the cottage, finding the duchess, and her assertion that someone else had been within the trees.

"And did the duchess see who this mysterious *other person* was?" Lord Edgerton asked, his sarcastic skepticism inspiring a few smothered grins from some of the other men. Dr. Ryder, however, maintained his somber expression, unimpressed by the baron.

"She saw a figure moving through the trees, that is all," Hugh answered.

The baron snorted.

"I spoke with your staff, Lord Edgerton," Wilkes said. "The servants within the kitchen imparted that Miss Smith received a message that morning, delivered to her by a man who, they claim, is employed here at Fournier House."

Hugh joined the rest of the jury as every head swiveled toward the duke. Fournier's aloof expression was only marred by the slight tensing of his brow. The previous evening, Hugh and Wilkes had taken supper together at the inn and had discussed the coroner's findings, as well as what Lord and Lady Finborough had revealed. Wilkes had not liked the coincidence that the second and third Countesses of Bainsbury had both been with child at the time of their puzzling deaths.

"Employed here in what capacity?" Fournier inquired coolly.

"As a stable hand," Wilkes answered.

The duke nodded. "I will speak to Gendron, my stablemaster."

Accepting that, Wilkes continued. "Miss Smith departed the

house after luncheon, though whether it was due to the message she received, they could not say. However, something Mrs. Landry, the cook at Haverfield, noted was of particular interest. She said Miss Smith mentioned seeing an unfamiliar man walking swiftly in one of the lower fields, between the woodland and a row of sheds on the property used for farming tools, on the afternoon of Lady Bainbury's death. At the time, Miss Smith wondered if he was simply a local farmer, but after hearing of the countess's odd death, she told Mrs. Landry. The cook was unable to discover who the man might have been, and in fact, none of the servants I spoke with made mention of a local farmer visiting Haverfield that day."

When Wilkes had explained all this to Hugh the evening before over their pints of ale and a thick venison stew, the first thing he thought of was the man Audrey had seen in her visions. Wilkes had, being a thorough investigator, visited the shed in question and found a balled-up sack coat and worn hat, stuffed into a large flowerpot.

"Was the coat missing a button?" Hugh had asked.

The coroner had set down his pint. "Indeed, it was. How did you know?"

"The duchess found one at the bottom of the quarry, where the countess came to rest." Hugh had kept the button in his pocket since Audrey gave it to him, and when he presented it to Wilkes, the coroner had nodded, confirming it was a match.

Ida Smith had seen the same man from Audrey's vision, and Hugh was nearly certain she had been killed for it. Had she discovered his identity?

After Wilkes explained to the jury the connections between the button and the coat discovered in the shed, as well as a shovel, its blade sporting a streak of blood, Lord Edgerton thundered, "Are you implying that a killer is among *my* staff?"

"Not necessarily, my lord. The man whom Miss Smith saw might have been trespassing and only using the shed."

"It looks as though the shovel might have been the weapon used against Miss Smith," Hugh added, gesturing toward the tool. It had been lain out on a table, along with Miss Smith's personal effects, including the basket and some bundles of herbs. Also on display were the coat, hat, and loosed button.

"Mrs. Landry's and Miss Smith's inquiries into the mysterious man might have alerted him that he'd been seen," Fournier said.

"If he heard it from others at Haverfield, that means he must be on the staff," Lord Renfry put in, side-eyeing the baron.

"Miss Smith was known to help some of the women in the county," Dr. Ryder said, speaking for the first time. "It is possible she related her concern about the mysterious man to someone outside the baron's staff."

"How did she help women?" Hugh asked.

"She was a midwife, of course," Dr. Ryder replied, sounding as if Hugh should have already known as much. The doctor wore yet another tall cravat, covering his birthmark.

Unable to dismiss from his mind the disjointed memories of a doctor bearing such a mark, and some attached scandal, Hugh had sent off a note to Thornton via messenger the afternoon of his visit to Dr. Ryder. He anticipated a reply soon and hoped to put the niggling thoughts to rest.

A few of the farmers nodded in reply to what the doctor said, and one claimed she'd helped to deliver all three of his wife's children.

Hugh and Wilkes exchanged a quick look. A midwife and a pregnant countess. However, Ida Smith had gone to the cottage a few days *after* Charlotte's death. Summoned there by messenger. Lured there, perhaps, by the mysterious man who realized he'd been seen.

"Thank you, doctor," Wilkes said, and when no one had more to say on the matters discussed, he moved that the jury present a verdict for cause of death. It was by no surprise deemed homicide. Taking advantage of the gathered jury, Wilkes then asked if they were ready to agree on a verdict of homicide for Lady Bainbury as well. They were.

"Two homicides within one week," Wilkes mused as the jury dispersed.

"And you have questioned all the staff at Haverfield?" Fournier asked, having remained in the icehouse.

"I have. I do not think the man is on staff. Otherwise, why stash the coat and hat in the shed? Why not bring his things to his own room?"

Hugh agreed. "There are several paths that lead into that section of the forest. The citrine quarry had a main road for laborers from town. Whoever it is could be familiar with the routes."

But *who* was the looming question.

"Renfry has been at the manor over the summer but has only just arrived again," he continued. "He has motive, albeit weak. I don't think he would be fool enough to hire someone to do in his stepmother while he was away fetching his bride."

"And if he chose to, his method would have surely been something quiet and easy, like poison," Wilkes agreed.

The duke widened his eyes, as if appalled by their theories. The door to the icehouse's third room opened, and Audrey swept inside. The abruptness of her step, the bright gleam of her stare as it met Hugh's, and the parting of her lips as if she could not wait to speak, alerted him that she had discovered something. That he knew her mannerisms well enough to interpret this filled him with concern. And yet, it also gave him a hint of delight.

"Audrey, what are you doing in here? Where is Cassie?" the duke asked as Wilkes bowed his head in deference.

Fournier's exasperation was more indulgent than it was irate, and Audrey ignored it.

"She is inside, deliriously bored," she replied. "I, however, have just spoken with Charlotte's maid. I know where she was going the day she died, and why."

As she explained about the maid arranging for a meeting with Ida Smith for herbs to induce cramping and terminate the pregnancy, Hugh went to the table of evidence. He picked up the bundles of herbs, tied off with twine.

"Miss Smith was summoned again to the ruined cottage the morning of her death," Hugh told the duchess. Holding up the herbs, he added, "The messenger came from this estate."

Audrey spun to look at Philip. The duke shook his head. "I will speak to Gendron and find out which servant and who sent him. However, Audrey, I must ask you to come with me. This is no place for you."

Her chin lifted an inch and indignance fired in her eyes. She wanted to refuse.

Hugh set down the herbs. "I'm going to Bainbury Manor. If the countess's maid summoned Ida Smith, she did so by using a messenger as well. I'll find him and speak to him."

"I will come with you," Wilkes said, an uncharacteristic grin touching his prim lips. "Bainbury might be more likely to let you trespass with me present."

Audrey didn't exactly pout, but her annoyance was plain. The duke touched her elbow, drawing her toward the door. "Come. I have a surprise for you. Cassie as well."

She peered at him. "A surprise?"

Hugh ignored the sharp twist in his gut at the sound of her curious pleasure. She sent a quick glance at Hugh before allowing Fournier to lead her from the room. As Wilkes drew the sheet back up over Ida Smith's face, Hugh pushed aside the irrational jealousy. The duke was right. This was no place for a duchess. Not just within this room, but within this investigation. Ida Smith may have died for what she'd figured out.

Hugh would not allow the same to happen to Audrey.

SEVENTEEN

A picnic. That was Philip's surprise.

Audrey didn't want to feel deflated or unappreciative, but as she and Cassie and Philip lounged on a large blanket on a knoll of green pasture overlooking the manor, she also couldn't help but consider the disparity between the lazy afternoon diversion and the seriousness of the recent murders.

It didn't seem real or right that they should be drinking lemonade and ratafia and eating salmagundi and berry pie while Hugh and the coroner were hunting down information on the killings. It was absurd, of course, to want to go with Hugh to Bainbury Manor, but she felt as if she'd failed when speaking to Dorothy. Why hadn't she asked *who* had run the message to Ida Smith? She supposed, at the time, it had not seemed a critical piece of information. But after Philip told her of the findings at the inquest, her blunder made her feel like a pure fool.

After Philip spoke to Gendron, the stablemaster rounded up all the hands to ask who delivered the message to Haverfield the day of Ida's death. None confessed. Gendron, embarrassed by the silence that had met the duke's request, had assured

Philip that he would find out who it was before the day was through.

There was nothing left to do but take their picnic.

The small grin Cassie wore when she'd come down from her bedchamber for the picnic had at least given Audrey a bit of appreciation for Philip's idea.

Cicadas hummed in the tall grass, and butterflies and bees swooped and buzzed from the broad flowering heads of wild carrot and bright corncockle. Two footmen had pitched a small canopy to shield them from the sun's direct glare.

As Philip poured them each ratafia, he'd made Audrey promise to discuss anything other than the investigation before he would hand her the small cordial glass. She had accepted with a small dart of her tongue just to cheek him, but she had held to the promise.

"Lysander," Philip said, reclining on one elbow, his second glass of ratafia nearly drained. "Lysander Philip."

Audrey barked a laugh. "That is a terrible name! Don't you dare suggest it to Michael. Can you imagine looking at a little cherub-faced baby and calling him *Lysander*?"

Philip had received a letter from Michael the previous day, and he'd mentioned that he and Genie had not yet settled on a name for their first child. So, for the last several minutes, she and Philip had bandied about names to see which one was most suitable for Michael's heir. It was, of course, an attempt to distract themselves from the much more unsavory topic that hung over them like a shroud. Cassie was listening in, smiling at the more ridiculous names.

"So, you do not object to the middle name, then?" Philip replied.

"Oh, I object to the middle name most of all," Audrey replied, trying not to giggle. "Philip is no more suited to a baby than Lysander."

The duke pushed himself into a seated position and nearly spilled the rest of his drink. "*I* was a baby named Philip, mind you."

"Yes, well, you weren't very cherub-faced, or so I've heard," she teased.

Cassie huffed laughter again, but it was a bit flimsy. She seemed distracted, just as she had been that morning while writing her letter to Genie. She sat upon the blanket, tracing the embroidery with her finger.

Philip poured himself more ratafia, though Audrey shook her head. The liquor was rather strong, and paired with the heat, it might cause them to take a long nap.

"I suppose even if he is named Barnabus Smockton, he will be perfect," Audrey said, recalling one of the other names Philip had advocated for, which had inspired Audrey to throw a slice of cold ham from their salmagundi at him. He'd simply plucked it from his sleeve and eaten it.

Cassie sighed then peered into her cordial glass. "I cannot wait to meet him."

"Or her," Audrey reminded.

"However, I wonder..." Cassie said, still looking at her drink. "I wonder if perhaps I should put off the Little Season and instead return to Aunt Hestia."

The words tumbled past her lips so swiftly, it took Audrey a moment to understand her suggestion. She sat forward in one of the wicker chairs the footmen had carried from the house. "Put it off? But the Little Season is important, Cassie. Why would you wish to return to Edinburgh?"

Philip, too, looked concerned as his sister shifted onto her knees.

"I just think it might be best after everything that has happened," she said without meeting Audrey's eyes. First, she had been having trouble writing to Genie. Now this.

"If it is the taint of scandal that worries you—"

"No, it isn't that," she quickly said. "I just wonder if it isn't the right time. What with Genie entering confinement and now with this mystery here in Hertfordshire surely making its way around London..."

Philip stood, and Audrey was glad to see he did not stumble. The ratafia had not dazed him yet.

"No. You will have your Little Season as well as your official Season, Cassie. It is what you deserve. We have isolated you far too much this summer."

"I chose to stay here," she argued.

"Because you are kind and caring of your older brother, yes. Allow me to do you the same courtesy," he said. "You are far too young to be playing nursemaid. You will go to London and enjoy yourself."

Cassie stopped twirling the stem of the cordial glass between her thumb and forefinger. "And what if I do not wish to?"

Philip blinked, staring at her in confusion. Audrey, too, was flummoxed.

"You've been planning for your debut for years," she said with a shake of her head. "Why would you wish to postpone it now?"

Cassie shrugged, still avoiding both Audrey and Philip's eyes. "It just seems silly and selfish to go have fun after all that's happened here recently."

Audrey had not realized just how deeply Cassie had been affected by the deaths, though now she felt insensitive for it. Finding a dead body had distressed her far greater than she'd realized. Or perhaps Cassie's reaction was natural. Which made Audrey question if her own, less affected reaction was not.

"I understand, but we must carry on," Philip said, sounding less understanding, as he'd just claimed to be, and more impatient. "Look at Bainbury, for heaven's sake. I can't stand the man and detest using him as an example, but even he is trying to move forward with the business of life. Renfry and his betrothed have arrived, and even though they now must include a funeral into their plans, they still intend to spend the week at Bainbury Manor before they wed."

A shrill and sudden whimper ripped up Cassie's throat, and she clapped a hand over her mouth. Her eyes squeezed shut, and for a moment, Audrey froze with concern.

"Cassie?" She started to stand and go to her. But Philip's sister jumped to her feet, her glass of ratafia spilling from her hand.

"I...I'm not feeling well. Can we return to the house?"

Philip gestured to the footmen, who immediately came forward to pack up the picnic, and then held his arm out to his sister.

"It must be the heat," Cassie said, as the three of them started down the knoll, toward the manor.

"Should we send for Doctor Ryder?" Audrey asked, still reeling and confused over the rapid change in her mood.

"No, no. That's not necessary. Truly, I will be fine."

Audrey nodded, following Philip and his sister as they walked arm in arm, returning to the manor. As soon as they were inside, Cassie broke off from him and went to her room. Philip stood in the downstairs hall, watching her disappear with a frown of concern. He turned his frown toward Audrey next.

"This has been too much for her," he said. "Do you think she is afraid?"

"So afraid that she would not want to take part in the Little Season? I can't see how. If anything, she should want to be away from this place even more desperately."

Philip slowly retreated into his study, and Audrey followed.

The room's dark wood paneling and drawn curtains had helped to keep the air cool in comparison to the atypical summer heat outdoors. Audrey sank onto the corner sofa cushion and wished they could still be on the picnic blanket making up silly names for their nephew.

"Do you think there is something wrong with me, Philip?"

Audrey hadn't expected the question to sound so plaintive. Philip, at the sideboard to pour himself a brandy, peered over his shoulder at her.

"Whatever do you mean?"

"Cassie is despondent after finding a body. I've found three now, in total, and I can't recall being so affected."

In addition to Charlotte and Ida Smith, Mr. Bernadetto, the theatre manager at the Theatre Royal, had been killed in the spring, and she and Hugh had come upon the newly slain body. She had swooned from the blood, but had recovered quickly, and the discovery had not given her any lasting distress. Wasn't that a bit odd?

Philip poured a brandy for himself and one for her as well. He then joined her on the sofa, sitting on the cushion next to her.

"There is nothing wrong with you." He handed her the snifter. She accepted the offering but didn't want it. Her stomach was in a knot, and she lamented even the small glass of ratafia she'd had at the picnic.

"Finding a dead body would affect anyone, but she is especially young and sheltered and impressionable," Philip went on. "I should have brought her up to London more often."

He had said this a few times over the course of the summer, but Audrey was at least thankful Cassie had not arrived at Michael and Genie's home on Grosvenor Square until May. She hadn't been in London when Philip had been arrested. Audrey would not have been able to move as freely as she had to investigate the murders of Miss Lovejoy and Mr. Bernadetto had Cassie been there for Audrey to chaperone and care for. Again, the stymied longing to be out there doing something to find answers for Charlotte's death, and Ida Smith's, grew hot in her chest.

She sipped her brandy, pondering whether Gendron had yet managed to force an answer out of his stable hands. One of them had delivered a summons for Ida Smith the morning of her death. There were over a dozen maids employed at Fournier House who might have wanted a meeting with the midwife and herbalist. The stable hand might have kept quiet to protect her identity. Or perhaps the stable hand had delivered the message for one of his own family members, or for another employee's family member. Any number of young women might be the one who'd been seeking Ida's herbal tincture.

Audrey and Philip sat in companionable silence while she mentally shuffled through the maids, but it was a pointless exercise. The only two women she knew well in the house were Greer and Cassie. Greer was far too busy during the day to run off to the ruined cottage. And Cassie...well, the idea that she might have needed Ida's assistance was easily dismissible. She was a debutante, and a sheltered one at that. Of course, there were a few handsome footmen, but Cassie paid them no attention whatsoever.

Besides, Cassie could not have been meeting with Ida. She had been with Audrey at the time. She'd found Cassie riding along the wooded path...

Her next sip of brandy went down her throat in an awkward gulp as she recalled Cassie's startled reaction when Audrey had come upon her. But now, she also recalled her sister-in-law's sharp tone when asking about the ruined cottage and her alarm at hearing the place had been mentioned at the inquest—a complete fabrication on Audrey's part. She'd been acting overly eager as they'd closed in on the small clearing, riding ahead and raising her voice to a near shout. It had not fazed Audrey too much at the time. She'd been focused on not revealing the reason why she wanted to be there—because of a vision.

But now...

She cleared her throat and lowered her brandy as a chiming tone filled her eardrums. *No.* It was absurd. Impossible. But as she stood and excused herself, telling Philip she was going to check in on Cassie, her nerve endings practically crackled.

Audrey took the stairs, and the closer she became to Cassie's room, the more her suspicion took root. Her reluctance to socialize this summer, her insistence that she stay put to care for a brother who no longer needed it, her changeable moods, her reluctance to go to London for her introduction to society...

She knocked upon the bedchamber door and waited, but no answering call came.

"Cassie?" She pushed open the door and peeked in. The bedroom was empty. "Cassie, are you in here?"

Walking deeper into her room, she peeked into the boudoir, but found no one. Turning from the boudoir, she leaped and let out a gasp at the sight of a figure in the bedchamber entrance.

"Your Grace? I'm sorry, I didn't mean to startle you," Ruth, Cassie's lady's maid, said. She entered the bedchamber with a few pieces of laundered and folded items.

"It is fine, Ruth. I was looking for Cassie. Do you know where she is?"

The maid frowned. "I haven't seen her since she left for the picnic, Your Grace."

"She wasn't feeling well and needed to come back here. She said she was coming to her room to rest." But apparently, she had not.

Ruth lowered her eyes and walked past Audrey, into the boudoir to deliver the linens. Something about the maid's expression and posture—the pinch of her brow, the intentional avoidance of Audrey's eyes—gave her pause. Like Dorothy had, Ruth would know the truth about her mistress.

"Ruth, I need to ask you a difficult question," Audrey said as the maid came back into the bedchamber. She went still, her attention still pinned to the carpet.

"I think you know what it is," Audrey said.

Ruth pressed her lips together as if trying to hold back some confession. Audrey felt a twinge of sympathy for her—her loyalty was torn between her mistress and the duchess, a woman of superior rank. However, now was no time for sympathy. Audrey required answers. The truth. And that required a blunt question:

"Did you arrange a meeting between Ida Smith and Cassie? Did you ask a stable hand to deliver the message to Miss Smith at Haverfield?"

The maid's shoulders dropped. She shuddered on an exhalation. "I am sorry, Your Grace, Lady Cassandra asked for my confidence."

Audrey's stomach plummeted. She swallowed, her throat going dry.

"I understand, however, I need your help now, Ruth. Is she...expecting?"

When the maid bobbed her head, a surge of dizziness took Audrey down to the edge of Cassie's bed. "She has...she has missed her monthly?"

She needed to know and yet was incapable of believing it. But when Ruth nodded again, she pressed her hand to her cheek and closed her eyes, trying to breathe evenly.

Who would do this? Who would *dare* seduce Philip's younger sister? She wasn't even properly out! And there had been no one —*no one*—at Fournier Downs all summer. A footman then? A stable hand? But Cassie was far too smart for such a stupid, reckless affair. Then again, she was quite impressionable and romantic. Someone must have taken advantage of her naivete.

"How many months?" Audrey asked, still feeling overwhelmed and dizzy. What would Philip do?

"Nearly three, Your Grace. She..." A few tears rolled down Ruth's cheeks and she gulped for air. "She said it must have happened in late May or early June."

That shocked Audrey out of her dizzy stupor. Cassie had come to them in June, after a month's stay in London with Genie and Michael. She'd gone to a few modistes and settled upon one that would design her entire look for the upcoming seasons. She was to spend a few more weeks with Michael when Philip became direly ill, and Cassie had practically flown to Fournier Downs.

"Who was the man?" Audrey asked, feeling ill.

Ruth shook her head. "I don't know, Your Grace, I promise I don't. She did not say, and it wasn't my place to ask."

Audrey stood from the side of the bed, needing to get her wits back about her. This was no time for hysterics.

"You sent a note with a stable hand to Ida Smith?"

Ruth nodded.

"Which day was this?" Audrey asked, though she thought she knew. When the maid broke down into fresh tears, she was certain. Ruth couldn't speak, so Audrey provided a guess.

"The day Ida Smith was killed?"

"Yes, Your Grace." She finally looked up and stared at Audrey with glistening eyes. "She felt responsible for what happened to Ida. I tried to tell her it wasn't her fault, but she's been so distraught, even before Ida was killed. Her moods have been fluctuating so powerfully, Your Grace."

Audrey breathed in and tried to exhale the shakiness

attacking her arms and legs. Cassie had to be overwhelmed. She probably felt trapped and scared and guilty.

She walked toward the window overlooking the rose garden and beyond, a lush green pasture. Where could she have gone?

"Search the house for her, Ruth. Say nothing to anyone. Not even the duke."

"Yes, Your Grace." The maid darted from the room, leaving Audrey alone to worry. Like Charlotte and Mary, now Cassie was pregnant and facing something terrifying, all alone. Audrey's stomach swirled as she bore in mind that Charlotte and Mary had both died. Mary, purportedly, taking her own life.

Something was wrong. Ruth would search, but Cassie was not in the house; Audrey's instinct told her that. *Most people have rather good instincts; they just fail to listen to them.* Hugh's earlier comment reached her through the beginnings of panic. She took an even breath and closed her eyes. After exhaling, she opened them again to see the nuggets of citrine lining the windowsill. Audrey touched one, the amber color golden and honeylike. Immediately, an image of Cassie pushed into her mind. Her eyes were red and puffy as she held the citrine nugget admiring it. How long ago had Cassie picked up the citrine to peer at it? And yet, she had been upset then too.

Audrey released the citrine. Her sister-in-law did love the gems. She scouted for them all through Fournier Downs, especially near the quarry.

Her stomach twisted with a wretched thought. She turned toward the bedchamber door and eyed the doorknob. Knobs were always filled with energy, what with hands touching them constantly. She usually would not allow the images to assault her when she gripped one, but this time, she made an exception. She opened her mind to what it had to show her: Ruth, rushing from the room just a few minutes ago. Then, not long before that, Cassie, wearing a bonnet, spencer, and gloves. Her eyes were puffy and red from crying again. It looked like she was going out for a walk.

Releasing the knob, Audrey bit her lower lip. *Trust your instinct.* Even if it proved wrong. And even if it meant finding Philip and telling him the awful truth.

EIGHTEEN

T he post road was well worn by the wheels of mail and passenger coaches, with dual ruts cut into the packed dirt and patches of grass and weeds lining the center hump. When Hugh spotted Tyson Perry up ahead, he was walking within one of the ruts. He had never met Tyson, but from the satchel slung over his shoulder and a cap that did not quite conceal his head of blond curls, Hugh was confident he'd found the wayward groom from Bainbury Manor.

He and Wilkes had gained entrance to the stables by the skin of their teeth. As Wilkes anticipated, the earl refused to allow Hugh to set foot on his property. However, the coroner impressed upon the earl that should their murder investigation be impeded, it would only draw out in length, and did not Lord Renfry have wedding nuptials coming up in a few days' time? The arrival of the lady's family, and the desire to maintain as much serenity as possible, was the only reason the earl had finally grumbled his agreement.

Derry, the Earl of Bainbury's longtime stablemaster, had met them with a skeptical frown. Tyson Perry was the groom who usually ran messages, as he was the fastest rider.

"Can we speak to him?" Hugh asked.

"You'd have to find him first," Derry had answered. "He hoofed it sometime last night. Bed empty this morning; things gathered up and gone."

The stablemaster went on to say it didn't make much sense —the lad had his wages coming to him in a few days. The only family he knew of for Tyson was a grandmother in Ryesburg. While Wilkes had asked Derry a few more questions, Hugh spotted Sir in a hayloft. The boy shuttled down a ladder, and on the pretense of grabbing another pitchfork near Hugh, whispered, "That's the one I didn't like, remember? The dodgy one. Blond curls like me little sister. Got real green around the gills when news of that murdered maid came around."

He and Wilkes had returned to Low Heath, and Hugh had hired a horse at the inn's stables. Tyson Perry couldn't have made it far if he was on foot, and Wilkes had left Hugh to the chase. First, however, Basil met him with a letter, sealed with a familiar signet ring pressed into red wax. "A private messenger delivered it just now."

Hugh's spirits lifted at Thornton's seal, and he tore open the letter to read his friend's reply.

For a man who opposes the ton so vehemently, you do recall a vast amount of gossip, Thornton had written. *The doctor you are referring to is Millbury. Several years ago, a viscountess birthed a son bearing the same port wine stain as her physician on his neck. The man was ruined. He failed to turn up to a duel issued by the humiliated viscount and fled London with his family. No idea what happened to him from there.*

With every sentence, Hugh had to hold himself back from kissing Basil's cheek in triumph.

Now, as he came up behind the groom, he called, "On your way to grandmother's?"

Tyson took one look over his shoulder, saw Hugh, and broke

into a run. Partly amused, partly irritated, he overtook the lad easily, bringing his mount around and cutting him off.

"You don't have much between the ears if you think you can outrun a horse, Tyson."

The young man backed up a few steps. Sir's depiction of him being green around the gills wasn't too much of an exaggeration. He looked on the verge of swooning, what with his sweaty brow and wide eyes. "How do you know my name?"

"I spoke to Derry. I know you ran the countess's message to Haverfield."

Tyson's eyes darted side to side, as if searching for an escape. There was none to be found. Hugh waited patiently for the stable hand to give up and meet his eyes again.

"You left Bainbury Manor abruptly," he commented.

"My grandmother is ill."

"Is that so? Then she could have used the wages you left behind for a doctor, I should think. Try again. Why have you cut and run?"

He stared up at Hugh, who was still in the saddle, and nervously licked his lips. He readjusted his satchel on his shoulder.

"You know what I think?" Hugh said. "I think you and countess were having some tumbles in the hayloft. You got her in the family way and panicked."

He did not, in fact, think any of that, but he needed to get the young man speaking. It worked.

"No! I didn't do anything like that!" he said, practically dropping the satchel stuffed with his belongings.

"Then tell me why you've panicked and fled."

"Why wouldn't I?" His voice cracked with emotion. "First, her ladyship dies. Then Ida. I'm the one what ran the message between 'em, aren't I?"

Hugh leaned forward, onto the horn of his saddle. "You think the killer has his eye on you? Why?"

His pale complexion tinged a shade crimson. "Because I know what the message said."

"You read it?"

Tyson hung his head and nodded, clearly rueful over his action. "I know what Miss Ida does—*did*—for women, you see, and I was curious. I'm keen on Dottie—"

"Dorothy? The maid?"

Tyson nodded and Hugh understood. "You thought perhaps Dorothy was summoning Ida for herself."

Tyson didn't need to answer; his look of shame was enough of a confession.

"Why would knowing the contents of the message make you a target?" Hugh asked next.

"I don't rightly know," Tyson answered, casting a look down the post road. "But with the two of them killed and that note linking them…What if the killer finds out I read it? What if he thinks I know something I don't?"

Was this how frantic and irrational Hugh had sounded when trying to convince Audrey to stay inside the walls of Fournier House? He hoped not.

"What did the message say?" He had an idea but wanted to know specifically.

"It just asked that Miss Ida bring the necessary herbs to the meeting spot at three o'clock that same day. There was a pound note included."

A pound? That was as much as some maids earned every month.

"And you gave this message to Miss Smith?"

He shook his head. "She wasn't there, so I asked Annie to give it to her. She promised to pass it along to Ida."

Hugh cocked his head. "Annie? Dr. Ryder's daughter?"

"Aye."

Hugh nudged the horse's ribs and turned in a circle, needing to move, needing to think. Thornton's note about Dr. Millbury and the scandal with the viscountess was still so fresh. Millbury fled London with his family in disgrace. How far had he gone?

Dust kicked up around him and Tyson. The stable hand watched him warily.

"What is it?" Tyson asked, looking green again.

Hugh drew his horse to a stop. The port wine stain. The babies.

"You aren't in any danger, Tyson. Return to Bainbury Manor and Derry might give you back your position."

Hugh nudged his horse's ribs and broke into a canter, leaving the stable hand in the dust. Low Heath was only a few miles west, and with answers falling into place, the time passed quickly. The doctor's quaint home came into view, and Hugh's temper started to simmer. He leaped from his horse and charged up the front walk to bang upon the door. When no one answered, he slammed his fist down again, until finally, the wood fell away. The same assistant who had greeted Hugh the previous day glared up at him in admonishment.

"Where is Dr. Ryder?" he asked before she could speak.

Movement in the hall drew Hugh's attention. Ryder came into the foyer, wearing his coat and hat, and carrying his leather doctor's satchel. "What is this commotion? Officer, what is the matter?"

As Hugh edged past the nurse, the doctor's eyes rounded in alarm. He had seen something in Hugh's expression, for he took a step back and stammered to his nurse that all was well, and would the officer like to speak privately?

Hugh stalked the man into his cluttered office and shut the door behind them.

"Your name is not Ryder," he said immediately. The doctor set his leather bag onto the desk before meeting Hugh's direct stare.

"Officer, I can explain."

"No need. I already know, *Dr. Millbury*."

He removed his spectacles, his hand shaking. "You must understand, I had no choice—"

"I don't care what happened in London. I don't care that you're a coward and wouldn't fight the man whose wife you seduced. All I care about, doctor, is what happened *here*, in Hertfordshire."

Millbury put his spectacles back on and stared at Hugh, as if perplexed. "How do you mean?"

Hugh surged forward and crowded the doctor against the desk. "You might have changed your name and started fresh here, but you haven't changed your ways at all, have you? This is what I think happened: Low Heath's newest doctor was a charmer, handsome, and found himself welcomed into fine homes, trusted by bored or unhappy ladies of quality—just like the viscountess and who knows how many others in London."

Millbury shook his head and flapped his lips to rebut the accusation, but Hugh cut him off.

"You seduced both Countesses of Bainbury—Mary *and* Charlotte—and when they became pregnant, you panicked. You couldn't have what happened with the viscountess repeat itself here."

A child, born with the same unmistakable and visible birthmark as Ryder.

"No, no, no," the doctor stammered, his head shaking violently. "That isn't what happened! I heal people—I don't hurt them. I would never hurt anyone!"

On his ride just now to Low Heath, Hugh had considered Mary and how she had died. A bullet to the head. Had the doctor broken her heart? Or perhaps he'd told her the baby would be born with the same marking and she panicked.

"You were forced to give up your life in London. You gave up your very name. Faced with the same consequences playing out again here, you went against your nature and did what had to be done to protect your secret."

Millbury squeezed his eyes shut and fisted his hands, placing them against his forehead. "No, *no*! I swear to you, officer. Yes, I made a mistake with the viscountess. I shamed myself and my family, and my wife..." He shook his head and nearly whimpered. "She took our children and left. She left me. I haven't seen her, or little Nadia or Joseph, in five years."

Hugh frowned as the man held back a sob. "But Annie stayed with you?"

The doctor unclenched his fists and lowered them, blinking at Hugh. "Annie? Oh. Yes, Annie. She...she isn't my daughter, you see; she is my sister, Andrea. We thought, with our age difference, we could assist our new identities if I was a widower and she, my child. But I promised her, nothing like what happened with the viscountess would happen here, and I've kept my word."

There was something in that confession, something about Annie being Andrea that tugged at Hugh, but he couldn't determine what.

"Bainbury wasn't the father in either case. You were," he pressed, even though he was not as confident in that supposition as he had been when he'd first entered the doctor's home.

"No, I wasn't! I swear it. Mary did not confide in me, but Charlotte did. It was Renfry, I tell you—*he* seduced her. And I'm almost certain he seduced Mary as well."

Hugh narrowed his eyes on the doctor as he recalled the glances Bainbury's heir kept throwing the sheeted body belonging to his stepmother in the icehouse. He felt ill as he commanded Millbury to divulge what he knew.

"Lady Bainbury—Charlotte—she confided in me...perhaps she'd taken too many drops of laudanum at the time...but she spoke about Lord Renfry and his relentless pursuit, and how lonely she had been. The earl was not as attentive, you see, and well...she gave in. But then, after he'd succeeded, the cad laughed at the conquest, boasting about how proud he was to have denigrated his father's newest wife."

Hugh clenched his jaw. Instinct told him that the doctor was not lying. Still, he asked, "Why should I believe you?"

"Because he is a profligate, a true blackguard. I know my own weaknesses, but that lout..." The doctor's expression twisted with anger now instead of fear. He held Hugh's stare and seemed to be weighing a decision. Finally, he said, "It goes against my strict code of privacy, but I do not think it can be helped. You must speak to Lady Cassandra Sinclair. She will tell you."

Stunned, Hugh stepped back. "Tell me what?"

But the doctor shook his head. "I am on my way to meet her now. A message arrived in the letter box earlier this morning. She said it was an emergency. You may come with me, and I will explain to her the importance of coming forward with the truth."

Hugh sent him a contemptuous glare, and Millbury was at least aware enough to recognize his own hypocrisy. "I will also admit my own secrets. I will...I will try to right everything."

"Why does the duke's sister wish to meet with you?" Hugh asked, ignoring the man's promise. If he came out with the truth, he would be run out of Low Heath. In London, he might have disappeared into the lower-class masses, but here...there would be no escaping the scandal.

His sister Annie—or Andrea—would certainly not be happy about that.

Hugh barely latched onto the thought when the doctor replied, "She, too, has an understanding of Renfry's wicked appetite." The significant look he pressed into Hugh made the Bow Street officer's blood simmer. The doctor's insinuation was unmistakable.

"How do you know this?"

"I recognized some of her symptoms earlier in the summer, while I was treating the duke. When I inquired, she broke down and told me what had occurred. The man is abominable."

Hugh did not doubt that Renfry was exactly what Millbury purported him to be. But Cassandra...why seduce the duke's sister? She was pretty. Young. Impressionable. It might have been one last conquest before wedding his betrothed.

"Where are you meeting her?"

The doctor pulled a folded piece of parchment from his coat pocket. "She has requested the citrine quarry. She was adamant I not come to the main house. There is an old road, direct from town to the quarry."

Hugh nodded, recalling the young woman mentioning her collection of the amber stones when they, and the duke and duchess, had been riding to the quarry. If she wanted privacy, it would certainly be a secluded spot, but it was an odd choice for Cassandra, especially when the body of Lady Bainbury had been found there less than a week before. Something felt off about the meeting, but Hugh joined the doctor as he went to the small barn behind the house, where his hired boy-of-all-work had readied Millbury's phaeton.

As Millbury directed the horse through a pair of stone pillars, onto a narrow dirt path that bisected a field, Hugh signaled his horse to slow.

"I will meet you at the quarry," he called to the doctor. "I have a stop to make first."

The doctor nodded and continued along the old quarry road. Hugh directed his horse onward, out of the village and toward Fournier House. If Cassandra had found herself in trouble with Renfry's child, meeting with the doctor and a Bow Street officer to confess her sins would be as unpleasant for her as it would be for Hugh. It would be better to bring someone she trusted.

The choice for a meeting spot continued to nag at him as he rode fast toward the estate. Why the quarry? Cassandra had been shaken quite badly after finding Ida Smith. Selecting the site of another murder seemed entirely irrational.

At last, he turned up the long drive toward the main house. As he reached the top of the knoll, where the drive circled around the lily pond, he tugged on the reins. His horse shuddered to a stop. Cassandra had been seated on the stone edge of the pond, trailing a finger through the water, until she saw Hugh approaching. Now she stood and swiped at her cheeks. She'd been weeping.

"Why are you here?" he asked, alarm stringing his muscles tight.

Taken aback by the gruff question, Cassandra blinked and parted her lips. "I... How do you mean?"

"You summoned Dr. Ryder to the quarry, did you not?"

She grimaced and shook her head. "No. Why would I have done so?"

Hugh dismounted and lowered his voice as he neared her, trying to calm his mounting trepidation. "He told me about your...predicament."

She jolted back a step and blood rushed to her cheeks. Before she could stammer a reply, he continued, "Did you not leave a missive in his letter box this morning? Or direct someone from Fournier House do so?"

Cassandra's shock and confusion was the genuine article. She shook her head furiously. "No, I did not. What is this about? Why would he tell you? He promised his confidence!"

Hugh felt like he'd been swept up in a storm wind. If Cassandra had not summoned the doctor, then who had? Who was he meeting at the quarry?

"I cannot explain right now. Something is happening," he murmured, taking the reins of his horse again. "Where is the duke?"

She sniffled. "I don't know. I went for a walk to clear my head, and when I returned my maid was out of sorts. She said Audrey had figured out my secret and was searching for me, and then the stablemaster said she and Philip rode out to look for me."

Cassandra dashed away a few more tears as cold fear ran down Hugh's spine.

"Where?" he demanded.

"I already said, I don't know!"

"Take your best guess, Cassandra, it's imperative. Where would *you* search for you if you were missing?"

It sounded like a silly riddle, but he had never been more serious. The duke's sister closed her eyes and scrunched up her face in frustration.

"I don't know! Maybe the wood. The quarry. But I wouldn't go there now, not after..."

Damn. He leaped back into the saddle. "I want four footmen to follow me to the quarry at once. Summon the coroner and magistrate. Send them out as well. You stay *here*, Cassandra."

With his heart in his throat, Hugh slapped the reins and tore toward the wooded path.

NINETEEN

P hilip rode at a fast clip, fury and fear propelling him through the forest.

"I cannot believe Cassie would put herself into such a position," he said for the fifth time, at least. "How could she have dishonored herself so thoroughly? So thoughtlessly?"

"We don't know what happened," Audrey reminded him as she kept pace with his horse. "The gentleman could have convinced her that he planned to propose, that he loved her."

Philip made a harsh grating noise in the base of his throat. "Gentleman. Hardly. It is indefensible! Love and promises..." He made another deprecating snort to emphasize what he thought about the excuse.

In truth, Audrey had no idea what her sister-in-law had been thinking or feeling. Reason did not seem to have a place in any of the theories she had conjured in the last half hour since learning the truth. And there was another possibility. One she had yet to verbalize to Philip, but one he must have considered by now as well.

"There is the chance, of course, that she was not given the choice..." Audrey felt ill and could not go on.

Philip brought his mount to a standstill in the middle of the path and looked hard into her eyes. "If that is the case, I will call the bastard out. And I will put him in the ground."

His vicious vow knocked Audrey back in her saddle. She had never seen her husband so thoroughly incensed before. It both frightened and impressed her.

He turned his mount back around and continued toward the quarry. After Audrey informed him of what Ruth had revealed, he agreed that they needed to go to the quarry first and foremost. The jump would certainly kill her, and if she was desperate...well then, there was no telling what she might do.

However, Audrey could not truly believe Cassie would do such a thing to herself, to her family. A few hours earlier, she had been declaring how excited she was to meet her first nephew. No, it did not make any sense.

"Who would do this?" Philip muttered, addressing the same quandary that was plaguing Audrey. "An unacceptable? Someone who wants her generous dowry but knows I would never approve a suit?"

The same theory had come to Audrey's mind too, but she'd dismissed it. "Why then would he disappear? Surely someone like that would persist until he had what he wanted."

Unless the man had already gotten what he desired—a mere conquest—and now wanted nothing further. She did not know which theory sickened her more.

As they closed in on the quarry, her neck and back broke out into a cold sweat. She drew on memories of the summer, of Cassie's behavior and the conversations they'd had. But again and again, her reaction when Philip mentioned Lord Renfry's upcoming wedding tromped to the forefront of Audrey's mind. There had been another similar moment during Charlotte's last visit to Fournier House. She and Charlotte had been taking tea on the verandah when Audrey asked after Renfry and the upcoming wedding. Cassandra had simmered with annoyance, commenting on how eager she was for Renfry to be gone from Bainbury Manor. Her coloring had gone a bit florid, but Audrey had blamed the sun and heat. It was possible Charlotte simply disliked Renfry, but as neither she nor Charlotte were gossips, when the countess offered nothing more, Audrey had let the topic drop.

Lord Renfry. Audrey had met him on a few occasions when she had been betrothed to Bainbury. He was tall and handsome, with the chiseled looks his father once possessed in his youth. It had been some time since she'd thought on it, but now, Audrey recalled several times the intense scrutiny of his stare had left her feeling uneasy. She also remembered a lewd comment made by none other than her mother—which Audrey had promptly dismissed and forgotten until now. Lady Edgerton had murmured that should the earl prove disappointing in the bedchamber, there would be a younger and likely willing version of him on hand. Audrey, disgusted with the advice, had buried the memory after she'd called off the wedding and married Philip instead.

"Thank God."

She snapped to attention at the sound of Philip's voice. They had arrived at the opening to the quarry, and she'd been so lost in her thoughts that she hadn't seen Philip, in his panic, dismount. He was now coming back from the edge of the open pit. He shook his head. "She isn't here."

Relieved, Audrey rode into the clearing, her mind racing, and her pulse trembling.

"I think I might have figured something out," she announced, though her brain still felt stuffed and jumbled. "I think I might know who the father is."

She brought her horse to a stop and dismounted. As she was coming down onto the ground, her horse blocking her view of

Philip, a female voice said, "That is entirely too bad." Audrey paused, startled, and during that moment of confusion, she heard a loud *thunk* and then a grunt.

Audrey hurried around her mount and found Philip crumpled on the ground. Standing behind him, wielding a gardening hoe, was a young woman.

"Philip!" Audrey started toward him, but the woman swung the hoe toward her, and Audrey scuttled back. She stared at the woman. "What have you done?"

"You aren't supposed to be here!" the woman cried. "You should have stayed out of it!"

Recognition flared. This was the maid from Haverfield. The one Audrey's mother had chastised for dropping the tea tray. "Annie? What are you doing?"

A trickle of blood seeped down Philip's temple. He wasn't moving. Panic clawed at her.

"Where is Cassie?" Audrey asked. "The duke's sister—*where is she?* What have you done to her?"

The maid sneered. "She isn't here. I didn't summon *her.*"

But clearly, she *had* summoned someone. She'd been waiting. Waiting to attack. Another look at her husband and her stomach lurched. It was so like the way Ida Smith had been found. In an instant, Audrey knew... The short and slight man in the coat and hat from her vision; Ida, reporting that she'd seen him entering the gardening shed at Haverfield; the hoe, now in Annie's hand.

"You..." She gaped at Annie. "You killed Ida Smith. You struck her on the back of the head."

And Charlotte...she'd pushed Charlotte off the quarry ledge.

"Shut up! He'll be here any moment," Annie said, agitated and nearly frothing with indecision. "You've ruined everything!"

He. She had summoned a man here. "Who? Lord Renfry?"

Annie twisted her face into something like revulsion. "No. Why would I want him here? My brother. The *fine doctor*." Her voice dripped with sarcasm. But then she went still and pointed the garden hoe at her. "You said you knew who the father was."

It came together then. All of it, all at once, and Audrey nearly lost the strength in her legs. The jumbled, muddled theories in her mind ironed out flat, and in doing so, a strange sense of calm quieted her trembling nerves.

"It seems I was wrong," Audrey said.

Annie laughed bitterly, her forehead and cheeks streaked with sweat. "You and everyone else. I shouldn't have trusted him when he promised to change."

"Your brother disappointed you?" she said as evenly as possible, latching onto what Annie had revealed a moment ago. Brother. Not *father*.

"He ruined my life once. I cannot allow him to do it again." She held the garden tool so tightly her knuckles turned white.

Dorothy had said *Annie* had been Mary's maid—an enviable position among the serving class. And yet now, she was an under maid, serving tea and cleaning grates. And somehow, Dr. Ryder was to blame.

"He and Mary had an affair. It was his child, wasn't it?" With the sensation of a fist pummeling her stomach, Audrey nearly lost her breath. "My God."

Had Annie killed her?

Asleep in her own bed, the maid could have easily entered Mary's room and pressed the small muff pistol to her temple. Then after, just as quickly arrange the weapon loosely in the countess's limp fingers before dashing out of the room. Perhaps even pretend to be the first to come running at the sound.

"Mary didn't shoot herself. Did she?"

Annie's nostrils flared, and she jutted her chin, but her eyes grew cold and detached. She did not deny it.

The rattle of wheels and tack reached them then, and a few moments later, a phaeton came into view. Doctor Ryder signaled to his horse and stood before the conveyance had come to a full stop. He stumbled and nearly lost his balance.

"Andrea, what in the world...what is the meaning of this?"

Andrea? So, not Annie then.

"I am protecting us, brother. Something you, as a degenerate, failed to do."

Audrey again tried to approach Philip's immobile figure on the grass, but Annie—*Andrea*—swung the garden tool. "Stay back! I'm afraid it cannot be helped now."

"Andrea, this is madness." The doctor leaped to the ground. "How are you protecting us? By assaulting the duke? Threatening the duchess? Have you lost your mind?"

"The only thing I have lost is any faith I once had in you!" she screamed. "I believed, after what happened with the viscountess, that you would reform, that you would not risk another disaster—"

"I have not!" the doctor cried. "I promised you, and I've kept my word."

The maid mocked him with a shrill, false laugh. Audrey tried to comprehend their disagreement, their words, but the earth seemed to be shifting under her feet every few seconds.

"Which viscountess?" she asked.

"The one who bore a son with a port wine mark on its neck —just like the one the good doctor has." Hugh's voice reached into the clearing, and straight into Audrey's chest. It squeezed her heart and brought such relief, she nearly stumbled as she turned, in search of him.

He stepped from the woods, a pistol in his grip. He had the weapon aimed at Annie.

"No!" Dr. Ryder darted toward him, foolishly entering the line of fire. As Hugh scrabbled with the doctor, a hand clamped down upon Audrey and spun her. When she came to a standstill, and Hugh had shoved the doctor aside, the sharp point of a knife pressed into the skin of Audrey's throat; the maid held her in a vise-like grip as a shield, her garden hoe discarded on the ground. Hugh locked eyes with Audrey, his pistol still raised.

"Andrea—" her brother began.

"You couldn't help yourself, could you?" she cried, her clutching fingers digging hard into Audrey's upper arm. "You think I did not know? Lady Mary had not shared the earl's bed in months! But you, always coming around, bringing her tinctures and tonics, and *then* she is suddenly overjoyed. Suddenly with child."

Hugh maintained his aim, though Audrey could barely breathe at seeing the barrel of his flintlock pointed right at her. A flashing memory of Fellows, aiming his pistol at her, the hot pain slicing through her shoulder, the cold water of the Thames closing over her head... She closed her eyes and breathed out evenly.

"And with that birthmark, everyone would know the truth," Audrey said, needing to keep her mind out of the depths of fear.

"You would be forced to give up your position at Bainbury Manor," Hugh added, his voice strained. "You and your brother would have to run again. Change your name again. And your dream of being housekeeper at a fine home would go up in smoke. *Again.* What did you give up in London, Andrea? Who did you forsake to help your brother start anew?"

Andrea whimpered, and as Dr. Ryder watched helplessly, she slowly backed up, pulling Audrey with her. The ledge of the quarry was not far behind. The point of the knife burned against her skin and something wet tracked down her neck. Blood.

"Stop moving, Andrea. Let the duchess go," Hugh commanded.

"Drop your pistol!" the maid cried. Pain seared Audrey's neck as the blade slipped and cut.

Hugh held up both hands and then slowly set the weapon on the grass. He met Audrey's eyes again, and she wanted only to be near him. He was safety—solid and certain and honorable. She needed more time. Needed to keep Andrea talking.

"You knew Charlotte was pregnant when her lady's maid sent that missive to Ida. You followed her to the cottage," she said.

"But Ida was going to help her end the pregnancy," Hugh continued. "Why chase Charlotte down and kill her?"

The answer burst into Audrey's head. "Because she changed her mind." She was seeing so clearly, so vividly, and she knew it was the quickly approaching ledge that was causing such clarity. "She wanted a child desperately after suffering those two miscarriages. She changed her mind and sent Ida away... But you followed her."

"She said I was crazy," Andrea said. "Said I didn't know what I was talking about."

"Because you didn't," Audrey replied. It was a risk to anger the person who was holding the blade to her throat, poised to cut deeper. But if she did and said nothing, she would still be in the same amount of danger. "You were wrong. Your brother was not the father. Lord Renfry was."

She felt the young woman's shock in the renewed pressure of the knife.

"You're lying," Andrea said as Audrey mewled in pain, the blade nicking her again.

"She isn't!" Dr. Ryder said. "The duchess is right, Andrea, it was Renfry. I promise you—"

"Your promises mean nothing!" She lunged backward, and Audrey had no choice but to trip along with her.

"He seduced his stepmothers out of hatred and bitterness

toward his father," Hugh said, raising his voice. "Your brother is not the villain here, Andrea."

"No!" she screamed in Audrey's ear.

"Ida saw you returning to Haverfield dressed as a man and it was only a matter of time until she found out it was you in that coat and hat, isn't that right?" Hugh pressed, wanting to unnerve her. Distract her. Audrey knew his intention and joined him.

"You followed her to the cottage when she was next summoned," Audrey said, realizing that Andrea likely had not even known *who* the midwife had been supposed to meet. "You sneaked up behind her, like you just did with the duke, and struck her down."

Philip continued to lay quiet and still. What if he was dead? Audrey's throat cinched tight.

"And today, you left that missive in the letter box for your brother to lure him here and make certain he did not ruin your future for a second time," Hugh said, to which the doctor muttered his shocked denial, that his sister would never do such a thing. His disavowals trailed off into silence when his sister did not deny Hugh's version of events.

"But you did not plan for the duke and duchess to be here. And now, a Bow Street officer. Also on their way are footmen from Fournier House, a coroner, and the magistrate. Andrea, release her. It is over."

"No," she said, her voice trembling. "You are correct. It is too late."

"How do you get away with this?" Hugh asked, spreading his arms. "She is a *duchess*."

"A lover's quarrel," Andrea said, her voice pitched high and breathless. "The duke found you together and...and he pushed her over the edge and shot you. Joseph, get the gun."

"Andrea, stop," the doctor pleaded.

"Get it!"

"No! I cannot. I will not. Please, you must give this up. No one will believe you."

The maid was shaking now. Her hands might be sweating. She wore no gloves. Perhaps the knife's handle would slip from her grip easily. Audrey considered how she might be able to manage such a thing when the maid guttered a laugh.

"Oh, but they will. Especially when they hear all about how the duchess was once sent away to an asylum for the insane. When they find out she's *mad*."

Hugh's eyes clashed with Audrey's. Her heart all but stopped. How had Andrea learned the truth? Did the servants at Haverfield know? Or had she gone through the baroness's things and found papers from Shadewell? The ground underneath Audrey's heels seemed to crumble, and with a limited twist of her head, she realized where she stood: right upon the edge of the quarry pit. *Now*. She had to act now—or never get another chance.

"So," Hugh mused, attempting to sound nonchalant, even though his eyes blazed with fear. "You kill a duke, a duchess, two countesses, and a Bow Street officer. It sounds like a losing hand of cards."

"This isn't funny!" she screamed.

Using Andrea's momentary distraction, Audrey gritted her teeth and jabbed her elbow back, into the maid's ribs. Her hold slackened, and Audrey tried to disentangle herself, but Andrea shoved her, hard. Audrey's heels slipped. She windmilled her arms, attempting to regain balance, but within a split second, she knew it wasn't going to work. It was too late. The open air claimed her and sent her plummeting below.

CHAPTER
TWENTY

"Audrey, no!" Hugh's heart tore in two, and his entire world slowed to a stop, as she disappeared over the edge of the open pit.

In the next second, a million thoughts attacked, though one rose to the top to torment him: he'd failed. He'd failed her.

Hugh lunged for his flintlock on the ground. Andrea still had the knife in her hand, and having regained her footing, she now ran toward her brother. The doctor had his hands up, shouting for her to stop, to see reason. Hugh aimed for the maid and for the first time in five years, he fired at another human being. His stomach dropped when the maid screamed and fell, the ball of lead having found its target. He ignored Millbury's cries of anguish and rushed to the ledge of the pit, his blood slowing in anticipation of the sight that would greet him. He dropped to his knees and forced himself to look. The painful cramping in his chest released when he saw Audrey on a narrow ledge about ten feet below. She moaned and tried to roll over.

"Audrey, no! Don't move!" he shouted, and when the duchess's eyes opened and found him above her, he shuddered with relief.

"Stay where you are, don't move!" he shouted again. "I'm coming for you."

Millbury was hovering over his sister, already treating her right arm, which was bleeding heavily. As Hugh scrambled for the opening in the cliff's edge that he and the duchess had descended a few days before, he found he did not care if the woman lived or died; she had murdered three women, two unborn children, and now, she had attempted to kill Audrey. If she did not die here and now, she would hang, and she would deserve nothing less.

Discarding any more thoughts for the doctor and his sister, Hugh shucked his coat and hat and started to descend the steep, craggy ledges. Audrey had landed on one that would not be easily reached. He assessed the best route to where she now sat, rubbing the back of her head, and wincing in pain.

"Did I hear a pistol shot?" she asked, her back pressed tightly against the quarry wall.

Hugh reached for a narrow ledge and jumped to it. He shinnied across, toward a second step, this one only slightly wider.

"Andrea isn't dead. Yet," he replied, pulling himself up onto another jutting rock. Sweat coated the back of his neck, and he refused to look down. "Are you injured?"

"Just my ankle." Then, more urgently, "How did you find out about Renfry?"

"I made the same mistake Andrea did—I accused Millbury, and he set me straight."

"Millbury?"

Hugh scaled another prominent shelf on the cliff wall, and finally came within reach of the duchess. Her ledge was just above him now. "Doctor Ryder's true name."

"How did you find *that* out?"

"Thornton. You see, I didn't truly discover anything for

myself, so will you at least allow me to redeem myself and rescue you from that ledge?"

"I do not need rescuing," she said, stubborn to the last.

He'd fully expected to see her broken body on the scree at the base of the quarry, so to see her alive, to hear her mulish retort, filled him with an indescribable emotion. It was more than just relief. Infinitely more.

But then, the duchess peered over the ledge, toward the ground below, and with a shudder, she squeezed her eyes shut. She pressed back against the quarry wall. "I...I can't."

"Yes, you can."

"Why don't you just lower a rope and pull me up?" Panic pitched her voice higher. Her coloring had paled, and her eyes were still closed. He knew what she was likely seeing: the countess's body, as she had discovered it.

"I don't have any rope," he said, trying to maintain calm and patience. He did not like the looks of the drop any more than she did. Any stumbling or missteps could send them both to Lady Bainbury's fate.

"I'll wait here. You can ride back to Fournier House and fetch some and—"

"Audrey. Look at me." She parted her lashes and met his eyes. He held her stare, unblinking. "I am not going to let you fall."

His heart thrashed as she nodded, and then, with stiff motions, slid toward him. She swung her legs over the edge of the rock. Hugh beckoned her to come closer, reaching up to grasp her legs firmly. He clutched her hips, and she braced her hands on his shoulders. Slowly, he guided her from the ledge above, to his own. Audrey kept her hands on his shoulders, wincing as she tried to stand.

He slid his arm around her waist and lifted, trying to keep

her weight off her injured ankle. "Do you see that wide rock behind me? About ten yards away?"

She nodded, even though her eyes were again squeezed shut. He grinned.

"We'll move slowly toward it together. Don't let go of me," he said.

She huffed a laugh. "No chance of that."

From the frantic digging of her fingers into his shoulders, he half thought he'd come away with bruises. Not that he cared, so long as he got her across the slim footholds to safety. They shuffled, Audrey opening her eyes just wide enough to view their progress. A few times Hugh had to lower himself to another outcropping while at the same time guiding Audrey with him, the effort enough to make him erupt in sweat. His whole body ached from tension by the time they made it the ten or so yards and finally reached their destination.

The wide rock ledge caught them both, and as soon as they stood upon it, Audrey collapsed against him. Hugh closed his arms around her and drew deep breaths. "That wasn't so difficult after all," he lied.

She looked up at him, her hand pressed flat against his waistcoat. "You are delusional."

As he peered down at her, grinning, rogue thoughts struck, like how perfect she felt tucked next to him. He didn't want to release her. Didn't want to move from the safety of this boulder. Hugh dipped his chin as he saw blood on her neck and upon the squared collar of her dress. "She cut you."

"I don't feel it," Audrey replied, her face still turned toward his. She made no move to withdraw from his arms, even when he lifted a hand to touch her neck. The wound wasn't deep.

"That was much too close," he said.

"I agree."

"We rarely do that," he murmured.

"I must have knocked my head harder than I thought," she said, and as he watched her lips form an impish grin, the last shred of resistance within him broke. He cupped her cheek.

"You are maddening," he said. She inhaled, quickly and softly.

"Hugh," she whispered.

He brushed his thumb across her lower lip, entranced. He waited for her to tell him to stop. To remember himself. Waited for her to pull away. She did none of those things.

Until the duke's voice rained down upon them.

"Audrey? Where are you? Audrey!"

She jerked backward, her eyes blazing with numbed astonishment. Hugh dropped his arms as the duke's panicked voice called out again, shouting for her.

"I...I am here!" Audrey called back, her voice cracking.

Hugh stiffened his jaw and jerked his head. "Up. Carefully."

Audrey clambered up the rocky path ahead of him, Hugh climbing behind her. How bloody stupid could he have possibly been? He forced himself to focus, especially with Fournier waiting for them at the top. When they reached the crest and the duke pulled Audrey up and into his arms, Hugh gritted his molars and cut his attention toward the doctor. He had loaded Andrea into his phaeton. The maid's coloring was waxy and pale, but she was still alive, her arm bound.

"I must perform an operation to remove the ball," Millbury said.

That he and his sister might instead ride fast out of town immediately crossed Hugh's mind. He wouldn't take the chance. "I'll come with you." Putting distance between himself and the duchess also appealed.

Millbury nodded tightly, as if disappointed, and he directed his phaeton back toward the quarry road. Hugh mounted his horse as four footmen came through the trees on horseback.

Blood streaked the duke's temple, and with Fournier likely concussed and Audrey's injured ankle, he was glad not to be leaving them on their own.

"See them safely back to Fournier House," he instructed the footmen. "The magistrate should be arriving soon. Have him send a bailiff to the doctor's home in Low Heath. The duchess will inform his lordship and Dr. Wilkes what has occurred here."

Though she filled his peripheral vision, Hugh could not bring himself to look at her. His chest burned and his throat constricted as he tugged the reins and followed the doctor's phaeton back toward Low Heath, feeling like a coward and a fool.

THE BAILIFF ARRIVED SHORTLY after Millbury pulled the lead ball from his sister's right arm. Hugh spent the length of the operation pacing the front hall of the doctor's home, contemplating the last time he had shot a person in the arm. When his half-brother, Lord Neatham, the new Viscount Neatham, had challenged Hugh to a duel five years ago, he had not wanted to participate. Bartholomew was his brother by all accounts and yet, he knew without a doubt that Barty would shoot to kill, not just wound. Allowing Hugh to live—allowing him to talk and divulge secrets—would only put the family's reputation in danger.

Though he despised Barty, he had not wanted him dead, so he'd aimed for his arm. At twenty paces, Hugh knew he could hit his target—the late viscount had taught Hugh to shoot, though he would often say Hugh was a natural and needed little instruction. Barty had always hated that, especially because their father would not heap the same praise upon him.

Thornton had been Hugh's second and after inspecting the pistol and walking the first ten paces with him, he'd frantically pleaded that he aim for the bastard's heart. Instead, he'd ruined the viscount's arm, shattering the bone, and rendering it useless forevermore. Hugh escaped without a scratch, though in many ways he'd been ruined too.

He had not seen or spoken to Barty, or Eloisa or Thomas, since. Eloisa was no longer in London. She'd disappeared after the scandal, and Thomas had bought a commission into the Royal Army as an officer of some sort. He didn't care enough to keep up.

All that felt like another life, though one that still followed him like a shadow. Audrey knew the gossip—that Hugh had ruined his own half-sister and had been called out for the atrocious offense—and yet she did not believe it. He didn't want to think about his behavior on the quarry ledge, so instead, he went over how Andrea Millbury had planned to make all their deaths look like some romantic tryst gone wrong. Bainbury had known Audrey had not been on the Continent and then at her aunt's home in Scotland for two years. He'd insinuated that it was something shocking and disgraceful, and it indeed was.

An asylum. She'd been committed to an insane asylum.

In the minutes after seeing Audrey fall from the quarry edge and his rush to bring her to safety, and then of course, after the rash and reckless near kiss, the memory of which formed a tight ache in the pit of his stomach, he had not given much thought to the maid's frenzied mention of the asylum. But he had seen Audrey's frightened reaction and knew it was true.

Fury simmered alongside the tight ache in his stomach as Hugh entrusted the bailiff to collect the wounded Miss Millbury and then left for the inn. He needed to inform Basil that they would be leaving first thing in the morning. His valet's pleasure tempered when Hugh also instructed him to hire a carriage and fetch Sir from Bainbury Park.

"Are you certain? The boy seems to be taken with country life, not to mention the cook's food at the manor."

"Go get him," Hugh had growled, his valet's show of dislike for the lad irritating rather than amusing, as it usually was. Hugh suspected it was artificial and that Basil simply did not wish to admit that he'd taken a liking to the boy, as Hugh had.

Though he was not eager to see the duchess, he could not put it off. He rode out to Fournier House, where he found Wilkes overseeing the removal of both Lady Bainbury and Ida Smith from the icehouse.

Wilkes stepped away from the footmen, carrying the carefully shrouded victims toward two carts. "Well done, Officer Marsden. From what the duchess has explained, it appears the two murders have been solved."

"Three," Hugh said. Wilkes grimaced.

"I stand corrected. Three, indeed. Would you like me to inform Lord and Lady Finborough, or shall you?"

The marquess and marchioness would not care who came to deliver the news that they had been correct in their theory. Their daughter had not taken her own life, but she was still dead. Hugh invited the coroner to visit Kilton House.

"I am leaving for London as soon as possible," he explained to Wilkes.

He needed to return, to get back to Bow Street and put all this behind him. There was plenty of work there. In the past few months, he'd been doing well, his focus clear. Until the duchess's letter arrived, beckoning him to Hertfordshire. Now, that same tangled and irritable feeling he'd grappled with in the spring had once again settled into his bones.

"Very well," Wilkes said. "It has been, if not a pleasure, then at least fruitful working with you."

Hugh accepted the stiff praise from the fastidious coroner and extended his hand. "If you ever come to London, Bow Street could put you to use."

"I will keep that in mind," Wilkes said, and then joined the footmen at the carts.

Hugh glanced toward the stone edifice of the grand home. There was no avoiding it. He would make his goodbyes and be off.

A footman saw him into the foyer, but as the butler, Verly, approached, the unmistakable sound of sobbing emanated from off the main hall.

"My apologies, officer," Verly said. "His Grace is unable to receive callers at this time."

The sobs continued. They belonged to a woman. Hugh could not tame his legs, and ignoring Verly, he swept past, following the distressing sounds toward a room ahead. Hugh's concern and temper rose in tandem as Verly called after him to stop. The sobbing drew him to the half-closed door to the duke's study. Hugh entered with a heavily panting Verly on his heels. Audrey sat upon the sofa, her arms bracing Cassandra's shoulders.

"Officer Marsden, Your Grace," the butler announced belatedly, after the duke had already seen him. He stood at the windows, a snifter in his hand and a dressing of linen wrapped around his head.

Hugh had already removed his hat and now set it on a table closest to the door. The wound on Audrey's neck had also been cleaned and bandaged. She met Hugh's eyes briefly before turning her attention back to her sister-in-law. Cassandra's eyes were swollen, and she pressed a lace kerchief to her nose.

"Marsden," the duke said, his voice ragged but calm. "What has happened to that maid?"

"She will live," he answered. "She's been arrested and will face murder charges. I have no doubt she will be found guilty."

It was no reason to rejoice and none of them did so. Instead, Cassandra's sobs continued.

Hugh did not know what to say. The young woman was ruined—just as thoroughly as Eloisa had been.

"The magistrate has gone to Bainbury Manor to speak to Lord Renfry to discuss his involvement with both Lady Charlotte and Lady Mary," the duke informed him.

"He will deny it," Hugh warned. And anyhow, there was enough witness testimony and evidence to secure Andrea Millbury's conviction without Renfry's confession.

Fournier slammed his snifter onto his desk. "He will answer for his actions. I will demand an offer for my sister, and to hell with his planned nuptials!"

Cassandra jumped to her feet, throwing off Audrey's arm. "No! I've told you I don't want to marry him!"

The duke lost his composure. "You have no choice! He has ruined you, Cassie! Do you believe there will be other offers from men of quality after this?"

Audrey stood as well, though she winced and favored her left ankle. "Philip, please. The man seduced his own stepmothers. You cannot force your sister to marry such a scoundrel."

"She made her choice, and now she must see it through," the duke bellowed.

Cassandra broke into fresh tears, and Audrey glared. "She does not deserve to be bound to someone so wretched for the rest of her life because she made one mistake!"

"This is your mistake as much as it is hers," Fournier shouted. She gaped, her color rising. "You were supposed to be watching her. How could you not have known?"

As Audrey's expression crumpled, loathing for Fournier, hot and potent, rose within Hugh's chest. Tears brimmed in her eyes, and she turned and limped as quickly from the room as her injured ankle could take her. Hugh watched her go, torn between wanting to follow her and staying to throttle the duke.

Cassandra stifled her tears at glared at her brother. "It happened in London, not here. It isn't her fault. You can be such a heartless, selfish bastard sometimes."

With that, the young woman turned on her heel and followed in Audrey's wake.

The study fell silent, the duke standing by his desk and Hugh by the door. He reached for his hat, wishing like hell he'd taken his leave from Low Heath immediately, rather than come here.

The duke picked up his snifter and swirled his brandy before setting it aside again. "I suppose you think I'm a heartless bastard too," he muttered.

"I think you could not care less about my opinion. But know this: if you weren't a duke, I'd knock out your teeth for making her cry."

Hugh held Fournier's astonished glare as he put on his hat, then turned and left.

TWENTY-ONE

After weeping for most of the evening, Cassandra finally fell into a deep, exhausted slumber. For hours, Audrey had sat with her in her bedchamber, soothing her, and assuring her that she would not be forced to marry Lord Renfry, who had, Cassie admitted, swept her off her feet in May. He had charmed her quite thoroughly after Genie introduced them at a dinner. Their flirtation moved swiftly, and encouraged by his words of devotion, Cassie believed it was love.

Renfry had promised to speak to the duke during the summer with an offer. She had believed herself as good as betrothed. However, soon Cassie overheard a few ladies gossiping of how Bainbury's heir was pressing his suit for the exorbitantly wealthy daughter of a merchant. When confronted, Renfry admitted it was true and that he would not be speaking to the duke after all.

In her fathomless humiliation, she realized he had never intended to offer for her. He had simply used her as a bit of sport, his words of love hollow and delivered with only one objective in mind. As Philip had professed a desire to do earlier, Audrey wished to call the heartless blackguard out. How a man could be so unfeeling and callous toward an innocent, untried young lady stupefied her.

When Audrey finally returned to her own room, she was thankful not to find Philip waiting for her. They were both angry, both overwhelmed, and though the murders had been solved, the turmoil was not at an end. Something would have to be done about Cassandra. Her mind would not cooperate, though, and so Audrey dismissed Greer and fell into bed, shutting out every thought that tried to gain entry.

Not unexpectedly, her thoughts were waiting for her as soon as she woke at dawn. The first through, without surprise, was the memory of Hugh Marsden crossing the uneven ledges at the quarry pit and bringing her into the safety of his arms. They had each lingered, neither of them moving to disentangle from their embrace. He'd touched her cheek. Her lips. As Audrey lay in bed, her eyes still closed, she allowed herself the briefest moment of freedom to imagine what might have happened had he closed the few inches of space between them and kissed her. It made every inch of her body overheat and thrum, and then, it had all been doused with a cold splash of guilt.

She opened her eyes and exhaled, a sheen of sweat covering her body. Though not from the fantasy of Hugh's mouth pressed against her own. No, it was already sweltering hot, and the sun hadn't yet fully risen. Audrey sat up and pushed the covers away. She had more things to think upon and worry about than a kiss that had not happened.

She put her mind to the task of bathing, dressing, and then seeking out Philip to advocate for a different fate for Cassie. She found him at the breakfast table, his wound dressing removed. He still had a throbbing headache, but he would be just fine. He was lucky. Andrea Millbury could have killed him with that blow to the back of the head.

"Mercifully, I have an infuriatingly thick skull," he said as he dipped a corner of toast into his soft-boiled egg. He peered at her, waiting for her to make a sarcastic comment. Audrey only arched a brow at the peace offering, then allowed a smile.

Philip pushed his plate away. "I am sorry I made you cry."

Audrey sipped her tea and nodded. "Thank you. And I'm sorry we have yet another scandal to endure."

"That is not your fault. I was wrong to say it was."

"You were," she agreed, but then shook her head. "But we'll say no more on it. Yesterday was challenging for all of us."

He rubbed the back of his head gingerly. "Can you even imagine—killing innocent women out of fear their babies would be born bearing a mark that would betray their father's identity? It is madness."

The oolong tea turned bitter on the back of her tongue, and she set the cup down. "I think she also felt betrayed by her brother. After giving everything up to stand by his side, to take on a new life and identity, she feared he'd again jeopardized her dreams and her security."

For women, so much of their lives depended upon the men who supported them. If those men failed to do so time and again, it would be natural to feel resentful and bitter.

"But she had been wrong."

Audrey nodded. She had been, and her fear had led her to do unthinkable things.

"Cassie must marry," Philip said after a momentary quiet. "Either that or she has the child in secret and gives it up before returning to London. There will be rumors—"

"She says Renfry does not know."

"And he will not know." Philip sighed. "But servants do gossip, and both Millbury and that murderess, as well as Marsden, knows."

"Mr. Marsden will not say anything," Audrey said. "And I'm

certain no one will listen to a single thing the doctor or his sister says now."

Then again, at the quarry, Andrea had revealed the truth about Audrey's stay at Shadewell. Hugh knew. So did the doctor. She wondered if Hugh had dismissed the maid's claims, but his pointed expression at the time told her he believed it. Moreso, that it had only confirmed what he'd already known. Had he known? She couldn't imagine how. Then again, he was a superb investigator, and on the carriage ride back from Kilton House, he'd nearly persuaded her to confide in him about her uncle's indicative remark.

Philip pushed back his chair and stood. "I'm sure you are right. If you'll excuse me, I have a letter to write."

She frowned. "To whom?"

"I have a friend in Sweden who might be persuaded to host Cassie through her confinement."

Sweden. Audrey's heart fell at what the young woman would endure the next several months. But it would be better than a loveless marriage to a revolting cad like Renfry.

The duke came to Audrey's chair and in a show of affection that took her by surprise, leaned over and kissed the crown of her head. Then, without another word, he departed for his study. She sat still for another few moments, startled by the display of warmth. Philip did love her. They were the best of friends and partners.

However, as she, too, abandoned her breakfast, she understood that it would never be enough.

As Dr. Wilkes would be visiting the Marquess and Marchioness Finborough to convey the news that their daughter's murderer had been apprehended, Audrey took it upon herself to make the trip to Greely Park, to inform Lady Prescott. Greer offered to go with her, but Audrey declined. She wanted some time alone, and as soon as she was seated in the brougham and on her way, she realized why. Tears quickly formed and fell as, at last, she accepted that Charlotte was gone. She wept for her friend, for the child she had decided to keep and bear, even if it would remind her of the horrible man who had taken advantage of her sadness and loneliness.

Audrey wept for Mary, too, and for Ida Smith, who had only ever helped women in need. There were some tears for Cassie as well, but the difference was that at least she had her life. She had another chance, no matter how complicated her future appeared to be right then. Audrey removed her gloves and dashed away the tears as she heard the greeting call of an approaching driver and the clattering of tack. Her own driver slowed and made room for the oncoming carriage. She peered out the window as it passed—and met with Hugh Marsden's momentary countenance.

His brown eyes brightened with alertness as he saw her, and then, he was gone, their carriages traveling onward in separate directions. Audrey sat forward, breathless.

"Wait! Kinson, stop!" she called.

Hugh was leaving Hertfordshire. Of course he was. He was finished with the investigation. Bow Street needed him back. As her driver slowed and she leaned her head out the open window, peering behind them, she expected to see his carriage shrinking in the distance, behind a cloud of road dust.

Instead, she saw his carriage had stopped as well. The door opened, and Hugh stepped down into the road. Her heart knocked along unevenly as she impatiently grasped the door handle and pushed it open.

The footman on the box seat leaped down and quickly lowered the step. She accepted his helping hand just as Hugh reached her. He wore a sly grin, and Audrey knew in that moment that she was lost.

"I was hoping you wouldn't leap down on your own and twist your other ankle," Hugh said as she joined him in the road.

"I am not that heedless," she replied.

"That has not been my observation, Your Grace."

Her smile thinned at hearing her title on his lips. It was only proper of course, but it was also a reminder of their different places.

At his carriage, a plain, hired coach and four, the young urchin known as Sir hung from the window, his arms dangling from the window's edge as he gawped at them shamelessly.

"Oh, so *now* you're in no rush to hightail it back to town," the boy shouted. Hugh ignored him.

"Don't mind Sir, he's just irritable to be giving up the food the earl's kitchen churns out. Apparently, my cook's ability pales in comparison to Bainbury's."

Audrey bit back a grin at the thought of Hugh's cook feeding the boy. That he'd brought him along in the first place showed how much he cared about him. It tugged at her heart.

She glanced at her footman, waiting dutifully by the brougham's door. Hugh noticed and gestured toward the roadside, where a rock wall bordered a grassy pasture. In silent agreement, they moved toward it.

"I am calling on Lady Prescott," she said as they reached the wall. "Have you been to see her already?"

He was due his fee, after all. But the last time she had mentioned anything regarding money, he'd seemed to take offense. He plucked a long stem of grass from the base of the wall. "Briefly. I need to return to London. I've cases there waiting for me."

She nodded, hating the punch of his curt words. "Of course."

He peeled the stem of grass in two then cast them aside. "How is Lady Cassandra?"

"I wish I could say she was well, but it would be a lie. You already know the truth."

Somehow, this man who had been a stranger to her just a handful of months ago, knew her every truth.

"Renfry's betrothed has cried off," he announced after a moment. "I heard tell of it this morning. Apparently, he and Bainbury nearly came to fisticuffs when Renfry confessed all. The lady and her family were appalled."

Audrey held her breath. "What of Cassie...?"

He shook his head. "He does not seem to know anything about that. And though Millbury is aware, Andrea might not be. If you recall, she did not sign the missive luring him to the quarry. Millbury only assumed it was Cassandra because of the mention of the citrine quarry. He must have known of her penchant to collect the stones."

Audrey exhaled, agreeing that sounded likely. But it was no guarantee that their secret would hold. She took a breath and bit her lower lip. Secrets and lies. They had plagued the last many years of her life.

The temptation to pretend nothing had been said back at the quarry about her stay at the asylum was strong. But pretending would not quiet the nagging voice in the back of her mind.

"At the quarry..." she began, haltingly.

Hugh turned toward her, and though it was a mere shift of his footing, the motion of it was powerful and swift. "Allow me to apologize. I took liberties and offended you—"

"You didn't," she said, stunned. It wasn't what she'd intended to discuss, but she realized now how much their embrace had weighed on him. The memory of his thumb sweeping across her lips blazed hot and defiant yet again.

He held her eyes, as if searching for truth. As if wanting her to be angry and to scold him. When she did not, he licked his lips and tucked his chin. "It will not happen again. It cannot."

Regret bit at her unexpectedly. She should not want it to happen again, even if she had let her imagination wander that morning, in the space between sleep and waking. "No, of course not."

And yet, Hugh would not release her from the same heated stare that had spellbound them on the quarry ledge.

"Besides," she said, "I'm sure our paths won't cross again. There can be no reason for them to."

He nodded, and at last broke their stare. Hugh turned toward the coach and four. The boy no longer hung out the window.

She tried again now that she could breathe. "What Miss Millbury said, about...where I was sent..."

"Edgerton sent you there?" Hugh interjected, facing her again. His sharpened stare was still intense but this time, with fury.

Audrey nodded. "With my mother's approval."

The memory of Shadewell's austere stone edifice, the barren moors surrounding it, the complete isolation of the sanatorium, and the endless cacophony that lived within its walls, made her unexpectedly nauseous.

"Bainbury knows," Hugh said.

Audrey stumbled. He grasped her arm as her mind continued to reel. "*He* told you?"

"He alluded to it. He suspects you were sent somewhere for, in his words, *seeing things that do not exist.*"

Hugh's fingers released her arm; they drifted down her sleeve, to her wrist, before brushing along her palm, to the tips of her fingers. When her arms swung back to her side, she felt untenably bereft. He took a step closer, then seemed to think differently on it, and stepped back again.

"I told you that you could trust me," he said softly.

"I do," she replied. "It's only that if you knew, I feared...you might change your mind."

He frowned. "Change my mind how? About what?"

"About me," she answered. It was too simplistic and not at all illuminating, but her mind refused to form more words.

Hugh took that step forward now, and though he did not reach for her, she felt the press of him, nonetheless. "Nothing will change how I see you, Audrey." His eyes darkened to a serious umber, her name on his tongue enough to make her chest squeeze. "Knowing where your despicable uncle and mother sent you does not change the fact that you are stubborn, exasperating, rash, entirely too curious for your own good, and have a knack for finding dead bodies."

With each additional affront, her eyes widened, and her lips parted.

"It does not change the fact that you have an extraordinary ability, that you are intelligent and brave to a fault. And though I wished it did, it doesn't change the ill-advised truth that I am drawn to you."

She stared at him, utterly perplexed and unable to take regular breaths. She trembled, but she did not know if it was from insult or pleasure. Or both.

"You are infuriating," she whispered and added weakly, "And not at all charming."

Hugh's mouth split into a grin.

"Oi!" Sir shouted from the coach and four. He was now seated on the edge of the window, waving his arm.

Hugh laughed. "I am being summoned."

They walked back toward her carriage and though the footman reached to help her up, Hugh's hand slid into hers first. He guided her into the carriage, and as she perched on the edge of the bench, he took his time releasing her hand.

"Well done, duchess. Another inquiry solved."

She could not fight the blush that warmed her cheeks. "Let us hope it is the last."

Hugh stepped away to allow the footman to latch the door shut. He pulled the brim of his hat in parting as the carriage shook and the driver urged the horses onward.

Audrey sat back as Hugh disappeared from view. She wasn't entirely sure she meant what she said. Another inquiry could mean another death, and there had been enough of those lately. However, there was no doubt she felt useful when helping in an investigation. Oddly enough, she felt more alive when faced with a puzzle to solve. And just as Hugh had confessed, she was drawn to him as well. Ill-advised, to say the very least.

She exhaled as the carriage rattled on toward Greely Park. It was all for naught anyhow. She and Philip had many things to see to before their return to London in another few weeks, namely what to do with Cassie. She would need to be Audrey's focal point now, and she would throw herself completely into helping her. There would be no time to think about murder investigations or Hugh Marsden or Bow Street. She was a duchess, after all. Even as she thought it, she recalled something Hugh had said: *A duchess can do as she pleases.*

Audrey bit her lower lip to stop the grin from forming completely. "Indeed," she whispered. "A duchess can."

THANK you for reading Death at Fournier Downs, the second Bow Street Duchess mystery! Please leave a rating and review on Amazon to help more readers discover the series. Audrey and Hugh's next investigation is on the way soon! Keep reading for a sneak peek at Silence of Deceit, the third Bow Street Duchess mystery, releasing April 22, 2023.

SILENCE OF DECEIT
A BOW STREET DUCHESS MYSTERY

Chapter One

November 1819
  London

The offices at number 4 Bow Street were an entirely different beast once the sun slipped behind the city's western horizon. During daylight hours, the magistrate's offices were generally sedate, with patrolmen either clearing out the overnight arrests or readying them for hearings at the magistrate's court. Come nightfall, however, those patrolmen were dragging in all manner of criminals, from petty thieves and pickpockets to drunken belligerents and unruly cyprians.

As a principal officer, Hugh Marsden no longer plied the streets to catch criminals in the act or answer the hue and cry of wronged citizens. He was accountable for more significant arrests and investigations that took time and patience to solve. Murders were, by and large, simple things to crack as most people did a rather shoddy job of covering up their evil deeds. People were sloppy. They were guileless and unoriginal. In short, they were predictable, which made Hugh's work relatively straightforward and boring.

Some cases, of course, broke the mold and diverged from the ordinary and mundane.

Last April, and then again in August, Hugh had come upon two such cases. In the spring, a delirious and blood-covered man had been found in leased rooms in the Seven Dials with a mutilated opera singer and the murder weapon at his side. That the man had been a duke of the realm had only further convinced Hugh that whether one lived in the slums, or in Mayfair, people were simple creatures.

Most people, at least.

The duke's wife had certainly challenged his theory. She'd rejected the clear-cut case and went about hunting down the true murderer, going against the grain and proving Hugh wrong. And then in August, the duchess had beckoned him to the country to investigate a woman's death. The unraveling of that case had been anything but straightforward, and once again, the duchess managed to untangle a host of well-concealed lies in lockstep with Hugh.

In the near two months since that case in Hertfordshire, Hugh had made arrests in several more killings in London, none of them very inventive or complex. And most of his investigating tended to happen during the day, when Number 4 Bow Street resembled a busy but orderly business firm.

Tonight, however, as he entered the offices near midnight, his eyes burning from lack of sleep and his mind slightly hazed from one too many drams of whisky, Hugh remembered the hassle of working at this hour, and he pitied the night officers and patrolmen. The main room was a madhouse of shouting and jostling bodies. A pair of drunken women screeched lewd and suggestive comments at the harried booking officer behind his desk while several patrolmen attempted to keep a group of ragtags from entering into fisticuffs. An old woman with blackened gums and teeth laughed hysterically as she bounced a baby, bundled in fouled linens, on her knee. And to top it off, in the corner, a stray, mangy dog lifted its leg over a potted plant.

Immediately, Hugh regretted his decision to leave his warm, quiet home on Bedford Street at such a ridiculous hour. He had no one to blame but himself. He hadn't been summoned, and earlier that afternoon, he'd resolved an investigation into several stolen shipments of snuff (an assistant to the tobacconist who reported the theft had, unsurprisingly, thought to sell it for his own gain). He had but some papers to sort through and reports to complete for filing. Nothing that could not wait.

However, Bow Street had been a better alternative to lying awake in bed until dawn, dwelling on what Miss Gloria Hansen had whispered in his ear that evening as they lay side-by-side, sweaty and spent. *"Who were you just making love to? It was not me."*

He'd stared at his long-standing mistress, baffled, and asked her to explain her meaning. Though now, he wished he had not.

The harassed booking officer caught Hugh's eye. He parted his lips, as if to call to him, and Hugh quickly threw up a hand in greeting and darted toward his office. Once inside, he closed the door, shutting out the chaos. He hung his great coat and top hat, both damp from a misty autumn rain, and sighed as he collapsed into the creaky chair behind his desk. The room was small and windowless, likely a closet when the house had been a residence during the previous century, before Sir Henry Fielding had started up the Runners. But it was his own space, and for that, Hugh was grateful.

He leaned back into the chair and stared at the stacks of waiting files on his blotter. Then sighed heavily. It seemed all he'd managed to do was change his physical location, for the memory of Gloria's bold question continued to plague him.

"You've been different lately," she'd elaborated with an insouciant shrug of her bare shoulder.

"In what manner?"

"Distant. Like you are thinking of something else. And yet..." She had searched for the right words, settling upon, "Yet, you are also more passionate. Desperately so."

Hugh had increased their once-weekly assignations to twice-weekly, and it had not escaped him that most recently, he had been asking her to visit a third time. Their exclusive arrangement seemed to please them both. As an assistant to one of the best modistes in London, Madam Gascoigne, Gloria earned a decent wage, however there was no question her agreement with Hugh benefited her greatly. And while most men of Hugh's circumstances would not bother to keep a regular mistress and would instead spread his seed among the many willing ladies of the *demimonde*, or even among lower-class cyprians, that sort of transaction had never appealed to him. Instead, for the last year, Gloria had warmed his bed. And apparently, she had a keen sense of observation.

"I apologize if I have failed to satisfy you," he'd said, sitting up in bed and eyeing the clock with an unexpected urge to flee. That usually didn't happen. Gloria's company was comfortable, and it kept his mind from wandering.

"Never that," she replied in her familiar composed and unaffected tone. He had always appreciated that about her. Emotions were not part of their relationship. "But lately, there is something...impatient about you."

"Desperate *and* impatient, is it? Safe to say my ego is wounded."

She huffed. "You make love to me like someone is trying to rip me away from you."

Hugh had thrown off the blanket and gotten dressed. He had no idea what to say to that. Gloria must have decided that to continue the conversation would be disadvantageous, for she dressed as well. Not even a word in parting when she kissed his cheek before leaving.

Who are you making love to?

Hugh sat forward, bracing his elbows upon the desk, and scrubbed his palm over his eyes. Three drams of whisky had not dulled his mind or made him at all sleepy, but perhaps this paperwork would.

A knock landed on his closed door as he picked up a folio and untoggled it.

"Enter," he called, knowing he sounded gruff but secretly welcoming the distraction.

One of the senior patrol officers stepped in, his clothing drenched from the waist down. His uniform's blue tailcoat dripped upon the floor.

Hugh frowned and guessed at the man's plight. "Not the finest night for a wade into the Thames, is it, Stevens?"

"It is not," he agreed.

"A body?"

"Yes, sir."

Hugh waited for the officer to say more, but Stevens's lips were twisted into a contemplative grimace. He had some sympathy for the young man. Hugh had pulled many a body from the river during his time on street patrol. The fresh ones were not always so bad, but the bloated ones were a trial to look upon. Often, the skin bloated to something grotesque, discolored to a putrid greenish color, and would even split open at times. It was not uncommon for the little critters in the river to begin feasting either. It turned his stomach just thinking of it.

"Is there something I can help you with, Stevens?" Hugh

pressed as the man stood there for a few more protracted moments. His skin appeared paler than usual, and a bit waxen.

He cleared his throat. "It's, ah... Well, I was about to send someone to Bedford Street to fetch you, sir. But Davis said you were here."

Davis, the beleaguered booking officer.

"Why send for me?" Hugh asked. And near midnight, at that. A dead body could surely wait in the bone house until morning.

"I don't quite know how to... You see, it's..." Stevens cleared his throat again, took something silver from his tailcoat's pocket, and then crossed the room. He set the object on the desk.

"A calling card case?" Hugh eyed the silver filigree lid, centered with an enamel posy of violets. He picked it up and sprang the latch. Inside was a clump of damp cardstock.

Just as he was deducing that the object had been found with the drowned body, he read the engraved contents of the top card.

Hugh went still. He stared at the card, then snapped his eyes to Stevens. "What is the meaning of this?"

The patrolman swallowed visibly. "Sir, the item was found in the waist purse of the woman we pulled from the river."

Hugh dropped the case onto the desk and pushed back his chair. The room spun around him, growing smaller. He heard the patrolman's voice continuing to explain that as soon he found the calling cards he immediately thought of Principal Officer Marsden—and that it might be best if he be the one to inform His Grace, the Duke of Fournier.

Hugh shot to his feet. "It is not her. It cannot be. Bring me to the body."

Stevens's eyes rounded. "You don't want to see it, sir. It's bad off, and she's...well, the face is..." He shook his head and suffered a bout of shivers. "You wouldn't recognize it."

Hugh stared at the card case. His ears began to chime. His whole body thrummed with the need to move, to run, to do *something*.

The body they'd fished out of the Thames was not Audrey's.

It could not be the Duchess of Fournier.

He had not seen her for two months, not since leaving Fournier Downs in Hertfordshire. He had no idea what she had been doing or whom she had interacted with. Other members of Polite Society to be sure, as there was no reason for her to socialize with anyone else. Especially someone from his part of society, which really wasn't considered society at all. But she had a habit of being reckless when she got a bee in her bonnet about something. Had she stumbled across another potential crime? Met someone unsavory? Hugh's heart rate increased, and a cold sweat formed under his clothing as he pocketed the card case and dismissed Stevens.

"Will you visit the duke?" the patrolman inquired as Hugh grabbed his great coat and hat.

He might have replied, but he couldn't be sure. He wasn't completely aware of the next several moments, for the next thing Hugh knew, he was on the street, hailing a hack. Violet House, Fournier's London home, was in Mayfair, an area of town he usually had no call to frequent. At this hour, just past midnight, the streets near Hyde Park were nearly empty. The rain-slicked roads glimmered yellow by the light of the gas jets in the lampposts. It was well past proper calling hours, but there was no impropriety Hugh could possibly care enough about right then to stop him.

The weight of the silver case was an anchor in his pocket as the jarvey directed the hack toward Curzon Street. All ladies and gentlemen presented their cards when calling upon

SILENCE OF DECEIT

another member of society whom they were not already familiar with. They were as much a form of identification as they were a social courtesy. The footman at the door would accept the card and present it to their employer, who would then decide whether they were in or out.

How could Audrey's case have found its way into another woman's reticule?

He closed his eyes and, for what could have been the hundredth or thousandth time, returned to the old citrine quarry at Fournier Downs. Hugh had just come to Audrey's aid on the narrow jutting ledges of the open pit. She'd fallen from the edge above and by pure luck had struck one of the craggy ledges instead of tumbling to her death some seventy feet below, onto rocky debris. He had been reeling with relief and gratitude that she was still alive, and in that moment of vulnerability, had nearly given in to the desire he'd been trying to bury since April. He'd come so close to kissing her that he'd felt her breath upon his lips. Thankfully, the duke had shouted from above, rending them apart.

As it should have been.

Kissing her would have been a gargantuan mistake, but try as he had, Hugh could not wipe the inane desire from where it had settled under his very skin.

The hack came to a stop out front of Violet House. An ill sweep of dread flooded his stomach as he tossed the jarvey his fare and then started toward the darkened front steps. He brought down the brass doorknocker three times and waited, knowing such a late-hour call would cause a ruckus. Arriving home past midnight would not be uncommon for the duke and duchess, if they had been attending the theatre or a ball. But had they been out, the exterior lamps would have been left burning and the front windows would have been bright with candlelight to welcome them home. A footman would also have been stationed near the front door to allow them in immediately. As Hugh stood waiting for a full minute, forced to employ the doorknocker once again, he concluded the house was simply asleep.

Finally, footsteps approached. Locks turned. The door opened to reveal a disheveled footman, a livery coat thrown on over his sleeping clothes and his powdered wig askew.

"Sir?" he blurted out wearily.

"Officer Hugh Marsden with Bow Street. I need to speak to the duke. Immediately."

The footman began to stammer a reply about the time of night and the duke being inaccessible, but Hugh cut him off. "Understand that this is an emergency. It involves the duchess." His throat cinched around the words.

A light appeared at the top of the staircase. "Marsden? Is that you? At this hour. What the devil—?"

Robed and fresh from his bedchamber, the duke descended the carpeted steps holding a candle. The footman stepped aside, and Hugh entered the foyer.

"Your Grace, I—" Hugh faltered. Cleared his throat. "I'm afraid I must ask...when was the last you saw the duchess?"

Fournier came to a stop on the last step and scowled at him. "What kind of question is that? It is past midnight, Marsden. Are you drunk?"

"No, I am not drunk," he bit off, barbs of irritation sharpening. "I am aware of the time. I've just come from Bow Street. There has been a...a body. Pulled from the Thames."

"What does that have to do with me? Or my wife?" Fournier held the candle in its holder higher, as if to inspect Hugh for any sign of drunkenness.

He swallowed what felt like shards of broken glass. "I have reason to believe it could be—"

"Hugh?"

Her voice reached him before a second candle on the upstairs landing registered in his vision. Dismissing the duke and footman, and propriety altogether, Hugh went to the base of the steps and gripped the carved wooden newel post. Audrey came down the steps, her hair draped over her shoulder in a thick blond plait, a banyan robe cinched around her waist. Her lips were parted, her cheeks rosy from sleep. She looked beautiful—and unequivocally alive.

"Mr. Marsden," she said, correcting the familiar uttering of his name, which she had likely done out of surprise at seeing him in her foyer. "What is happening?"

He closed his eyes and exhaled, a hundred stone lifting from his chest. "It is not you."

"What isn't me?"

"A dead body, I presume," the duke said tightly, his patience thinning rapidly. "You best explain yourself, Marsden."

The duke could have launched into a vitriolic diatribe right then, and Hugh would not have cared. The body Stevens found was not Audrey's. He nearly swayed on his feet with relief. She stood before him on the stairs, her eyes shining with concern in the dim candlelight.

He reached into his pocket and revealed the silver calling card case.

She took another few steps toward him, her eyes locked on the case, her hand reaching for it. "Where did you find that?"

"A patrolman fished a woman out of the Thames tonight. This was in the waist pocket reticule," he answered. She quickly retracted her hand, leaving the case in his palm. She didn't wish to touch it, and Hugh thought he knew why. Objects held onto memories; memories that Audrey could see in her fascinating mind whenever she touched them. She would not wish to see whatever memories this object retained.

She frowned, her brows pinched together in confusion.

"I misplaced this case weeks ago," she said, shaking her head. "I don't understand, how did it get into the pocket of a—"

Her pinched brow smoothed, and her lips parted on a gust of air. She stared at the case in her hand with dawning recognition.

"*Oh.* Oh no. I think I know who it is."

～

Pre-order Silence of Deceit (Bow Street Duchess Mystery #3), releasing April 22, 2023!

ABOUT THE AUTHOR

Cara is an author, history lover, and Netflix junkie. She loves to read and write across genres, but her heart is reserved for romantic historical fiction and mystery. When she's not writing, she's freelance editing, driving her kids everywhere, burning at least one side of a grilled cheese, or avoiding doing laundry.

ALSO BY CARA DEVLIN

The Bow Street Duchess Mystery series

MURDER AT THE SEVEN DIALS

The Sage Canyon series

A HEART WORTH HEALING

A CURE IN THE WILD

A LAND OF FIERCE MERCY

THE TROUBLE WE KEEP

A Second Chance Western Romance